Obsessive Messages

CAPTIVE WRITINGS
BOOK TWO

M.L. PHILPITT

Note

Obsessive Messages is the second book in the Captive Writings series, which is best read in order. Obsessive Messages is a stalker romance with content some readers may find triggering. You can read the content warning list on the last page.

This book uses Canadian spelling. This means words will have U's in them, "re", or double LL's. (colour vs color, centre vs center, signalling vs signaling, etc.) These are not typos.

Playlist

"Every Breath You Take" by Chase Holfelder
"On My Own" by Ashes Remain
"The Devil Within" by Digital Daggers
"Disturbia" by Rihanna
"Stockholm" by Bianca
"Almost Touch Me'" by Maisy Kay
"Marionette" by Antonia
"Hush Hush" by Asher Monroe
"Please Take Me" by Beth Crowley
"Wonderland" by Taylor Swift
"Love Me Like You Do" by Ellie Goulding
"Twisted Games" by Night Panda & Krigare
"Monster" by Beth Crowley
"Irreplaceable" by Madilyn Paige

For everyone who found love in unconventional ways

Preface

He ensured I would pay for my brother's sins by claiming me for himself. A few messages are all it took before I fell down the hole his web of lies formed. One that seemed impossible to climb out of and could easily bury me alive.

It started when Tristan Pence first snuck inside my house, at a seemingly random point in my life. He's as beautiful as he is a villain—my villain—and with every pretty word, every stroke of his finger, and every consuming orgasm, he claimed more of me for himself. But with every visit, with every touch and kiss, I chose to hand more of myself over to him until I lost myself completely.

In the daytime, he's someone entirely different. At night, he plays the ultimate game with my sanity, and guess what—he wins. But it's both versions I end up craving.

Until the night it all changes. When he reveals his true self and the plot he's orchestrated, making my role one I never saw coming...

There's a true villain in this story, and it's not Tristan.

One

NATALIE

LIFE'S PREDICTABILITY SUCKS SOMETIMES. For other university students, it means going out with friends. Or perhaps simply curling up on the couch and watching a movie while gorging on unhealthy snacks. Or for those like me, who prefer to remain focused on their studies, it means keeping up with the mountain of school work professors feel we would benefit from having in our lives.

Or it *used* to be like that for me, anyway.

Until two months ago, when the strange phone call came, providing me with a date, time, and location—that was it. It was something like fiction, but for some stupid-ass reason, I went. Curiosity, fear... *something* drove me to follow the instructions.

And then my life changed in ways I only ever dreamed about.

Which is why, instead of studying, I'm standing on the front step of my now paid-for townhouse, waiting for the fancy black sedan to arrive, as it does every Friday evening since that life-altering day.

I cross my arms, blocking the evening chill from touching my bare chest, thanks to the lowered neckline of one of three dresses I own. I wear them on a cycle each week, and it's this one's turn. I ought to go shopping soon, before he notices my lack of diversity in elegant clothing and tries to fill my closet with more.

When the black car pulls up to the curb, the typical turbulent reaction I get each week flows through me. Nerves, per usual. I've never felt at ease in his company; the unknowns and newness of it are too anxiety-triggering, but there's also a slight excitement at the disbelief that *this* is my life now.

Billy, the driver, steps out and, like a well-practiced machine, he opens the back door, gesturing toward the darkened cabin.

The first time he did this, I almost shit myself.

The second time, it was just as scary, but I knew it wouldn't result in anything fatal, such as my dead body being tossed into a dumpster.

The third time, I felt less afraid and was able to say, "Hi, Billy," which has become my usual greeting.

Like every other time since then, he grunts his reply, but his lips twitch, telling me he's okay with my acknowledgement. I figure, make friends with the driver because if this ever does go south, he'll be the one to drive me far away and leave my body somewhere no one will find me. The other month, one of my literature classes studied the original tale of Snow White, and I suppose her plan inspired mine.

Billy shuts the car door behind me, confining me in the dark back seat. The only light present comes from the streetlights and the glow of my cellphone, which I use to keep my mind busy during the hour-long drive, mindful that, upon arrival, I'll need to shut it off. My host is a tad paranoid about people hacking phones and listening in on conversations.

I play along, because it's how the rich think, and it's not like I ever had the opportunity to know if it's a thing or not—being as I didn't grow up wealthy. That, and because he's paying for my education, living arrangements, and other bills, funding my aunt's centre, and oh, because I'm terrified of him.

So, why do I go? Why am I leaning back against the rich, textured leather of the vehicle, sighing as I stare out at the town? Because I'm scared of what happens if I say no. We've always lived two different lives, and while I'm grateful for his new place in mine, I'm too petrified to test what will happen if I turn him down. So far, it's been fine—new and weird, but fine.

Even a little bit nice. If this works out for the best, he may be able to take away some of the loneliness in my life. It'll be enjoyable to have someone else in my life. Someone to just listen as I talk, and maybe spend time with outside these dinners.

They say blood is thicker than water, so I can only hope he believes the sentiments behind the phrase as well.

After a while, I glance up from my phone, noting how the town's lights have faded away, leaving behind the dark walls of trees lining the highway. Our destination is Cortville, the city nearest Bridgetown—also known as, home. Or, more specifically, outside of the city, because it's the only area a house the size of his has the land for, while still remaining near the city and his company's downtown office.

With Billy's approach to the mansion's property, the two wrought iron gates, ones the height of my townhouse, creak and slowly open, allowing us passage into the otherworld—a place no mere mortal goes, simply because they cannot afford it.

He claims the company is a multi-million-dollar business, and when he inherited it, he got everything that went along with an income of that magnitude, such as this house and the land it occupies. I've never inquired further, because it's not exactly something you come out and ask a newcomer in your life.

Billy continues up the long driveway, past the perfectly manicured lawns, past the fountain I'm sure is the size of a coffee shop, and parks in front of the grand entranceway, less than ten feet away from a staircase belonging outside Cinderella's castle.

I lock a deep breath in my lungs, knowing it'll be the only one I take for the rest of the night as I sit uncomfortably on the edge of knives, waiting for the truth to be revealed. It's *bound* to be divulged eventually. It's not that I want to think badly of him and the improving financial situation he's gifting me, but it's strange how he's known about me for a while but is choosing only now to reconnect. Or... connect, since I never met him before. For Aunt Jolene's sake and my own self-preservation, I smile and nod, and wait for him to eventually disclose if there's a more sinister purpose for bringing me into his life or if it's simply what he's claiming—to try to resolve old mistakes.

Billy immediately climbs from the driver's seat and comes around to my door. I learned on day one, only Billy opens the vehicle's doors. Not me, even if I'm not helpless like his staff assumes I am. As I climb out, steadying myself on the rich cobblestone, Billy's attention drops to my hand.

"It's already off and inside my clutch." I hold up the tiny purse.

It only took two visits before he had Billy stop checking my phone. Two visits for him to trust me, but this is coming from the guy who believes my phone may be listening in on our non-secretive and boring, all-about-life conversations. Yet another fact I lodge away for another day; another piece I'll use to crack the case of what is happening in my life.

"Very good, Miss Miller."

Pretty sure I've only been referred as that by, like, professors and such. I'm not an elite person, and no matter how hard I try, no one here calls me by my first name.

"Natalie!"

Except him.

I smile, his joyous tone wiping away all the previous worries. Like usual, my concerns seem to only exist during the car ride here, and then later, when Billy takes me home. Once I'm in his soothing presence, nothing else matters. So what if all this is a bit sketchy, strange, and even eccentric? There's no concrete proof of anything menacing, therefore I have no actual reason to fear him. Not when he's simply being a good guy.

A good brother.

Alex Miller, my never-known-about-until-two-months-ago biological brother, skips down the dozen steps and is by my side quickly. Despite wearing a suit that belongs in a boardroom, boyish charm rolls off him, and it's instantly energizing, uncoiling my nerves and easing my tightened back muscles with his beaming expression.

Billy steps back against the car, his attention lowering to his feet. "Sir," he greets, but Alex ignores him and stretches his hand toward me.

"Good drive here?"

Maybe it's fear. Maybe it's respect. Perhaps a bit of yearning to be cared for. Either way, I lay my palm in Alex's waiting hand and allow him to lead me up the stone steps, and through the double glass doors that are propped open and waiting for us to enter.

If I'm honest with myself, the entryway doors are my favourite element of this house because of what they represent—as though anything is possible once you broach them. They stand taller than two normal-sized doors stacked on top one another, resulting in me feeling even smaller than I am. They're entirely made of glass, with black iron filigree between the panes.

Aunt Jolene tried to give me a good life, but given her career, it was only enough to sustain herself. She never counted on the addition of me in her life, so money was tight for a while. The second I was of a suitable age to be hired, I began working my first part-time job in the evenings and on weekends to help with the house's finances and save whatever free cent I could for university. Jolene always wanted me to attend and make something of myself so I won't struggle when I'm older.

When you own a house like Alex's, with doors like these, it screams wealth, and wealth means anything is possible. The world becomes bigger when you have the money to afford more, and Alex can *clearly* afford everything.

Jealousy gave me a splitting headache the first time I came here because I should have had access to this lifestyle, and not have had to place extra stress on Jolene, but after one dinner with Alex, I decided my life was better than his. As elaborate and lovely as his existence is, it's too distanced from the rest of the world—figuratively speaking.

While this may seem like *the* life, it's not for me. This is a world where wearing a dress and heels for a nice Friday night dinner with your brother is normal. Where staff wait on you hand and foot. Where trying to put your own plate away gets you reprimanded. Where climbing in and out of the car isn't allowed until the door is opened for you.

If I was raised in this life, I'd be an entirely different person—rich, spoiled, and probably more worried about making it to my nail appointment than finishing an essay assignment. The distaste this possibility brings causes me to shudder.

Alex leads me down the silent hallway, past the sitting room, the piano room, the hallway that eventually connects with the kitchen, and into the dining room. Before Alex, I believed dining rooms to be only a room attached to kitchens. Here, it's a separate room with a table that can easily seat at least fifty people. Candles line the centre of the table, stretching up to the two place settings at one end.

"You know," I call out, "I'm fine eating at a smaller table. This is a lot of work for your staff to set up." Not even counting the electricity bill he's paying to light this entire room for nothing.

Alex scoffs, continuing to our places. "You're cute, Natalie. You need to get used to the better life. One day soon, this could also be your home."

Interest. Piqued. "Yeah?" I squeak, surprised he's finally giving me a hint of what he sees our future as being.

He says nothing more and pulls out my chair. My hand swoops

beneath my bottom, ensuring my dress is tucked properly for when I sit. He pushes in the chair and then takes his own seat.

Staff are immediately by the table, pouring red wine into our glasses. This is one of the best parts of the evening. When Aunt Jolene would buy wine, it was the cheap, grocery store kind, and it was usually only to celebrate something. I never enjoyed the taste though—too bitter—but the stuff Alex serves is plain magic. It must be from another world entirely and I take a large sip, uncaring if it's improper etiquette.

His attentive gaze watches my large gulp, but he says nothing and leans back against the chair. "Natalie, how was your week?"

His question forces me to put the glass back in its place on the shiny tabletop. "It was good."

"Do anything fun?"

I shrug. "Fun and me don't really get along. I mainly studied and watched TV."

"Hmm." Alex's hand comes up and props his chin. His eyes scan me—study me, is more like it—and under the weight of his scrutiny, I wither into the padded chair.

I'm not pretty by any means. Not like the women he brings around here, I'm sure. My plain, brown hair falls limp down my back, the curls I spent an hour meticulously creating are already unraveling. The power behind perfectly, natural straightened hair is a curse at times. I'm average height, taller with these three-inch heels clasped to my feet. My dress is simple, cheap, mid-thigh length, and plays nicely with the additional weight I can never seem to get rid of—I think, anyway. My face is done with minimal makeup, enough to heighten my features, but nothing over-the-top or unnatural.

Alex is classically handsome. His dark hair remains trimmed to the top of his head, his facial features similar to mine, but much more symmetrical. No stress mars his face. Up close, you spot the similarities in our appearances, but in times like now, it's obvious we've had entirely different lifestyles.

Self-conscious under the weight of his stare, I touch the tips of my hair. "What?"

"Next Friday, I was thinking we could do something different than our usual dinner. I'd like to host a party in your honour."

"A party?" The word comes out more like a surprised squeak than I mean it to. "Like... here?"

"Where else?" His lips curl into a polite smirk—not mocking, just amused. "I'd like to introduce you to influential people. Business partners, and the like. You know how it goes."

More people in his life. I straighten, dropping my hands in my lap, and murmur, "I guess it could be fun." My fingers knot together, so I don't rub at my skin where my nerves are making it itch.

His eyes, brown like mine, sparkle under the candlelight, telling me he believes my lie. "Good. I know this is overwhelming, Natalie, but I do want to give you everything you're owed. Helping Jolene, your housing situation, and paying for your education is only a fraction of what you deserve. I also have personal and political connections I can share with you. I want you in my life completely. I want my colleagues to meet the sister I continue to mention in my calls." He smiles. "I can further your future in ways you won't even believe. Plus," his hand falls from his chin, "I'd like you to meet my girlfriend."

I jerk at the new fact about himself he's sharing. "You have a girlfriend?"

"Oh yes. Teagan. We've been together since high school."

Huh. He's never mentioned her before. A relationship that's been going on for that long would have been mentioned to me sooner, no?

Stop second-guessing him. Maybe he simply needed to ensure you're trustworthy before he opens more of his life to you.

I realize then, that while this entire time I've been believing Alex has sinister purposes behind all his generosity, he's likely as nervous about me being in his life as I am of his.

Alex places his glass back down, his playful glint dropping and darkening his expression. "I'm sorry for everything in the past. Our parents weren't the wisest people, to say the least, and I *am* trying to make up for lost time. For what Mom took from you and what Dad should have given you. A family. Mental and financial well-being."

Aunt Jolene, being my mother's older sister, told me what she knew when I was old enough to understand, which unfortunately isn't much. About a year after my birth, my mother arrived on Jolene's doorstep, begging her to take me in and raise me as her own. Jolene agreed, though with a lot of questions that went unanswered. Then after my mother delivered me, cops found her strangled to death in a forest, some miles out.

Jolene said there was never evidence as to who the culprit was, which I found weird, considering DNA should have proved who did it. Ten-year-old me researched everything I could about the case, but came up empty. Police labelled it as a cold case and closed it. Perhaps it's what got me into crime dramas. On TV, there's always a bad guy who gets caught, but in real life, the bad guys get away.

Jolene never informed me who my father was though, no matter how many times I begged her to. She said it was better I didn't know, since he never wanted me, and though her answers only created more questions, I didn't dig any deeper, not having the means to learn the truth. By the time I was twelve and understood the struggles Jolene had been experiencing to care for me—the extra shifts, the second job, the long hours, and sleepless nights—I didn't want to toss her generosity and love in her face all to chase a ghost of my past. Children are raised without both parents all the time—and in cases like mine, no parents—and they turn out fine. Therefore, I'm no different. My past didn't want to find me, so there's no point in seeking it out.

Until Alex sent that obscure message, and upon arrival to the designated meet-up spot—here—I found a brother I never knew I had and a history more interesting than I could have ever imagined.

Our father was a ruthless businessman who grew his company from the ground up, starting it back when he was our age, before pulling from the company and retiring in Newton to become a principal at the high school. Which is so fucking *random*, but okay. Alex claims the company went under some bad press, so our father took a break. Our parents had Alex, and less than a year later, me. But our father never wanted a daughter, apparently, and our mom knew that so she ran away with me.

Alex found me a year after our father died. I have yet to visit his grave, and I'm not sure I ever will. Jolene is my family, and now Alex. I've spent most of my life without a father, so there's no reason to visit the man who created me.

"I know." I smile softly at Alex, recalling his last words about caring for me.

"So, the party?" he probes.

"Sounds nice." *Sounds horrible.* Parties and I do not get along, but if Alex wants to continue to mend fences in the only way he knows how, then I'll suck up being awkward for the night and buy a fancy dress.

Ever since Alex came into my life, not only did he buy me a townhouse to get me out of the dorms, pay for Jolene's care, but he's also kept my bank account padded. At first, I wasn't sure how I felt about it, but in the end, it allowed me to quit my job and focus on my grades, since working and going to school is challenging to do at the same time. With his money, buying a dress that will allow me to fit in with his crowd will be simple.

"I'll send over my personal shopper."

"Oh, no," I counter, "I can buy it with—"

"Nonsense," he cuts me off, slashing his hand in the air. "I'll be sure she knows to dress you appropriately."

"But... okay." Rule number one when dealing with near-strangers: don't fight them. I'm sure I'm being dramatic and Alex would never hurt me, but I've only known him a whopping two months, so I don't truly *know* him. Not really; not past what he's shown me.

Alex smiles, his teeth blindingly bright against the dimly lit room. "Good. Now then, are you hungry?" Without waiting for a response, he flicks his fingers.

Although we're the only ones in the dining room—or at least, that I can see—two people come forward, each carrying trays. They're rested in front of Alex and me before the covers are lifted, revealing a perfectly cooked steak, crisp green vegetables, and roasted potatoes. Steam drifts from each freshly prepared item, somehow perfectly timed for when Alex randomly demanded food.

I'd love to know how they managed to accomplish this feat.

"Enjoy, Nat."

Nat.

I pause, the fork pinched between two fingers. He's never referred to me by using a nickname before... but I don't really mind it. It makes me feel wanted. Appreciated.

Less lonely.

Like parties, relationships and I have a difficult time. Romantic, family—clearly—friendships... Perhaps I'm too awkward. Perhaps I don't say the correct things at the right times. Whatever the reason, I spend ninety-nine percent of my time alone or surrounded with strangers whose gazes pass over me as though I'm not there at all.

Maybe I simply need to breathe more. Maybe, despite the weird, unnerving twist at the base of my stomach, Alex is simply a stand-up guy with a lot of money and he's truly trying to make up for lost time.

Maybe I should stop freaking out and allow our relationship to expand in the ways he's aiming to build it.

Maybe having a brother will be a good thing.

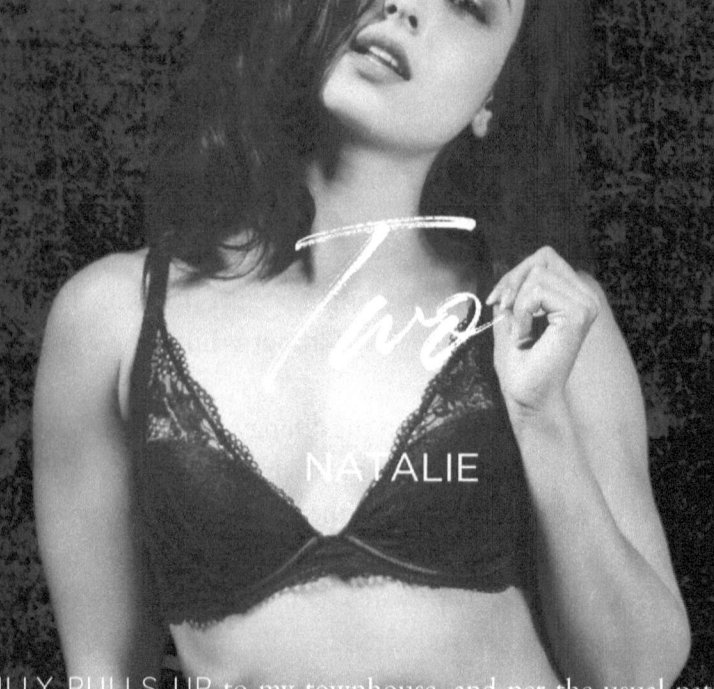

Two

NATALIE

BILLY PULLS UP to my townhouse, and per the usual pattern, he opens my door for me. I take his hand, using him to lift me out from the low vehicle, and once I'm situated on two shaky legs—*damn tasty wine*—I release him, taking a step toward my house.

My ankle wobbles, and for the briefest second, I'm looking at the cement sidewalk through fuzzy eyes.

"Whoa, there, Miss Miller. How about I walk you to the door at least?"

I blink, noting I'm right way up again, and the clamp around my elbow is the only thing keeping me from teetering. "I think that might be best. Thanks, Billy."

"Your safety is a priority. Your keys please."

Boy, that sounds like something recited. I roll my eyes, unknown to him since his back is to me as he gets to unlocking my front door.

As he helps me through the entranceway, he says, "I suggest you take your shoes off, Miss Miller. You don't want to have an accident."

"Smart." With the help of his steady hand, I manage to kick them off in the most undignified manner, knowing the price of these things have probably just killed me twice over for treating them as such.

Before Alex, I didn't own heels, and the lady at the shop continued to go on about the quality of high-priced stilettos versus cheap ones, so they're the only thing I've splurged on with Alex's money.

"Have a good night. Be safe," is the final thing he says before shutting the door and leaving.

With the strength of the wall, I manage to switch the lock on the door before limping upstairs and toward my bedroom, falling face-first on my bed. I should get undressed, wash my face, and even charge my phone, but that wine is too powerful for my own good. When it tastes as delicious as it does, it's hard to stop at one glass. Or even two. Or three.

Note to self: ask Alex to cut me off after two next Friday. With a party full of, however many people he's planning on inviting, I'd rather have all my inhibitions.

And with that thought, I welcome the darkness, passing out until late morning the next day.

ONE OF THE greatest relationships I do have is with Alex's expensive wine because I wake up hangover-free. Unfortunately, evidence from last night is strewn all over my bedspread. I rub at the burgundy lipstick stains, cursing myself for wearing something so dark. All my touching has merely spread the red, creating a blotchy mess overtop the lavender comforter. Scowling, I strip the bed, thanking Alex once again for the townhouse, and more importantly, the washer and dryer down the hall. I ball the comforter up and as I turn away, at the last moment, something on my pillow catches my eye.

A folded-up piece of paper, and something that *definitely* wasn't there yesterday.

I drop the blanket, stepping around it and reaching for the note, my mind scrolling over the endless possibilities of what this could be. I unfold the paper, finding a messily written message that electrocutes my nerves into flurried action.

You're beautiful, Natalie Miller. Watching you sleep will soon become my favourite activity.

The message falls from my hand as I spin, eyes darting to every corner of my room. The windows were closed throughout the night, but I never bother locking them because unless someone is scaling the side of my house, there's no way to climb through them. Downstairs? I locked the front door before bed, and I don't ever open any other windows.

Who the hell was here? My gaze falls to the paper at my feet. The writing is unrecognizable, but then, the chances of me recognizing someone's handwriting is slim.

Alex? Other than Elena, he's the only one who knows where I live. The message referred to me by name, so whoever it is knows exactly who I am.

A fact that has my stomach bottoming out and fear climbing my throat with the worst taste possible. A faceless, nameless stranger knows where I live, who I am, and according to the note, was *here* while I was asleep.

What the fuck do I do? I could report this to the police, but there's no proof in one note, and they'll likely pass it off as a prank.

A prank. I snort, crouching to lift the paper up again, only to crumple it and toss it in the garbage can in the corner. That's all this is. A prank. A prank won't be stopping the day I have planned out. Once I put the comforter in the wash, I'm heading to the school's library to get some research and outlining completed for an upcoming essay.

This is fine. Completely fine. Everything will be okay.

After taking care of my comforter, showering, and getting ready, I grab my laptop and cell, shove them into my bag, and head down the road to the university.

I'm struck with the same wonder I do every time I approach campus. History seeps from between the grey stones, stacked a million high to make up the main building. Around it, smaller ones circle it, each housing lecture halls, science labs, professors' offices, or other school administration offices. I turn left, heading for a building on the edge of campus.

The bones of this one is as old as the others, but in recent years, they have remodelled the building with glass walls. I believe it's the university's way of making studying less dreary and the whole place less jail-like.

Before entering, I survey the street around me, scouting for a cop car.

Again, maybe it's simply because I watch too many crime dramas, but ever since the other day when Elena warned me away from whoever it was hanging around, I've been cautious. At first, I believed she was joking, but the seriousness in her tone said otherwise.

Then the next day, he appeared outside my classroom. He might have been looking for her, but I gave him my back and allowed myself to be swallowed by the crowd of other students, taking the long way to my next class, just in case.

When I see no one sketchy hanging around, I enter the library.

Three

TRISTAN

NATALIE WALKS THROUGH THE UNIVERSITY CAMPUS' gates and beelines straight for the library. My lips twitch in amusement, watching her approach the glass building. I can sense her eagerness, even from here.

At the doorway, she stops and scans the area around her, but she won't find what she's looking for.

Ever since Elena spoke to her that one day, she consistently fears I'll be around, so I needed to shift my plans. She thinks I've left her alone, when all I've really done is park my cruiser down the street, the opposite way she walks to the school, and hide in the shadows.

Even on the weekend, Little Bird remains studious and focused.

It's cute, and I suppose a part of me envies her. In high school, I didn't love any one subject, but I also didn't hate them. I didn't ace my courses, but I also didn't ever fail any of them either. I averaged B and C grades. Witnessing Natalie be able to focus for hours on a particular assignment, and then move to a new location and pick up exactly where she left off, continuing to work for the better part of a day is something quite amazing. With her focus, she'll no doubt exceed in whatever it is she's planning on doing with her life. It dawns on me then, I'm unaware of her degree, and suddenly, I want to know it.

In time, she'll tell me.

For now, I turn away and head back to my car. The nice thing about being an officer in a small town is that no one bats an eye when you drive your cruiser on days off, and with Natalie occupied for hours, I lead the vehicle out of town and toward my heart, making it there in record time.

I stride through the front entrance, stopping briefly at the front desk to jot my name down on the clipboard they use to track visitors.

Zelda, the aged receptionist, turns around. "Tristan, nice to see you. We weren't expecting a visit from you this week."

"Slow Saturday. Plans change."

"Fair enough." She waves her hand toward the hallway I'm already heading down. "Have a nice visit. She's had a good week."

"I'm pleased." I smile before moving past the desk and take the trip I've done so many times before, walking the familiar hallway I've practically grown-up in.

At the end of the hallway, her door is propped open a few inches, so I knock lightly, peeking my head in between the space.

"Cheryl?"

Mom.

From the closet's darkness, I can see Mommy still on my bed, her legs spread, blood dripping down one of them. Instead of checking on her, I crawl deeper in the shadows, wishing those men never came.

Her screams went on for so long, and I still hear them in my head. Finding the farthest corner, I bend my legs and drop my head on my knees, wrapping my arms around myself until the memories of her screaming passes.

My mother raises her head from the puzzle she's focusing on at the small table across the room. Her eyes take a moment to focus before—

"Tommy, what brings you here?"

17

"I had some free time and thought you earned a visit."

Mom pushes away from the table and comes toward me, a smirk lifting her wrinkled mouth. "*Earned?* Big bro, between the two of us, you were always the one who were more of a troublemaker. If there's anyone who needs to be earning anything..." She trails off as she approaches and lifts her skinny arms up.

As always, her reference to me being her brother—to being Uncle Tommy—is a firm kick to the gut. After all this time of pretending, it's never gotten easier.

Her body is swallowed up in my arms, her feet lifting off the ground. It becomes the moment I know I can't feel guilty for doing what I am to Natalie. Whether she's aware of her brother's extra activities or not, it doesn't change what he's doing. What his actions can do to a family. I doubt he's thinking about these women's families at all, as he's slicing into them.

I breathe in her scent—the scent of home, even if she hasn't been it for a long time. Uncle Tommy and Aunt Lisa raised me, gave me everything I could ever ask for; they really stepped up to be there for Mom and me, but there was always a major element missing from my life.

I release her, almost unwillingly, and step back, forcing the solemn thoughts back to where they emerged from. Mom doesn't know who I am, and doctors don't want us triggering painful memories by reminding her, so I put on my Tommy-face again and smile easily.

"Show me this puzzle you're doing."

Mom doesn't move, and her eyes scan me in ways only a mother can—calculating. Knowing. She may not remember me, but something inside her—some deep-buried facet of her biology and instincts recall motherhood—and it's times like these it's so obvious.

Her lips purse as she continues her examination of me. "What's wrong with you, Tommy? You seem... troubled. Like your brain is somewhere else."

"I'm fine."

I'm not. Of course my brain is elsewhere. It's asking all the questions I wish I could out loud.

Why can't you remember who I truly am?

Why can't you overcome one dark moment in your history to have a brighter future?

Why is your mind content to remain in a facility its entire life when it could be experiencing more?

Why did those scumbags break in and steal you away from me?

Why do filth like them and Alex Miller get to live their happy lives when you're stuck in a lie?

Where the fuck is Alex keeping these women and why is no one else searching for them?

Her eyes narrow again, but she takes a step backward. "Fine. Don't think you're fooling me, Tommy. But if you don't want to talk, so be it."

It's more I can't *tell you. Not I don't want to.*

I follow her toward the small wooden table she was seated at and pull up the only other free chair. Seated, I scan the partially-completed puzzle of a cat hiding in a teapot.

"Cute," I comment.

"Help me finish?"

"Of course." I glance at the time on my phone, doing a quick mental calculation of how long it'll take me to get back home. No doubt Natalie will be in the library for a long time.

Mom picks up a piece before scanning the puzzle, searching for its rightful spot. Watching the determination on her face has me biting down on a chuckle. But it's the warmth inside my chest reminding me why I'm here.

Why I'm doing any of this.

No child deserves to hide inside a closet and be forced to watch their future get yanked away. I refuse to allow more children like me be affected by Miller's cruel, selfish, and evil acts.

FROM THE PARK across the street, I appear like a casual onlooker relaxing on the bench, watching the world and people pass by. But behind my shaded sunglasses, my gaze stalks the woman walking down the street. Her hands are fisted around the bag on her shoulder, while her head remains down, hair blocking her face from view as she returns home from the library.

Oh, Little Bird. If you only knew how close I am to you.

Natalie approaches her front door before unlocking it and taking a quick scan of the area. I drop my head, appearing to be staring off elsewhere until she enters the townhouse.

With the sun still up, I won't approach until later, and I can't wait for our date. The message I left her last night worked perfectly, but I'll need to do more to get her running to Alex. With it, I created fear, but now it's time to up the ante.

The alarm on my phone pings, reminding me I'm late for Ryker's impromptu meeting, so I leave the bench and head toward my car.

The one thing I'll never admit to Ryker is that having Natalie as my mark is no challenge. She may be a job, but she's a fucking gorgeous one at that. She hides underneath baggy sweatshirts and leggings, but it's what she chooses to wear that makes her so lovely. Other women insist on doing themselves up in immaculate clothing and a heavy layer of makeup, but not Natalie.

Fortunately for me, it seems her beauty is skipped over. I've been watching her every day, and no one seems to look twice at her. It's a damn shame. She's a shadow passing through the crowds, unnoticed, as guys chase the skinny, fake girls instead.

I let myself into Hawke's house with the key he's given each of us, and then head down the stairs into the unfinished basement we've been using to meet in. It's safe and private, making it an ideal location to store any documents and files we dig up on Miller.

"Finally," Ryker comments from his seat at the end of the table. Perched on his lap, Elena sits, facing away from the rest of the room. With my entrance, Ryker returns his attention to her.

I take a chair at the opposite end of the table, observing them for a moment. He's been obsessed with her since high school, and fuck, I knew they'd eventually end up together. It was only a matter of time their fucked-up story got the proper fairy-tale ending they deserved, even if it took Ryker going to prison to do it.

Elena and Ryker are two people that just *work*. Not sure why, but they do.

They're happy, and it's all that matters. I haven't had a relationship in a while, and though I have nothing against them, I refuse to get into one until Alex is behind bars. After all, how do I tell a woman I'll be late for our date since I'm busy stalking my Little Bird?

Natalie.

Fucking beautiful.

She seems so damned innocent, I wonder if she's a virgin.

And then I ask myself why I care? Why watching her has not only my cock stirring, but also heat pooling in my stomach?

"Learn anything yet?" Brent asks from the other side of the table. His arms are folded over his chest, chair kicked back. Paired with his blond hair and blue eyes, he's the golden boy of the group—and one of many reasons he was chosen for Elena.

Kudos to him for being able to still be in the same room as them. There's being able to separate your emotions, and then there's what he's doing. Considering he spent years fake-dating Elena, I'd think emotions would have gotten tied-up in there somewhere. Yet he's now able to look at both her and Ryker as though their past doesn't matter.

When I claim a woman as mine, she's mine and no one else's. I'd never be able to do what he did.

"No. Elena has made my job a bit more challenging." I flick my attention at her turned back, jutting my chin even though she can't see me.

The speed she twists around throws her hair into Ryker's face. "I did what?" Her tone raises to a screeching level that has Brent flinching from across the table.

God, she was more fun when Ryker was fucking over her life.

"You told Natalie to stay away from me. That I'm a bad man. When she sees me, she turns away, so I had to take it a step further."

Elena stands, her body going into a protective stance. Cute. "What is 'a step further?'"

"Dolly," Ryker rumbles, reaching his hand out toward her wrist. "We've talked about this."

She shakes him off, her attention remaining firmly on me. "Tristan, I swear, do not hurt her." She straightens out of attack mode, backing up a step until her legs touch Ryker again. "I'm sorry, but she's a good person. Innocent."

"We don't know that yet," Hawke chimes in from his corner. Being the newest in our group, and as quiet as he is, I often forget he's even here. "Tristan, keep it up. The sooner we know anything, the quicker we can end this. Just don't tell us what you're doing, so no pointless fights begin. How 'bout we leave it at that?"

"Deal." Focusing my concentration on Elena, I add, "I won't hurt her. Elena, you should know better than anyone how we like to play with our toys. She will lead us to the monster, you can trust me on that."

With those words swirling around the basement and shutting Elena up, I leave, skin tingling in anticipation at seeing my Little Bird again.

If Natalie thinks I'm stopping at the one message, she's insane. I'm fixing her brother's mistakes, starting with her. One whimper at a time, I'll make her beg for a reprieve, but never give in.

Alex Miller is no better than the fucker who hurt Mom. It's men like him who leave children without a mother and a lifetime of nightmares. How many of the women Alex trapped have had their minds snapped? No one was there to help them tape the cracks back together before he reaped their lives.

Alex will die for his sins. But first, it's time to play with his sister.

Four

NATALIE

NOT ONLY DID I complete my research and outline, I also wrote my introduction, so when I get home from the library in the evening, I'm feeling accomplished.

I triple-check my door this time, hating how simply standing in the entranceway has me second-guessing coming home at all. Prank or not, they got into my *house*, and that's fucked up.

My phone buzzes in that second, taking me away from my partial debate, as I glance down.

ALEX

It was good to see you yesterday. I'm sorry if I seemed a bit excited about the party, but it'll be nice to spend time with you outside weekly dinners.

ME

I agree. It's okay.

My fingers hesitate over the screen, and I wonder if my next words are forcing too much fake-excitement, but it'll show him I'm trying too. I type,

I'm looking forward to it too.

Friday night will be thrilling in new ways. I feel it inside me somehow. With no friends, other than Elena Sparks, my social life is abysmal at best. As for Elena, she and I are barely friends. Just people who occasionally hang out on campus or in the evening.

It's like neither of us are willing to refer to what we have as being an actual friendship.

Friday night could be the start of something, like Alex is promising.

I climb the stairs, taking careful steps to look around every corner, every dark room, inspecting and despising the need to even be doing this. Times like this remind me how alone I am—vulnerable and waiting for something bad to happen.

When I make it to my bedroom, relief is instant when I find nothing. A whoosh of breath releases from my lungs with the knowledge that, for now, I'm safe. It's enough of a reprieve I'm able to grab a quick snack before bed, and sleep with both eyes shut.

WHY THE HELL *did I chug water before bed?* I mentally grumble, sliding from the cozy blankets and heading for the bathroom down the hall. Sleep cakes my eyes, but memory guides my body to where it needs to go.

When I return to the bedroom, my feet come to a faltering stop. Despite my half-asleep senses, the air feels different. Thicker. My skin tingles in awareness and I rub my fists against my eyes to rid them of sleep. I rapidly blink, ensuring I'm alert to fight whatever crazy my brain is currently cooking up.

Everything in my room is the same; nothing amiss. Clearly, I need more sleep. A deep breath works its way through my lungs, sucking in the air that still feels different, and I stalk to my bedside table, tapping on the screen of my phone.

Three in the morning.

Creak.

This house doesn't creak. Alex made sure I got a townhouse built within the last couple of years, so there would be minimal maintenance issues.

Someone is here.

In the silence of the room, nothing indicates that fact. Nothing but the sound of blood rushing to my ears and my own heart pounding so hard it'll break through my skin shortly if it doesn't calm down. I grasp my cell, aware it's my only form of communication and assistance, if this goes south.

"Hello?" I call out.

No answer. Which, why would they talk and make themselves known?

If someone's even here.

No, someone is definitely *here.* With their arrival, they've changed the air. Electrified it with their presence, and my house was warning me the entire time.

Since I despise morning wake-ups by the sun, I invested in blackout curtains, and now, having them shut means not even the moonlight shines in, giving me zero light. I'm blind in the darkness, requiring me to switch on a light.

This could be to my benefit since he won't see me reaching for my lamp.

I inch to the right, stretching my arm out for the hanging string, hoping I don't swing it to hit against the lamp post. When my fingers make purchase and tug on the chain, I huff in relief.

Nothing happens. No light basks the room.

What the fuck?

I tug again, this time rougher.

"Little Bird, that was cute."

Oh my God.

My body dies, freezes, stops working—all of the above. It's the only explanation for the voice in my room. I'm dead, and it's all in my head. But then warm breath coasts along my bare neck, reminding me that I'm in panties and a tank, no bra, and completely exposed to whoever this creep is.

None of this is in my head. There's someone actually here. I straighten from my attempt to switch on the lamp, feeling the smooth chill of leather, I think, brushing my arms.

"The lamp. I unplugged it."

"Wh-what do you want?" I'm thankful he's—the voice is way too deep to be a female's—behind me and can't see the blatant fear from my expression. The way my eyes shut tightly and re-open, praying he'll be gone by the time they open. Or the way my throat moves painfully over the large lump lodged in there. Or even how my hands curl at my sides.

"What do I want?" Amusement coats his words.

"That's what I asked." I bite my tongue, hoping he doesn't take my comment as rude. My appreciation for crime shows and documentaries suddenly becomes extremely useful.

Lesson one: Never piss off the bad guy. It doesn't end well.

"I'm here for you, of course." His breath ghosts over the back of my neck, followed by his touch. His finger strokes the skin there, lifting my hair out of its way, and coming around to my neck bone. I twist my head, aiming to look at him, but he steps behind me once again.

He's not wearing a face covering, or else he'd wouldn't be scared to stand in front of me, knowing my eyes will eventually be able to see through the darkness, allowing me the ability to pick apart his features. I scroll through anyone I know, specifically recalling any male staff I've heard at Alex's house, but no one's voice sounds like this one. It reminds me of that chocolate syrup for ice cream, the one that hardens nearly instantly. Rough and hard but velvety and smooth beneath the surface.

"After all, I never introduced myself."

"You wrote the message," I deduce, the words coming out strained. Who else would happen to write me a creepy note and then also enter my room in the middle of the night? I'd have to have *really* shitty luck for that to have been two different people.

"I did." He chuckles, and it's pleasant. Not like a serial killer's laugh. I want to allow it to ease me, but logic has me continuing to play with the edges of my shirt as anxiety works its way through my body.

"Are you here to hurt me?"

"That depends."

Oh, God. No please. I roll my lips together, forcing air through my quivering body. "On?"

"On how well you behave, Little Bird."

"Little Bird." My intruder is giving me a nickname. Nicknames mean he's interested, which could be good for my life; he won't kill me. I think. "Why are you calling me that?"

"It's what you are. You're a small, terrified bird stuck in a birdcage."

"Would that make you the cat?"

"Very good." I can hear the smile in his voice. "We need to get to the finish line together. During this game, you can either play along or fly helpless through the streets. A fair warning, either scenario will see me as the victor."

A game. That's all this is. But he's right about one thing. I'll play along—I'll use his own words and give him the responses he so clearly wants.

"Then why should I play?"

"Because how we get to the finish line matters."

Spoken like a true crazy person.

"And if I go to the cops? Trespassing, threatening, stalking, breaking and entering are just a few of the charges you'd have against you."

"Would they believe you? You have no proof of me being here. You could have written the note yourself."

Fuck, he's right. But I won't tell him that. Instead, I keep my mouth clamped before I say anything else that will backfire on me.

"Besides, you'll come to love this game very soon."

"I very much doubt that." This time, I allow my tone to come across as snarky.

"We'll see," he murmurs in my ear. With my eyes focused on the wall across from us, waiting him out until he leaves, hopefully sooner rather than later, I don't feel the soft touch until a line of heat shoots itself down to my core. His fingers trail along my shoulder, following the path to the curve of my breasts before stopping on a nipple.

His thumb strokes once, then twice over my tank, and by the third pass, my nipple is a hard bud. *Why does this feel good?* Being touched by the stranger who broke into my home should *not* feel like this.

"I-it's biology," I counter, a stagger threatening my voice.

"Or," he purrs in my ear, "you like this. Your breathing is ragged. Your pulse, right here—" his tongue flicks out, swiping the spot, and I almost die from pleasure, "—is thumping erratically. It's a delicious sound, Little Bird. If I bite down, I bet you'd come from sheer excitement."

"It's called fear."

"Call it what you want, but your body certainly wasn't behaving like this moments ago. But if you don't believe me, we won't fight about it." Abruptly, his hand drops away from my body, taking the breath I was holding in with it and I nearly beg for his touch to return. "Yet."

The heat from his body grows fainter, and I hear his feet step away from me. He obviously wants me aware of his distance since he's already proven he can approach silently.

With his distance, anger pulses in my head, overtaking the pleasure because he's fucking right and, sadly, I can't deny it. I spin, ready to call him out on all his shit. But...

He's gone.

How the hell did he disappear so fast? I didn't hear anything. A scurry, a door closing—nothing. I go to the window, pushing aside the curtains and peering outside into the dark, but the streetlights give nothing away.

Quickly, I rush through the rest of my house, ensuring every window and door is shut and locked, and they all are, exactly as I had them earlier. *Weird.* And terrifying. If he can leave silently, it means he can also enter soundlessly, like he's already proven.

He claims he won't hurt me, but he doesn't tell me what he *does* want.

I tuck myself back into bed, pushing the blankets tightly around my body and creating a wall between me and the outdoors. A completely penetrable wall, but it makes my body relax enough to lie down.

But I don't sleep.

NATALIE

"NATTIE, YOU LOOK TIRED." Aunt Jolene pats my hand with her thin, frail one. Her cool skin still warms mine though. "School keeping you up at night?"

"Something like that." In reality, the complete stranger who's chosen to torture me is at fault for my sleepless night. After his exit, I didn't dare shut my eyes, in case he came back. He never did—was likely watching and saw I was still awake and stayed away. The very real possibility of it had me wanting to sew my curtains shut and hide in my closet for the rest of my life.

Irrational, I know. But the fucker invaded my life and *touched* me. Regardless of his claims that I enjoyed it, I didn't. I don't.

Liar.

My hands fist by my side as annoyance burns hot through me at the fact that his touch is the only action I've gotten in some time. Regardless of what books and movies portray, nerdy, chubby girls are *not* the ones the hot guys go for.

My visitor had the voice of a hot guy. Deep and baritone and...

Ugh, stop! No, I *can't* be thinking about his touch, or how damp he made my panties with his barely-there teases. I'm horny and that's all

31

there is to it. When the mood strikes, I dig out my vibrator, or if the craving is bad enough, an app to find a quick hookup. There are enough people in this town, who don't mind a girl with extra fat in certain areas, for a single night's activities at least. Either option will solve this new dilemma of feeling *anything* other than vicious hate toward my stalker.

"Get some sleep soon, okay?" Jolene's soft voice pulls me back to the present. "Either way, I'm happy you came for our visit."

"Of course." I smile. "It's Sunday and you know I always stop by on Sundays."

"Still, it's nice you make time for me."

She's always made time for me. A nurse approaches then, smiling at me and then Jolene. "Jolene, it's nearly lunchtime, if you'd like to come in soon?"

Aunt Jolene nods and stands, taking me in her arms. "I'll see you next Sunday, yeah?"

I wave and step back, giving the nurse plenty of room to take my spot and walk beside her. I wait until they're back inside the facility before letting myself out through the guest entrance's gate.

"Nice seeing you again." The door attendant tips his head as I pass through.

The employees at the mental health facility are angels, and seeing Jolene far more relaxed than she used to be makes me appreciate Alex's arrival in my life so much more.

A year ago, when she was driving home after work, she got into an accident and smashed into a pole. She told the police she blinked and lost focus for a moment, and after doctors started to throw out fancy medical terms and tests, ending with the summary of a heart disease commonly known to cause fainting and black-outs, they suspended her licence. With medication and care, she's fine but unable to live alone, in case it happens at time that could be more dangerous, like when she's climbing a staircase or cooking. With me at the university during the day, it was worth the price to have her live a facility with staff who can assist in her full-time care. The first one Jolene and I found wasn't nearly as nice as this one and had me working overtime to pay for my rent, tuition, living expenses, and her care.

Then Alex appeared in my life some few weeks ago and deemed the facility not up to standards and had her transferred to the best one in the area.

I scan the pretty gardens surrounding the glass building, noting the water fountain in the front by the entrance, and the various gardening staff currently working to maintain the oasis the residents adore spending so much time in. The nurses are sweet and caring, and Jolene's had extra pep since arriving, commenting about the various activities made available for the patients. Better yet, their visiting hour policy is fairly open—much better than the previous place—so seeing her last-minute is as simple as a quick phone call.

I can never be mad at Alex for the switch.

Ever since I told Jolene about Alex finding me, she hasn't said much about it, opting to remain tight-lipped. Even up to today, I'm unsure how she feels about him. She's never asked to meet him though, and he's never mentioned wanting to either, so for now, they each remain a part of my life, never crossing paths with one another.

My route home takes me by the police station. I stop in front of it for a moment and consider my stalker's words again. I could go in there and ask for... something. Something to protect me from the creep coming through my door—or window—or a fucking crack in the ceiling for all I know—but other than a crumpled-up piece of paper in my trashcan at home, I have no concrete proof. I doubt they'll be rushing to assist me when there's a possibility I'm wasting their time.

I grumble, despising the frustration burning at the base of my stomach and move on, continuing home.

On my doorstep, I hesitate before unlocking the door, gathering the courage I need before entering, hoping to find my space still *my* space—unblemished and uninterrupted.

Nothing seems amiss and everything is where I last had it. I then jog up the stairs to my bedroom, scanning the space and especially the bed for a message or anything of that nature.

There's nothing.

When I'm breathing easier, I go back downstairs and put on a movie to lose myself in for a few hours.

"MISS MILLER, *we need you to come down to Bridgetown General Hospital," the voice on the other end says.*

I halt mid-step, uncaring when other students bump into me, some grumbling at my abrupt stop. None of it matters, save for the hollowed-out feeling in my stomach. There's only one reason—one person—that would require me to go to the hospital.

"What happened?" I ask, voice pained, strained.

"Your aunt was in an accident."

My aunt. Accident. No. *She's the only family I have; the only person in my life. She's my everything, and I can't lose her.*

"I'll be right there," I manage to push out before hanging up and shoving through the crowd toward the building's main entrance.

I'm always punctual and have never skipped a class, but today could be exams for all I care and I'd still not attend. In the back of my mind, as I'm flinging open the front doors, I make a mental note to email my professors, apologizing and explaining the situation, but that'll be later, after I know what happened to my aunt.

For now, Jolene needs me.

I'm uncertain how I make it downtown so fast, but when I do, I immediately throw myself at the front counter of the ER's lobby, eyes frantically searching for the first available nurse.

"Hi, my name is Natalie Miller. I'm Jolene Conner's niece. I was called not too long ago to come down here. What happened?"

The nurse—Beth, I read from her nametag—flicks blonde bangs from her face and scans a paper in front of her. *"Ah, yes. Down the hall,"* she points, *"first right. Follow the other hall to room one-ten. Your aunt is there."*

"Thanks." I push off the counter and follow the nurse's directions, flying past all the doctors and nurses loitering in the hallway, going to and from the various rooms until I find the one numbered one-ten.

At the door to my aunt's room, I pause, gathering extra breath in my lungs before I rush too quickly into the unknown. The muscles in my neck remain tight and unyielding, so I step inside, later realizing this single step will change so much of my life.

A doctor stands by the bed, jotting something down on the clipboard he's holding. He glances up as I enter, his eyes doing a quick sweep of me before coming to the conclusion, *"You must be Natalie."*

My head nods—jerks, more like it—as I scan the middle-aged doctor, noting how the skin around his eyes isn't tight and his shoulders have a slight slump to them. He's relaxed. It's a good sign.

Then I finally allow myself to look toward the bed—toward where Aunt Jolene's life is single-handedly being decided. Cuts mar her face, lines of dried blood on her forehead and cheek, most noticeably. Other than that, she appears to be fine and sleeping.

"What happened?"

"She was in an accident. Her vehicle smashed into a pole, and thankfully, it took most of the hit. The police reported her car's air bags being deployed, so to be frank, they did save her life." He places the clipboard back in its slot at the end of her bed. *"Your aunt was awake when she was brought in and claimed to have a vague recollection of the moment. She said she remembers turning a corner, but nothing else after that."*

"She fainted?" I ask, horror coating my tone.

"Based on what she described, it sounds like a brief blackout." He

smiles kindly and steps by me, toward the door. "When she wakes, we will be conducting tests to determine the cause and possible frequency."

His steps take him to the doorway while his words register in my brain and I finally squeak out, "Frequency?"

The doctor stops and smiles again before tucking his hands inside his coat's pockets. "Miss Miller, a woman of your aunt's age doesn't simply blink and forget what she's doing or where she is, without there being an underlying issue. We will need to examine all possibilities. For now," his graze drifts toward the bed, "let her sleep. She has been given medication to ensure an undisturbed and painless sleep. I will be back in a bit to check on her."

"Thank you," I murmur before he walks off, leaving me to face my an unknown future.

With brick-heavy feet, I drag them toward Jolene's bedside, towing a chair closer to her. I slump into the hard plastic and lean over the edge of the bed, placing my hand overtop Jolene's. The temperature of her hand is a stark difference to mine, but beneath the chill, I'm thankful there's still life.

I sigh, scanning her sleeping form. Other than the cuts, she appears fine. But the doctors words ring in my head. Words about underlying issues and further testing, and I sigh again, this one long and drawn out.

"I'm happy you're okay," I whisper. "Don't leave me, Jolene. I don't know what I would do without you. You mean the world to me."

Of course she doesn't respond, but it doesn't stop me from repeating the words over and over until she eventually wakes up and we're given news of a diagnosis changing both our lives.

Six

NATALIE

DINNER AND TWO MOVIES LATER, I'm yawning. With it being Monday tomorrow, I have an early class in the morning, which means before Monday kicks my ass more than it already will, I shut everything down, check my doors and windows, and head up to my bedroom.

Holding my breath, I enter my room slowly. Perhaps I should sleep downstairs, but somehow, I think that would be worse. I flick the overhead light on, eyes continuing to scan the room at the same time.

Empty.

But then I spot it, on my pillow, and the simple, folded-up piece of paper lowers any sense of victory I was previously feeling.

He didn't go through the front door; I was downstairs the entire evening and would have heard it, which leaves the bedroom window as the only other likely way of entry. He could have Houdinied his way in, but it still doesn't change the fact that I need to figure out what the fuck he wants from me.

The only recent change in my life is Alex, and in the grander scheme of things, I don't know him that well. Alex is hiding something, I'm sure, like that girlfriend of his he's only recently mentioned. Considering the insignificant amount of time we've known one another, it's probable he feels the same cautiousness around me that I feel toward him and is keeping certain things to himself.

Is someone trying to get to *him*? Maybe this is about Alex, but not in the ways my mind initially jumped to. Although, with me being a part of his life for such a short time, it'd be more advantageous for them to target someone closer to him, like his girlfriend.

Whoever and *why*ever they're doing this, it doesn't rid the paper from my pillow, so with a long, ragged sigh, I step forward and lift it to read the scribbled message.

LITTLE BIRD, I'M SADDENED I'LL BE UNABLE TO COME TO YOU TONIGHT. OTHER DUTIES CALL, BUT DO NOT FRET BECAUSE I WILL BE BACK SOON. REST UP. I NEED YOU STRONG FOR OUR GAME.

I crumble the message in my fist. *He's fucking delusional.* This is two now and—my thoughts cut off, a brilliant idea slipping into place instead.

I uncrumple the paper and twist toward the garbage can in the corner where I tossed the other one. If he's going to keep sending them, I'll keep taking them, and soon, they'll be joining me for a trip downtown to the police station. Whoever this psycho is will not win, no matter what "game" he wants to play. With two messages as proof, maybe they'll believe me, at least enough to help in some way and monitor the street for him or something.

But as I tower over the small garbage can, I find it's empty.

That fucker. He's like a damn mind reader!

"Ugh!" I'm back to having only one note and debating whether or not to just go and see what the police say and/or do—if they'll laugh me out of the place or believe me. At this point, he'll never allow me to keep more than one note, so going in with the one is better than nothing. I tuck it inside my drawer, thankful for my closed curtains. Because even if he claims not to be around, why would I trust my psycho stalker, who's probably out buying what he needs to murder me with?

I shiver, turning away to prepare for bed. When I'm finally sliding underneath the blankets, I curse the fact that I have no tall bookshelf or dresser to place in front of the window, to block that possible entrance.

Besides, that's simply one *window out of several throughout the house.*

The moment my body gets settled into my familiar groove in the mattress, my eyes slide shut. The lack of sleep last night has one positive effect at least, and exhaustion quickly drags me under.

HIS TOUCH IS LIGHT, *tentative, pulling a small breathy moan from my lips. His fingers tighten, pinching my nipple to the point of pain, but tingles of pleasure soon overtake any ache. Apparently, I like it rough.*

"Seems like you're enjoying this. Yes?"

"Yes." The agreement slips out so easily. Fighting the claim is impossible when every part of my body is crying out for his touch.

He releases my nipple and glides his hand down my bare stomach and toward the waistband of my pants. I lean my back on his chest, allowing him easier access to my body. Whatever will get him to where I'm craving for him to be faster. His chest against my back moves lightly with his breaths; the same breaths blowing heat over the side of my neck.

His hand reaches the waistband, and my hips roll, aching for him to touch me soon or I may explode. His free hand wraps around my throat, guiding my head backward and landing on his shoulder. His tongue flicks over my pulse, feeling how it jumps beneath my skin.

"Someone's excited."

There's no denying or hiding how my body reacts to him, so I beg, "Touch me."

The waistband is pulled away from my skin as his fingers slide inside my pants, edging toward my clit—

I gasp, shooting up in bed. *Fucking Christ.* I should *not* be fantasizing about the same creep who insists on interrupting my life in the most unsettling way possible. My mind is already broken if this is who it insists on allowing inside my dreams.

I'm horny, that's all this is. It's what I concluded this morning, so it must be true. There's no other possible reason for me to fantasize about my stalker in such a way.

Reaching over to my nightstand, I open the drawer, pulling from it my familiar pink vibrator. It's simple, not one of those fancy ones, but does the job nonetheless. I lie back down, relaxing under the blankets while I slip the vibrator beneath my damp panties.

I twitch at the initial touch, but soon the familiar sensation has my eyes shutting and my mind escaping to somewhere else—a forbidden place.

A place where a stranger's touch excites me in ways no other guy ever has.

In the night and under the power of a small device, my mind revisits that dark place, and this time, I don't fight it. Maybe it's fucked up, but if imagining him gets me off, who am I to fight a fantasy?

Besides, it's a fantasy for a reason, right?

I move the vibrator around my clit, enticing a small gasp as my mind imagines it's him touching me instead, his thumb flicking against my nub while another finger enters me, shooting off fireworks. When his mouth clamps roughly down on my pulse, I cry out. The contrast of the two sensations are so different from one another, but so welcoming.

The vibrator presses firmly onto my clit with the addition of pressure—pressure I haven't added.

What? I jerk, my legs catching on the weight hovering above me. Once again, my blackout curtains work against me, providing me with unclear vision, but I know who's here.

"Wh-what?"

"Oh, Little Bird," he purrs, "this isn't at all how I thought I'd find you. Not that I mind one bit." His breath blows over my bare hip bone, his hand clamping down over mine, pinning the vibrator on my clit.

"H-how?" Am I so horny my imagination is producing the real thing? My eyes go to my window again. It definitely didn't open...

"Surprise. I finished early and wanted to check in on you. I assumed I'd find you asleep but, Natalie, fuck..."

Regardless of the vibrator's continuous ministrations, his sudden appearance killed the high my body was reaching for. I focus my eyes through the room's thick darkness, until catching an outline of him, crouched over my hips.

With the haze covering my mind now gone, I release the vibrator, my hand shooting out toward him. He's quick, of course, and avoids my touch. My other hand reaches out toward my lamp, aiming for light.

One flash is all it'll take for me to get a good look at him.

He's faster than quick; he's a blur, and suddenly, his legs are on either side of my waist, his hands pinning both of mine onto the pillow under my head and his weight pressing down on my stomach.

"That's not how the game works, Natalie. You can't be knowing who I am just yet."

My furious heart slows at that last word. "Yet?"

He chuckles, his breath gentle over my face. It smells like mint, and it clouds my mind. He's close—close enough if I lift my head, I'm sure I would end up kissing him. I blink, focusing through the dark and will my eyes to adjust faster. It's difficult to see more than an outline, and somehow, that's more terrifying than the fact that, once again, he's gotten inside my house.

"Your fucking scent." He inhales the air between us. "It's intoxicating. Makes me want to bottle it up."

"Get out," I bite, hoping conviction overpowers the fear.

"Not yet, Little Bird, not yet." His weight presses down, nudging the vibrator straight over my clit again.

"Oh!" I jerk with the sensation, but before fog clouds my brain once more, I shake it free, pulling at my locked wrists. "No, get off me."

I buck upward, hoping the motion will shake the grip he has on my arms. Instead, all I do is rub against the vibrator, enticing another moan from my lips. My mind continues its fight for freedom, but I'm losing my body to the sensations.

"That's it," he murmurs. His jean-clad legs tighten by my hips, causing the vibrator to remain in place.

My arms go limp under his hold as my core and everything else inside me concentrates on the pleasure he's wringing from my body. My eyes shut, blocking out the outline of his body, and I fall into the sensation, hating that a complete stranger knows how to work me so well.

"You're fucking beautiful, Natalie."

His whispered reverence has my heart skipping a beat. His words are so gentle, so soft, as if he hadn't planned on speaking them at all. And maybe he didn't, but nonetheless, my pulse leaps because no man has ever said those words to me before. Maybe it's fucked up I'm enjoying this so much. Maybe sweet words are a part of his plan, but during this haze, I'll accept them.

In a crime drama, this would be the point when the girl gets murdered and her body chopped in pieces and left around town but fuck the risks. Even if I'm insane for pushing aside the possibility, all for *this*.

It's there, underneath a stranger humping my vibrator into me, I orgasm. My cry fills the room, full of abandon and recklessness and while spiteful hate blows through me too, I still don't completely care about any of it because stupid horniness rules over my senses.

"Fuck." His sweet breath blows over my face and I realize he's also panting. "Little Bird, there's so much more to you than I initially realized. You're goddamn addicting, and now that I've heard your cries, have felt how your body accepts what I'm giving you, can *smell* your arousal, I don't think I'll ever be able to stop."

His words deepen the flush coating my skin. Its possessiveness is new to me; an emotion no one's ever had around me, and though I'm sure it's merely a form of Stockholm Syndrome, I still allow myself to smile.

"Maybe if you introduced yourself to me like a normal person, rather than stalking me, you would have known that."

"Where's the fun in that?"

The bed shifts as he removes one hand from my wrist. Despite having one arm freed, I don't move it from my pillow. Not even as he reaches between us and tosses the vibrator to the side before moving back over me, his hand reclaiming my freed wrist. His jeans rub on my damp panties and—*oh*. He's hard. Like, insanely hard. Like, he can fuck me now and I'd feel it until next week hard.

I search through the dark for his eyes, scanning the rest of his face —the small amount I can make out anyway. Even though there's nothing distinguishable about him that'll make him easy to identify in the daylight, I still search.

"Yes, you made me hard. How could I not be after a show like that?" He repositions his body, his head moving closer mine. I press back into my pillow, keeping spare inches between us. "You have no idea how much I want to finish what we've started and fuck you into oblivion."

With the vibrator gone, the fuzz over my senses dissipates too, and I'm able to ignore his enticing words. "We started nothing," I spit. His grip tightens on my wrists, digging into the skin and I cry out, this time from pain. "Fuck, *ow*."

"Stay still."

"If I do, will you stop hurting me?"

"Yes."

I huff, lowering my attitude to prevent the pain. "What do you want?"

"Time will tell. Told you, we're playing a game."

"In which you'll win?" My brow hikes, even though he likely can't see it.

"Depends."

"On?"

He chuckles again. "I should leave. But right now, your fucking delicious pussy is staining my jeans and I can't find it in me to pull away. Not when there are so many more orgasms I can give you."

"Yeah?" I find myself asking breathlessly. "How?"

Fuck, girl, what is wrong with you? It's him. He's addicting somehow—controlling any and all logic inside me. I'll be dead by next week if I don't stop.

His scent casts a spell, throwing me under the power of his charms. It's the only answer I can think of for why my senses and judgment disappear when he's around.

"Your little vibrator is child's play compared to what other toys are out there, waiting for us to use for your pleasure."

That doesn't sound half-bad, not that I'll ever admit it to him verbally. Instead, my body tells him in the way my hips roll under him, using the roughness of his jeans against my clit.

He notices, of course. Not that I'm exactly subtle. "You have no idea how delectable you smell. I'll have you rubbing that sweet cunt along my lips, chasing the high you'll undoubtedly beg me for, and I can only imagine what your taste will do to me."

"What would I do?" I whisper, following the rabbit he's set forth in this fucked-up maze he's designed for me.

"You'll transform me." He lowers himself, his face coming closer to mine until his lips are just a hairbreadth away, but this time, I don't try to create more space. "I firmly believe after tasting you, I'll awaken as a new man. A man who'll dedicate every waking moment to exploring the inside of your pretty pussy, to allowing my fingers and tongue to become intimately familiar with your clit. I'll bind your hands, of course, giving you no other choice but to lie there as a helpless feast for my taking." His soft groan follows, mingling with the one edging on my lips, holding onto the very last fragment of sanity before I fall. "I bet you're super fucking tight too, and it'll be challenging to fit even two of my fingers inside you, but we'd make it work. Oh, Natalie," his voice lowers into a purring whisper, "I could describe every way I plan on making you come undone beneath me, but I don't have that kind of time right now."

"I do."

He sighs. "But I don't, and I'm the gamemaster here. Until my next visit, you will not pleasure yourself. As of now, I'll be the only one to touch your body. Understood?"

Without waiting for a response, his hands unclasp mine at the same time his weight goes away, my bedroom door shutting behind him.

"Wait," I call, scrambling out of bed. The blanket he tossed off me tangles in my legs, slowing my speed, and by the time I'm free, I hear the front door shut from down below.

I don't trust he's gone, so I do a quick pass of the house, coming up empty before I return to bed. I tuck the vibrator away, back in its drawer, shame making my neck hot, and I feel like he didn't satiate my desires, but rather worsen them because I want more.

The hottest action I've ever gotten was from a stranger who broke into my home.

And I don't even know his name.

Seven

NATALIE

MORNINGS BRING FORTH A NEW DAY. One with new chances, new beginnings, and new tasks, but for me, it also brings new clarity.

What a damn moron I've been.

I fly through my house, getting ready at a speed of mock ten. I cast a dirty look toward the drawer in my nightstand, as if the vibrator could be at fault for what happened—for how I *allowed* a stranger to get me off. Worse, a stranger who broke into my house and has been leaving me messages.

He was *here*. He was watching me pleasure myself and then *helped*. My face warms at the memory of last night, but anger soon replaces the other horrible and pointless emotion moving through my body.

I was not myself last night. I'm not *that* girl. Not the one who rubs on the first available guy who gives her attention. When my needs are bad enough, I seek meaningless one-time things, and after losing my virginity back in high school, there's only been a whopping four other guys who have touched me.

Five in total. My stalker probably has five a week.

"I'll have you rubbing that sweet cunt along my lips."

Only one guy has ever tried. Most don't seem interested in more than getting off themselves, and the one who tried didn't succeed.

No. No, this is over. Monday or not, I'm skipping class because this is ridiculous. I snatch his latest message from my dresser, thankful he didn't nab it last night like how he did his previous one and shove it in my purse.

The police *will* listen to my story, even if I need to scream it at them a few hundred times before they do anything.

I lock the door behind me, triple-checking the lock, and before I step away, my eyes scan every inch of the street around me. My town-house faces a park—a wide-open area. How have I not realized how vulnerable I've been this whole time? That's probably where he watches me from, waiting for my bedroom light to go out or me to depart home—like now—so he can leave me another message.

An average person would feel disgust, but instead, I feel only anger. I'm angry at his invasions, at the "game" he claims we're playing. My hands curl into fists at my side, shoes pounding a bit harder at the pavement beneath my feet as I step away from my house.

Fucker, I've left. Your turn to go on in.

Damn, I can't wait until the police put a damn restraining order on you or something.

I make it three steps before my phone buzzes, forcing my attention downward to the cell in my hand.

ALEX

Have a good week, Nat.

Alex. He has money, and everyone knows money makes the world turn a bit faster. Alex claims to want to help me—to allow me access to what should have been mine. The Miller family and associated power is what I need right now. If anyone will make this go away, it'll be him.

Time to see if Alex is all words and no action.

I'm gambling with whether the police will believe my claims, but I know that Alex will most definitely believe me. If he wants us to be a happy family, he better believe me.

ME

I need help. Can we meet?

ALEX

I'll send Billy to pick you up at your house right away.

Once again, having a brother is proving to be a good thing. I lower myself to the front step of my townhouse and wait for Billy.

THE DOOR OPENS and Alex slips into the car's back seat beside me. Though the skin around his eyes crease with worry, he appears quite at ease with his graceful smile and lowered shoulders. He leans back against the leather seat, which perfectly matches his black suit and tie.

Beyond him and the car's window, his company's building stands sky-high. Billy drove me straight downtown into Cortville—a place I haven't been to in years. I don't count my trips to Alex's house as visiting the city, since we're only ever on the city's edge. Thanks to growing up in small towns, it's not often I have the opportunity to fully appreciate what a city provides. While I'm safe inside the car, it's like we entered a whole other world. Suddenly, Billy was weaving in between other vehicles and bikers, who seem to enjoy cutting off cars when they zoom through the bumper-to-bumper traffic. Delivery trucks double-park, blocking the road and creating more hold-ups, but even those didn't stop his skill from getting me to Alex in a decent amount of time.

"Natalie, talk to me. What did you need help with?"

Right. I drag my purse onto my lap and dig out the piece of paper from my stalker, handing it to him.

Alex takes it right away, unfolds it, and reads. As he does, I explain, "The other day, I came home to a note left in my room. Not this one—another one—which I no longer have. But then this one arrived yesterday. I don't know who they're from." Well, I know who they're from but not *who* that someone is.

His gaze whips back up, dark eyes manically searching mine as something protective switches on inside him. "Someone's breaking into your house? Are you okay?"

"Yes," I tell him truthfully, willing my mind away from the sinful and devious memories it wishes to relive. "Twice now."

That I know of.

"And—" I stop, the rest of the truth hovering in the air between us. I could—*should*—also mention the two times I've spoken to him—the two instances he's touched me—but it's a truth I'll leave buried for now. If the messages and break-ins end, then so will the touching, and Alex doesn't need to know about my unwise past decisions when I didn't stop the stranger from exploring my body.

"Have you gone to the police yet?"

"I wasn't sure they'd believe me, but I planned on doing it today. It was where I was heading when I got your text." I peer at him, leaning an inch closer as I study his dismayed expression. "Do *you* believe me?"

He sits stiff, the paper poised between pinched fingers. His nostrils flare as narrowed eyes read it over and over.

"Of course I do. I'll get this dealt with. Sick fucker, breaking into women's houses like this."

His reaction lessens the tension in my shoulders and I rest back against the leather, thankful I made the decision I did.

"I'll take care of this, Nat, I promise. Go home and hang tight. I have a few calls to make." His fist crumples the message, and he flings open the car's door. Billy, upfront, scrambles to catch it in time, but

Alex is already striding across the sidewalk. Despite the busy downtown street, he easily pushes through the crowd, heading back to his glass tower.

A few calls... I have no idea who he'll call to solve this, but I'll do as he asked and sit back and hang on, grateful for his assistance and obvious concern for me. It's nice. Different.

After Jolene was diagnosed and hospitalized, I had to become an adult quickly. Thankfully, I was eighteen at the time, legally an adult, but no one tells you the part about how being a legal adult and an *actual* adult are two different things. When money was tight due to rent, tuition, Jolene's care, and food, a bill would go unpaid, and it became my problem to resolve. I had no one to run to—no one to help me.

With Alex in my life, he's taken up the mantle of being my big brother, and it's lovely to have someone to rely on. To not be alone in my fights.

Billy bends down, popping his head into the back seat of the car. "Back home, Miss Miller?"

I glance at the time on my phone, doing a brief calculation of the trip's length. "To the university. I have an afternoon class I can make."

"Very good." He nods, shutting the door Alex recently exited from before getting back into the driver's seat.

As Billy pulls away from Alex's company, I imagine him sitting somewhere inside, likely on the top floor of that fancy glass building, looking at the world below.

And hopefully also making a call to rid my house of the stray cat insisting on hiding there.

Eight

TRISTAN

DID I mean to touch her the first time? Hell no. After sending the initial message, I needed to ensure she took my threat seriously. Tossing away the paper as she did was a mistake on her part, and I had to show her that. Petting her chest was to prove how easy she is to get to; that she's not safe.

She must fear me enough to cry to the police—to me. One conversation is all I need for her to realize I'm not the bad guy Elena made me out to be. Eventually, we'll be friends, and I'll be in her life before she can even blink. I'll learn all about her sibling relationship, and more importantly, where her fucker of a brother is hiding out. Because despite how publicized the Miller name is, finding his house is something else entirely.

Part of my training involved learning to work in the pitch-dark, therefore I've honed my night vision quite well. Even though her back was to me, I saw *everything*. The way her eyes diluted, the way her chest moved up and down with her rapid breaths, and when she stopped breathing altogether.

She's beautiful. It's never been a debate, but seeing her up close is much different than watching from afar. I was able to fully appreciate every inch of her flawless skin. The way her curves meld to her body so perfectly, I wanted to hold her to my chest. There's so much of her that she chooses to hide away from other people.

Women and I have quick flings, but there's never been anyone I wanted to keep for more than a night or two. But with Natalie—and I realize this is stupid to even think—something switched *on* in me that first time. My arms itched to hold her, to fuck her... to keep her.

But I can't, because once she gives me what I need, she'll hate me. She's not mine, and never can be. Two messages, one visit, and that's all it should have been before she came running for help.

So why did I return the second time? I ask myself this, but I already know why. When her nipples budded, when her breaths came out heavier, and when her pulse jumped beneath her neck, I knew I was absolutely fucked.

Fucked with a capital F, because my wants were no longer a matter. My *needs* were, and I knew they had to be met in the short time she and I have together.

I took the message from her garbage can, leaving her with only one facet of proof. Why? Because even though it's stupid and selfish and possibly ruined the plan I so perfectly designed, I couldn't move on to being her friend just yet—not when I hadn't seen her orgasm.

Still, I planned on avoiding her, despite my needs, because thankfully, a small fragment of logic kept me in check. I was on patrol, but fuck me when I couldn't hold back from visiting her that second time.

I cross my legs under the safety of my desk, using it to hide my thickening erection from the rest of the force with my wayward thoughts. Given the time, Natalie should have been sleeping, not pleasuring herself. Not giving me a scene to forever be branded in my mind.

I bite down on my tongue, recalling her shut eyes and parted mouth. The way her hands worked the vibrator on her own clit, and then her surprised gasp at my assistance. When pinning her arms down and controlling the device between us was the only thing to ensure I didn't toss it aside and let her finish on my tongue. I wanted—*want*—to taste that sweet cunt of hers. To feel her come and lick up her juices. I nearly did it; nearly let my hands go to where the vibrator was after I tossed it aside. In hindsight, I should have.

I groan, biting down on my fist as I shift again, eyes bouncing above my monitor, ensuring no one's paying attention to me.

Natalie is sour candy. Delicious, sweet, but consuming. She scares me.

Not because of her family, not anymore. Once, it was a possibility Natalie knew what Alex is doing, but after observing her for the short while I've been, I really don't think she does. She's too... innocent, is the best term I can give her. She has no secrets in her eyes. Still, we need her to hand over details about her brother.

"Pence!"

The chief's command yanks me away from my wandering thoughts, and I shoot to my feet, twisting toward the direction of his office.

"Sir."

"Office. Now." The large burly man turns, heading to the back room he came from.

I follow, shutting his door behind us, curiosity swirling in my brain.

"Sit."

Ever the man of many words. I sit, staring at the police chief across from me. He leans back in his cracked-leather desk chair, his arms crossing over a protruding stomach. As chief, he spends little to no time in the field anymore, and it shows.

"What's wrong, sir?"

"Nothing's wrong. In fact, for your career, something is very right."

I straighten, interested, pushing all thoughts of my Little Bird from my head. Ryker may have designed a long game; the Academy may have been one step in many to help us get here, but it's also something I've come to enjoy and plan to keep as a life-long career.

"You're young," he continues, "like, what—twenty-five or so."

Not what I expected him to ask. Tension knots at the base of my neck with the unknowns of where this conversation is heading. "Or so," I reply, going with the second option he gave.

"Hm." He purses his lips, leaning forward before resting his hands on the desk. "How would you feel about working undercover?"

"Sir?"

His eyes flick behind me and back, his tongue reaching out to wet his lips. He's anxious—nervous—but about what? "The department has a private investor. He provides us with a... top up, if you may, to what the city's funding allots to us. So it's a relationship I'd like to maintain. He's reached out, asking for a favour. His sister, Natalie Miller—"

My mind blanks as mini fireworks shoot up inside it. Natalie Miller. Private investor.

"What about her?"

His eyes narrow. "Shut it, and you'll hear what I'm saying. The girl claims she's being stalked. Messages are being left in her house, which means someone's getting inside to put them there. He's requested someone from the department pose as an undercover bodyguard to protect her. To survey the entrances at all times, and to not leave her house unless she goes too. He wants us to catch this guy." His brows lift. "You hear me, Tristan? Our investor is important and he wants someone competent to protect his sister. Don't fuck this up for me— or you. Do this right, do this well, and you'll be seeing a promotion sooner than later."

No mention of my nighttime visits. Interesting.

"Yes, sir." I nod, renewed energy coursing through me, empowering my senses. Talk about the goldmine of opportunities. Fuck becoming her friend and playing the slow game. Alex handed me the perfect cover and reason to be by her side.

"Good." His shoulders relax as he sits back again. "I've gathered some notes on her, from what he's told me. She's a university student. Lives alone in a townhouse. Fairly quiet girl. This should be an easy task. She doesn't have any idea who the guy is or why he's targeting her." Chief shakes his head slowly. "You're one of the youngest on the force, and of the young ones, you're my best. You'll fit in by her side." He flicks his fingers, a smirk pulling at his lips. "Lose the uniform and go back to school, Pence."

"Yes, sir," I reply, fighting to maintain composure and not show him how much of a gift this is.

Am I surprised Alex is paying off the local police department? Not in the slightest, since we suspected this. It's why I'm working this job, after all.

"Good. You will receive all your orders from me so keep your phone on you at all times. Lose your uniform but take your gun. We don't know who this guy is, or how dangerous he is."

"Has he hurt her?" I ask, feigning professional interest in the case.

Chief shakes his head. "There was no mention of it. Now go. You start right away. I'll text you her address."

I scoot, digging out my phone as I rush by my desk and out the door, not saying goodbye to anyone else. Eagerness thrums through me. I'll go home, I'll change my clothes, and then I'll play an entirely new round of the game. A round, I never dreamed even possible.

I text the group conversation first.

ME

I have the biggest 'in' possible. Give me a couple more days. I should have his location then.

Ryker responds with a thumbs up.

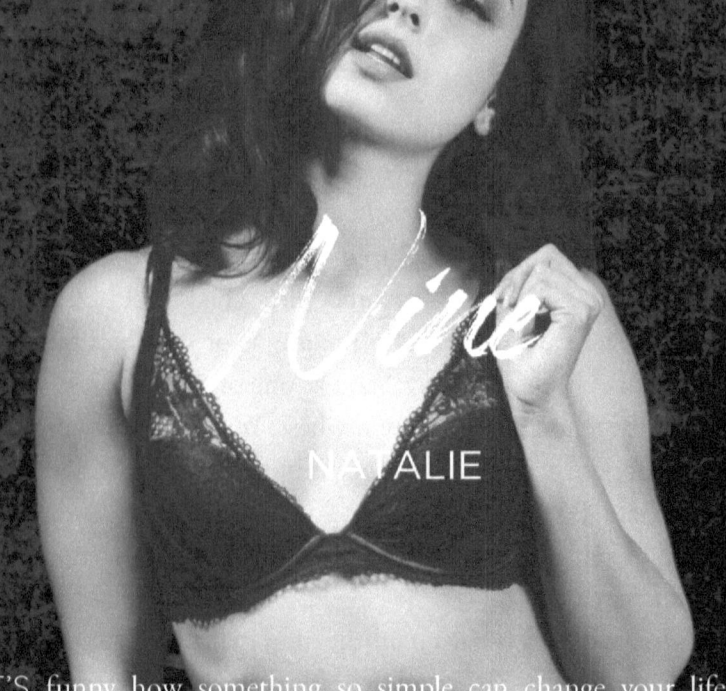

Nine

NATALIE

IT'S funny how something so simple can change your life. How everything after that is altered; how you see friends and foes differently. How it puts you on an entirely different path, one you didn't know existed, leaving you to wonder why you're so easily fooled by lies.

Three simple messages signify my life-changing event. First, the two from my stalker, and now, one from Alex.

ALEX

I hired a bodyguard for you. He will be anywhere you are. Your professors have already been notified. This is until he catches the intruder.

A fucking bodyguard? *That's* what he meant when he said he'd be taking care of it?

Annoyance, anger, it singes my nerves. I'm not a people-person, and he knows that. A bodyguard will be here all the time. Every step I take—to class, home, and the library—he'll be right there, acting as my shadow.

ALEX

Please acknowledge me.

ME

Do I have a choice? I shoot back right away,
fingers flying over the screen.

ALEX

Not really, no. It's the best way to keep you safe.
He's a cop, and someone I was assured would be
perfect for the job. He'll be at your house by the
time you finish class.

I sigh, not that he can hear me.

ME

Thank you.

This conversation must end because I can tell Alex won't budge on this, and in the end, he's correct. If having someone in my house ensures my stalker never returns, so be it.

I turn the final corner toward home and stop at the sight.

A man—can't tell his age from this far—stands on my doorstep, leaning on the adjoining brick wall. His attention remains focused on the phone in his hand, his fingers scrolling over the screen. He's tall, standing closer to the top of the door than I'd ever be able to reach, with a messy mix of dark and light hair.

My hands fist my purse strap. Socializing with strangers is bad enough, but now I'll be temporarily living with one. My attention falls to the small bag at his feet. A bag, no doubt, filled with his personal items and extra clothing.

At my approach, he looks up, twisting his head in my direction. His lips pick up in a cocky smirk and—

Wait. I know him.

"What are you doing here?" I barrel up the steps, placing myself between him and my door.

Up close, I realize my small form is nothing against his overly large one. His leather jacket stretches taut over his arms, showcasing clearly formed muscle. I suppose, being a police office would require it.

But it doesn't explain what he's doing here.

No. Why the hell did it take so long for my brain to catch up?

He smirks again, as if knowing where my thoughts finally reached. "Nice to meet you as well. I've been assigned as your bodyguard."

His voice, deep and sultry, has my next words pausing on the edge of my tongue. He sounds... familiar. As if I've heard it once in passing before, but all the times I ran into him outside the university, we never spoke, so...

I shake my head. Other more important things are a priority. Not if a guy's voice sounds familiar. It probably reminds me of another guy in my past. After all, you hear one guy, you've heard them all, right?

I fold my arms across my chest, aiming to appear as threatening as I can. "You're the same guy Elena warned me away from. She said you're not a good person."

He rolls his eyes and kicks off the wall, standing straight now. "Elena and I go way back, to high school. She's always had her problems with me."

"That doesn't exactly encourage me to allow you inside my house. If Elena has her problems with you, then who's to say I won't as well?"

He shakes his head, amusement further tinging his expression. "She used to have a thing with one of my friends, like, way back in high school. She's been cranky with me ever since. That's all. Now when she sees me, I remind her of the past."

I mull on his words, slowly lowering my hands back to my side. I suppose that makes sense. I mean, she did seem pretty worried about him when we spotted him by the curb that one day, but it was also the day she had a meeting with school staff, so perhaps she was feeling a bit overly anxious.

My breath huffs out with my decision. "Fine. If that's the truth, I guess I can see why she'd say what she did."

"Scout's honour."

"You're not a scout."

He laughs, a pleasant sound drifting straight to my core. "You're right. Police honour then?" His brow quirks, enticing my own giggle before I can hold it in.

I might not enjoy other people, but laughing feels good. Easing in a sense I hadn't realized my body was lacking in. If this is how it'll be with him, maybe it'll be okay*ish*.

It may even be good for my own wellbeing.

"I'll take it for now. Well, um..." My hands knot, and suddenly, I don't know what to do. How does one invite a stranger to stay with them?

He gestures toward the door, wondering the same thing. "Are you going to let me in?"

Eventually. Does he not realize how odd this whole thing is? Inviting a stranger whose name I don't even—

"Not until I know your name."

"Tristan."

Tristan. I've never known another Tristan, but somehow, I know his name suits him well. He looks like a Tristan.

"Natalie," I reply back.

"I know." His responding grin lights my insides on fire, and my mouth goes dry, staring at his perfect face.

Maybe my response is due to my midnight visitor, or maybe last night didn't fully take the edge off, but here on my porch, I respond to another stranger stronger than I ever have anyone else. I lean in, getting closer to his intoxicatingly clean scent. It consumes my senses, making my head go light.

"Natalie?"

I jerk back, his words waking me up. "S-sorry." Shame heats my face, and I twist around, unlocking the door as I go. Being forward with someone is not me. I'm not the girl who makes the first move.

I push open the door, flicking on the light as I enter, even though the bright daylight streaming through all the windows illuminates the house better than a single switch ever could. I kick off my shoes and start down my skinny hallway, leaving Tristan to shut the door and follow behind me.

"This is the living room." I gesture to the small space—the faded couch against the wall and the TV across from it. "I guess... you're living here?"

"For the time being," Tristan rumbles, coming up behind me. "I'll try to stay out of your way."

I peer over my shoulder at him, noting his tall form, charming smile, god-like physique, and hair my fingers are itching to touch. Nothing about him says it's possible for him to stay out of my way.

"I doubt that," I mutter wryly, twisting back to gesture to the space. "Well, the couch is yours, I guess. Bathroom's upstairs."

"Can you show me?" he purrs close behind me. I don't feel his breath reach me, but I shiver nonetheless, still hyperaware of his voice. It's a tone that nearly has me ready to lose all composure and tear off my clothes.

My gaze falls to his large hands, imagining them on my hips, my stomach, my breasts... clutching the strands of my hair as he puts me on my knees and—

"Natalie?"

I blink, eyes shooting back up to his. My cheeks heat, and I wonder if my thoughts were transparent.

I've known Tristan for all of thirty seconds, and already he's setting my blood on boil. If I'm not careful, in time, it'll bubble over.

He's like my midnight visitor, I realize. Two men who flick something on inside me.

"Um, yeah. Sure. Um, yeah, follow me."

I lead him out of the living room and gesture down the hallway. "Kitchen. Help yourself to anything in there."

I continue toward the stairs, maintaining a three-stair distance to keep some space between us. When we reach the landing at the top, I edge to the wall, making as much room for him that I possibly can while I point around the space. "Bathroom, and there's my room."

Tristan slips by me, heading straight for my bedroom, without any invitation.

I scurry behind him, mentally recalling how I left my room this morning. Dirty laundry picked up? Check. Sex toys tucked away? Check.

"This is where he's leaving the notes?"

"Yes."

Tristan heads straight for my window, scanning the edging, his hands following the path his eyes take. "And you don't know how he's getting in?"

"No. When I'm downstairs, I think he uses that window. When up here, I guess the front door. I keep everything locked, so it really makes no sense."

"Spare key?"

"None."

He turns away from the window, lips pursed as he studies the rest of the space. Not as if he's just looking to look, but examining to investigate. "He might know how to jimmy locks and windows," he says absentmindedly, eyes still passing over all my personal effects.

My stomach flips. "People do that?" My words come out a bit more screechy than I intended them to. "I thought that was only on TV."

Tristan's seriousness takes a momentary break to throw a wink toward me. "Where do you think media gets it from?"

I suppose that makes sense.

"So, what—you're going to stay awake all night and wait for him to maybe show up?"

"Until we catch him, yes."

I tilt my head, scanning his flawless face. "And when will you sleep?" It'd be a shame for his pretty face to be graced with dark bags beneath his eyes.

"During the day." He shrugs. "He only comes at night, when no one can see him, so I'll sleep in the early evenings and late mornings, before and after your classes."

I frown, guilt washing over me. This will be such a shitty job for him. "Sleep when I'm at school," I offer, but he's already shaking away the suggestion.

"He's likely watching you during the day."

Oh. I shiver. "But you being by my side won't change anything. He can still watch me from afar."

"At least he'll know what he's up against." His chest puffs, arms crossing his wide chest, as if he's trying to prove himself to me, except there's no need. The visual of his body is enough to reassure me he'd definitely be fine up against my stalker.

"I guess. Did you choose this job?" I ask, curious, clenching my hands behind my back. No doubt he's regretting it now if he did, and if he didn't, well, he'll hate his life soon enough when he realizes how boring of a person I am.

"I was chosen to protect you, first because of my age, and second my abilities. But I can't say I'll mind it one bit."

"Why's that?"

Tristan approaches, passing me on his way out my door. His leather-covered arm brushes mine as he walks by, leaving his fresh scent lingering in the space he just left. His intense gaze flicks over my face, settling on my lips briefly before he murmurs, "Because anyone who would cry about this job is a fucking moron."

He leaves then, but the fire he's ignited inside me doesn't burn out for many hours to come.

Ten

NATALIE

ALEX

All going good with the cop? If you don't like him, I can have the chief send someone else over.

ME

It's fine. He's fine.

FINE IS TOO CALM a word for the awkwardness that surrounds us as I make dinner. Tristan is a silent shadow who stalks me while I prepare a large pot of pasta. Too large, but I haven't cooked for more than myself in years. Occasionally, he leaves and surveys the house, looking for something, I guess, or to make himself seem useful. Those couple of moments he's gone gives my body the much-needed reprieve to catch my breath and ease the tension in my muscles before he returns, and my insides clench up all over.

My visceral reaction to Tristan is something bizarre and unnerving that has butterflies constantly taking flight inside my stomach.

Attraction.

It's heady in the air—at least from my end—and how can it not be? He's so damned hot.

63

Girl, stop. That's not why he's here.

A day ago, I allowed a stranger to bring me to orgasm, and now I'm seeking the high with another new guy in my life. It's like something out of a movie and something is *so* wrong with me. Maybe I'm hornier than I realized, and I need to revisit the trusty hookup app and satisfy my craving before I make a mistake with Tristan.

ALEX

Any update on the situation?

Right. Alex was messaging.

ME

Nothing yet.

"Natalie," Tristan starts, announcing his arrival back in the kitchen.

The way my name sounds in his mouth is way too delicious for me not to respond to, and I shove my phone back into my pocket.

"Mhm?" Keeping my back to him, I continue stirring the pasta. Doing so is the only way to hide my expression from him and keep some sort of professional normalcy between us.

"Tell me about yourself. We'll be together for a while, it seems."

I pinch the wooden spoon between two fingers while I work to keep my nerves in check. The hot guy wants to know about me.

Instead, all that comes out is, "Um."

There's a shuffle of his feet against the tile and suddenly, his heat wraps warmly around me. He feels very similar to—

No. Tristan, the respectable and helpful cop, does *not* feel anything like my midnight visitor.

It's lust, that's all. My mind is combining them together.

His next words are close to my ear, his breath covering the skin of my neck. If I simply straighten, my back will be pressing into his front.

"If stirring the food and speaking at the same time is too difficult for you, I can help."

His condescending tone blows away the cloud of fog hanging over my head and I snap, "Dick. But if you want to help, drain the noodles, please. I need to finish the sauce."

"My pleasure." His whispered words drip with sex and I bite down on the inside of my mouth, willing myself to focus on my task before sauce ends up exploding all over my kitchen. I'm *not* going to survive this experience, so my stalker better be found quickly so Tristan can return to the station. "Natalie, I asked you a question."

"I heard you. I just don't know how to respond."

After tasting the sauce, I slide it from the stove and begin dishing the drained pasta onto two plates. He steps out of my way and sets the tables with the required silverware. Like we're some domesticated couple, and not two strangers thrown together due to an unfortunate circumstance.

I finish up, serving two portions from the pot and hand him his plate before taking my spot at the table. Immediately, I push pasta on my fork and shove it in my mouth, the taste of the food reminding me how hungry I am.

I glance up from my plate and catch Tristan watching me, amusement lining his lips. He takes a bite too, commenting, "This is very tasty, Natalie. But you still haven't told me anything about yourself."

"Maybe I don't want you to know my secrets."

"Touché." He makes a gesture with his fork. "What if I tell you about me? Will that loosen your lips?"

I take another bite before responding, "It might."

"Well, okay. I worked my ass off to get through the police academy and get the job. So far, it's working out well." His gaze flicks over my form, a smirk edging his mouth again. "I live alone too, so I understand how weird me being here may be. I have three close friends, two of whom I went to high school with."

"Parents? Siblings?"

His eyes flash with something I can't place, but it's ominous and has me lowering my fork. His next response is quieter, his tone guttural and chilling. "No siblings. Never knew my father."

But no mention of his mother. Understood.

"Your turn." His tone lifts back to nearly what it was before my final question.

"Well, I'm working on an English Literature degree. It's my final year, and all that, so I'll be busy writing more essays than you can count on two hands. I don't really hang out with people other than Elena. I prefer the quiet and am usually alone. Don't know my father, only of him. I don't remember my mother. She dropped me off with my aunt when I was a baby and was found dead a short while later."

The fork drops from Tristan's hand. I'm sure he's only being kind, but the look of concern masking his eyes has a pain forming in my chest. Not knowing Mom means I don't have emotional ties to her, so speaking about losing her is easy despite the heavy topic.

"From what, if you don't mind me asking?"

"Strangulation." My eyes remain pinned on my plate, not wanting to glance up and find sympathetic eyes. "No prints though. Whoever did it was never discovered."

"Hm," is all he replies as he picks up his fork. "And your aunt?"

A much happier topic so I look at him, smiling. It's easy to when thinking about her. "She was my mother's older sister. Happy, alone, never wanted children, but took me in. Raised me as her own. She was my mother in every sense of the word." I pause, letting the upsetting truth back inside me. "She's in a facility now due to a medical condition. With me away during the day, I couldn't risk her blacking out and injuring herself." Or worse.

"I'm sorry," he rumbles. He pushes his now-empty plate away, completely focused on me. On the table, his hand fists and the sudden craving—the need—to hold it becomes so strong that I have to take another bite of food to rid myself of the feeling.

When everything happened with Jolene, it was only her and me. No grandparents or other aunts. I shouldered it alone—the money issues, the sleepless nights to ensure she didn't hurt herself. When she went into the facility, it was such a bittersweet relief, but then I was alone and I had to learn to enjoy it.

Perhaps it explains the feelings I'm getting being around Tristan. It has nothing to do with his bad boy appearance or the way he sets my nerves ablaze. He's a person; someone to interact with. To talk with.

I shrug. "She's happy, and I visit her each week."

"You have any siblings?" He moves on.

"One." I say no more, debating how much to go into it. "He's the reason you're here, in fact," I supply instead, hoping this new detail will give him something to mull over.

"So it's your brother I need to thank?" The dark colour of his eyes glints in the kitchen's overhead lighting.

"Why's that?" I ask and finish off my final bite, also nudging the plate away.

"For introducing me to you."

This is getting dangerously close to flirting, and the mention of Alex has me considering how pissed he'd likely be to learn my bodyguard became my sex toy instead. My horniness isn't worth getting Tristan in trouble. Instead, I scoop up both plates and take them to the sink.

"Leave them," he orders. "If you have work to do, I can wash them."

His simple offer has my heart fluttering. "It's fine. I'm not doing anything tonight. Besides, I'm the host."

The chair scrapes as he stands, his steps bringing him quickly to my side. Not that the room is exactly large so he didn't have far to walk, but still.

"The unwilling host," he counters, taking the plates from my grip. "I'm serious, Natalie. Go chill. You cooked and it's the least I can do."

The firm set of his mouth and eyes tell me he's determined to stick to his word, so I instead say, "Thank you," before backing away and giving up a bit of control. "I typically stay home and watch TV. I'm a boring person. You up for a show?"

"Sure," he responds right away, switching on the hot water to fill the sink. "What do you have in mind?"

"On Monday nights, my favourite crime drama airs. It'll be that, unless you have a preference for something else?"

His brows lift, his gaze finding mine from over his shoulder. "You like crime dramas?"

"Yeah, they're, like, my favourite. Anything in the genre."

"Me too. Do you watch documentaries as well?" he asks, turning back to face the sink.

With his back to me, I take the chance to stare at the other parts of him I haven't really checked out yet. He took off the jacket before dinner, leaving his arms bare. Muscles I hadn't realized were there now showing. I'm not a girl who typically appreciates a man's backside, but damn, Tristan has definitely put work into his and it's paid off.

"Sometimes, but not often. Why do you ask?"

"Curious," he calls out. "My favourite documentary is one about a guy who was so in love with a woman, he stalked her until becoming friends, and she fell in love with him that way."

"That's fucked."

He shrugs, not twisting around. "It is what it is. According to the episode, they remained together until cancer eventually took him in his senior years."

"And she never figured out the truth?"

"Never."

"Huh. Well, I suppose if they were happy."

The splashing stops and he turns, his hands propping him up on the counter behind him. Water and suds drip from him. "You don't see it as a fake happiness?"

"I mean..." My back falls against the wall and I cross my arms, mulling over on the sudden debate he's thrown my mind in. "I suppose we can blame my Romanticism era lit courses, and sure, it's fucked up, but if they became true friends and she fell in love with *him* and is happy with that decision, then how they met matters less. In the end, she made her choice."

Tristan's head tilts. "But would they have met if he hadn't stalked her?"

"I guess not. I mean, it's not as if I approve of stalking or anything." I wave my hand, gesturing toward him. "Obviously, or you wouldn't be here. But..." My teeth dig into my lip, my mind drifting to last night.

A game, he called it. But what if there's more to his visits? My entire life was simple a mere few months ago, and now I have Alex, a stalker, and Tristan, the man protecting me from said stalker.

At the centre of everything is Alex. He's the new thing in my life, and now I wonder, what if I'm right, and someone is using me to get to Alex and his money. What if *I'm* the game—the chess piece he'll play until he checkmates Alex.

"But," Tristan probes.

"Maybe there's a reason. I don't condone him coming in here and leaving me notes, but what if it's for a greater purpose?"

Tristan flinches. I suppose, from a cop's perspective, there is no good reason for stalking. A crime is a crime, no matter the reason behind it.

I shrug, pushing the entire conversation away. "Anyway, my show's about to start, so I'll set it up. Sound good?"

"Great," he replies, his eyes stuck on the wall past my head. His jawline is tight; he's pissed.

Whatever. It's not *he* has a stalker.

Eleven

TRISTAN

NATALIE LEAVES THE KITCHEN, giving me space to catch my breath, and I chuckle.

My Little Bird has no idea how close she is to the cat chasing her. With everything she says, the maze only gets more complicated, her cage shrinking smaller.

I've pieced together enough of her background from the bit she's told me. She was raised by her aunt after her mother dropped her there, only hours before getting herself killed. Knowing Alex's villainy, no doubt their father was evil too, and their mother recognized that and kidnapped Natalie before she got sucked in. And then was killed by their father.

Talking with Natalie seemed to reaffirm my gut feeling that she doesn't know the truth about her brother. She knows too little of her history. Of course, she can merely be an excellent liar. But my stomach tells me it isn't the case.

Alex cares enough to hire a personal bodyguard for her, but one kind act can't resolve his sin-ridden soul.

The dishwater feels chillier against my skin when the memories of every photo I've dug up flashes in my mind. For years, I've witnessed cases get open and shut within a day, and each time, it's involved an ex-employee of Miller Inc. Photos of the dismembered corpses get locked away the moment they're revealed, and it took illegal access for me to uncover them when Ryker was in prison.

His lawyers buried every connection his company has to the murdered women. Stark blood flashes over my eyes, momentarily blocking my vision from the pot I'm washing.

There's one goal here and Natalie will not make me lose sight of that. Even if she doesn't know what her big bro is up to in his spare time, she knows where he lives, where he hangs out, what he fucking likes to eat. All information I'll need, so I know what to poison his ass with when we do find him.

I told her to buckle in for the game, but it's a game I need to play as well. I drain the water and stalk down the hallway, toward the living room she pointed to earlier. Each time I've been inside the house, I've noticed how nice it is, but being here during the day shows how truly well-maintained it is. Natalie hasn't mentioned a job and in the couple weeks since I started following her, she's never gone to one. Obviously, Alex came to the rescue again.

Buying her off like this could be his way of getting Natalie under his thumb, exactly like he seems to do with everyone else in his life.

CHIEF

Pence. Updates.

Case in point.

ME

Hello to you too. I've found nothing yet, sir.

After a moment, I receive a read receipt on my text, but Chief doesn't respond, so I tuck away my phone in time to make it to the living room doorway, where I peek in.

Natalie stands by the couch, hands on her hips as she positions a pillow at one end, before swapping it for the other end. I press my lips together in amusement to prevent from laughing. She's fucking cute.

And damn sexy.

And she's attracted to me.

Despite what women think, a man knows when they're wanted. The woman's back naturally arches from pure instinct. Her breathing hikes while the pulse beneath her skin jumps erratically. Her skin warms, blasting hot energy, acting as some kind of mating call.

And fuck, I wanted to respond to Natalie's.

I want to dirty her—drag her down to the depths of depravity my soul bathes in and drown her there with me. Only a dirty soul would love what I'm doing to her.

Thankfully, she has no fucking clue who I am. I make my voice deeper to hide my other persona, and so far, she hasn't picked up on it. Even during the instances I've cursed myself for repeating similar actions, like stepping near her back when she was cooking. It's a behaviour she knows from my nighttime guise and I need to be careful how much of me she feels.

Like the documentary that started me on this path, I need to remain only her friend in the daytime. But at nighttime... Night is when the cat can come out to play.

My hand twitches, watching her now position a blanket. She may view herself as an introvert, but I'm learning now how much I like the quiet ones. A personality trait, I'm saddened I avoided in high school, because fuck her quiet energy is addictive. As she turns her couch into a bed for me to sleep on, the only thing I want to do is fuck her for her thoughtfulness.

Maybe later tonight.

I'll wait until Natalie goes to bed before I visit again. I need more of her, regardless of how bad of an idea it is. Being inside her house doesn't mean I can stop sending the messages; if I don't, she might find a reason to no longer require a bodyguard and there's no way in hell I'm leaving now that I'm here.

Leaving means I have my answers and I'll need to let her go.

And I'm not ready to do that yet.

Not when I haven't made her mine.

I'll make her mine, I'll use her, and then... well, we'll see.

HALFWAY THROUGH AN EPISODE about a serial killer, Natalie suddenly murmurs, "Thanks for being here. Even if you don't have a choice in the matter."

I shrug, aiming to appear as if I don't mind staying here while I peer to the right, where she's seated on the opposite end of the couch. "It's all good. My checks have been clear tonight so maybe my presence is already working."

My fake-checks around her house and the outside have only been short breaks to allow me to breathe in air that doesn't smell like Natalie.

When she said she enjoys crime dramas, she wasn't kidding. Every flinch, she's there for it, grinning. Every reveal has her shifting to the edge of the couch. While it's quite cute, it's also a bit unnerving because, after all, I know her family. She's interested in the wicked, even if it's in a healthier manner.

"I suppose I may as well tell you, since you'll be following me every-where, I go to my brother's every Friday. His driver picks me up. This time, it'll be for a party."

I straighten in my spot, fighting to keep my body and expression in check and trying not to display the pleasure her words have brought me. Friday. This will all be over Friday. She'll lead me straight to the devil's door.

Alex is smart, and I doubt he'll let just anyone into his safe space, but it'll be easy enough to put a tracker somewhere on her person. By Friday, I'll have his location. Once inside, it will be a matter of finding evidence of where he's keeping the women.

"Okay," I reply, keeping my voice low and neutral.

"Although," she muses, her lips pursing, "I can't see Alex wanting you there. I'll be with him, and safe, so I suppose you get a night off. That'll be exciting, right?"

My lips twitch. Exciting, yes, but not for the reasons she thinks, and it'll definitely not be a night off.

"Great," I supply, before locking my eyes back onto the TV screen.

Friday. Only four more days.

Twelve

NATALIE

MIDNIGHT.

That's the time my clock reads.

I left Tristan downstairs on the couch three hours ago, wishing him a good sleep. It's bizarre as hell to know a stranger is sleeping on my couch, but weirder knowing I'm still awake and waiting for another one.

Yes, waiting.

Because sleep continues to evade me and so far, he's been two for two in his nighttime visits. Why the fuck have I not told anyone about these visits? I admitted to the messages, and it would be so easy to walk downstairs and confess the rest to Tristan.

What is wrong with me that I'm still awake, waiting in anticipation?

What if he doesn't come? What if Tristan's presence scared him off? While that's the goal, the thought has my heart sinking in despair.

The sound of my window clicking shoots me upright in bed, clutching the blanket to my chest, the only barrier between the insanity I'm about to hand myself willingly over to.

The figure shimmies my window open and as he climbs through, I spot the switchblade in his hand. *Tristan guessed it.* He closes the window, placing the curtain back in position, and blocking the little bit I got to see of him. He's in a hoodie, but with the curtain shut again, I lose my vision. At the same time, there's a whoosh of the blade closing.

My throat tightens at the realization I'm a stupid love-sick schoolgirl who's read too much Jane Austin for what's normal. He could very well kill me this time.

Still, I don't yell out. Tristan is one floor under me, and easily accessible. But lust accompanies my stalker's very presence—the knowledge he's *here* and for me—has my teeth biting down on the words that'll end this.

"You're awake." But he doesn't sound surprised.

"Yeah," I breathe, tightening my fingers around the blanket, staring at the shape of his form.

"You have a guard dog."

By no means would I ever call Tristan a dog, but again, I say, "Yeah."

There's silence, and then suddenly, the bed meets my back, my eyes struggling to catch up to his quick movements. He straddles me, his hands going for my wrists again and pinning them to the bed.

"And yet you welcome me into your bed, Little Bird. Naughty girl."

My heart hammers against my chest and I'm almost positive he can feel it from his position overtop of me. "Yeah."

He makes a murmuring sound. "Have you touched yourself in my absence?"

The sex dripping from his voice has my legs clamping together. "No," I say, finally finding another word. And then boldly, "I was waiting for you."

He chuckles, a sound going straight into my chest. "Yeah? And if you've waited, what is it I will find then, hm?"

Please check.

"If I release your hands, will you touch me?"

"No," I tell him truthfully. If touching him ends this, then I'll tie my own hands to the bed.

After another beat, his fingers unpeel from my wrists, one at a time, testing me. In good faith, I keep them in their current position over my head.

"Good girl," he murmurs, sending heat straight to my core. "You've surprised me, Little Bird. You're playing the game better than I believed you ever would. Waiting for me, pussy wet and wanting. Only a skilled player does that."

"How do you know I'm wet?" I challenge, voice weak with desire.

"Because." His eyes flash in the dark as they near me. Through the obscurity, I try to make out what I can of him, but his hood is pulled too far over his head, causing it be difficult. "I know you, Natalie. I know your body is craving my touch."

"Because you watch me."

"I watch you because you're fucking beautiful, and smart, and I spend the entire day waiting for night, so I can be near you again."

"Why wait for nighttime?" I probe, wondering if he's just given away his reason for stalking me.

"Because people like me don't play in the daylight."

"People like you?"

"People—"

He cuts himself off, lowering his face until he's an inch away from my chest. His tongue flicks out, licking at my flesh there, before trailing a line into my tank. He stops and grasps my tank with his teeth and tugs it lower. The cool air nips at my stiff nipples, straining in the air for his touch.

His tongue continues its torture, skirting down and around a bud, but not actually touching it. A breathy sound halfway between a moan and a groan escapes me and my hips roll into his body, desiring more.

"Because," he starts again, "guys who come into women's houses to play games with them are not people who live in the daylight."

"Lucky for me then," I murmur. "I don't want those guys." He chuckles, his heat blowing over my bare chest, and I groan again. "Touch them. Please."

"Touch what?" He blows another breath, making my nipples tighten to the point of pain. My hands fist together by my head, keeping them pinned to the spot.

"Me. My nipples."

"Because you asked so nicely." But he doesn't touch them. He *bites* them. His teeth sink into one so hard, I'm sure he's about to draw blood. And then he does the same with the other, and I feel like I'm dying in the best way possible.

"You're quivering under my touch, Little Bird." There's a level of amusement buried in his voice. "Looks like you also like to play in the dark."

"Yes."

"I promised myself I wouldn't leave until I got to taste you," his tongue flicks out at my nub, "because yesterday was a cruel tease to the senses."

"Yes," I repeat, completely agreeing with him.

"Natalie."

"Hm?" I murmur after a moment, when he says nothing further.

"You're going to use your hands to keep your mouth shut. We can't have your bodyguard downstairs coming for you. What would he think to find you whoring yourself out to the villain like this?"

He'd think I was disturbed. Because damn, I'm pretty sure I am.

"And while you work on keeping your noises down, I'll be driving you to make them." He shifts, sliding down the length of my body, his fingers hooking on the band of my sleep shorts as he goes. "I'm going to eat your cunt now. I'm going to feast on you until you beg me to stop, or until we're interrupted by your guard down below. That way, if I'm caught and he kills me, I'll go to Hell with the taste of you on my tongue."

I whimper, not knowing what else to say to his insane, vile, delicious words.

"You like that, Natalie, don't you? God," he tosses my shorts to the side, "the smell of you is something I'll remember long into my time in Hell. But it's okay, because I'll have my retribution."

The word is odd, especially for the scenario and has me asking, "Retribution?"

"While I'm remembering your scent long after my death, you'll be remembering the feel of my tongue when I make you come harder than you ever have before. And that, Little Bird, is the retribution I'll leave behind on this earth."

Oh, how I want that. My hands tighten on the pillow. If he continues to talk like this, he'll make me orgasm from his words alone.

Even through the darkness, I *feel* his eyes on my centre, but I want more than his eyes there. My legs fall open, inviting him into my body.

A staggering breath whooshes out of him. "You're spreading your legs for the villain. How does that make you feel?"

Powerful. Excited. Like I'm living on the edge of danger.

"Answer me," he demands, his voice hardening.

"Powerful," I supply. "I have the villain on his knees."

He groans, a sound making me tingle right down to the tips of my toes. "Oh, you have no idea."

I wait, with bated breath, for the next part. When that first lick comes, my spine jolts off the bed. When the first probe into my centre occurs, I hand him my entire being.

"Drag me to Hell with you," I whisper. "That way we can do this all the time."

He doesn't respond, but I know he hears me since his tongue sinks inside me, his fingers grasping my open thighs and pinning me down as he gives me what I begged him for.

Him. Desire. To lose myself on the madness of his tongue and let him drink it from my body as we become one.

I whimper, stuffing my fist in my mouth because he's right—alerting Tristan would create a hella a lot of questions, ones I can't—won't—answer. My teeth dig into my knuckles, hating that I can't cry out like I crave to, but also finding the secretiveness of our rendezvous both reckless and thrilling.

His tongue wreaks havoc on my insides before circling my clit once, then twice, and sucking it in his mouth. I jolt, hips bucking against his mouth as another whimper escapes me. With my moan, his ministrations turn more vigorous. Playing with my clit—sucking it, biting it—until I'm forced to throw my head to the side and into my pillow to keep my cry from echoing through the entire house.

My wicked stranger pulls back, chuckling, but in no way is it a happy sound. Rather, it's a dangerous chuckle. One that says he officially has taken my soul. "Fuck, Little Bird, seeing you undone like that makes me want to steal you away and keep you in a cage of my own."

Stealing me away to continue these orgasms every day, all day is not the worse kidnapping scenario I could imagine.

"For now, though, you'll continue to fly free."

Until when? That's the question I wish to ask, but instead, I'm distracted by the bed jostling. His form comes over me, his face nearing. White spots, the result of clenched eyes disrupt my view. But I'm learning, it's not the view that matters. It's what he says.

And does.

His body presses me into the bed, his lips brushing mine. He's kissing me, and I still under the command of his presence.

"I want you to taste yourself. Taste how you truly feel about my visits."

His mouth claims mine roughly, his tongue breaking through my weak defences and flicking against mine. I do taste myself—sweet and different than anything I've ever tasted before. I kiss him back, positioning my hands on the bed and pushing my face into his, seeking more—deeper, harder—*more*.

For a moment, we're not two strangers.

He's not a man, whose name I'm still unaware of, despite him bringing me to orgasm twice.

He's not a man who's snuck into my house multiple times, simply to bring sin into my life.

He's not a man who's stalking me.

We're simply two people, on their way to Hell together.

He pulls back, far enough the hood once again covers his face. I wish I could see it. See his expressions and be able to distinguish what he's thinking—see *him*.

"I'll be back tomorrow night. Keep your window unlocked."

And like a thief in the night, he's gone, the window shut firmly behind him.

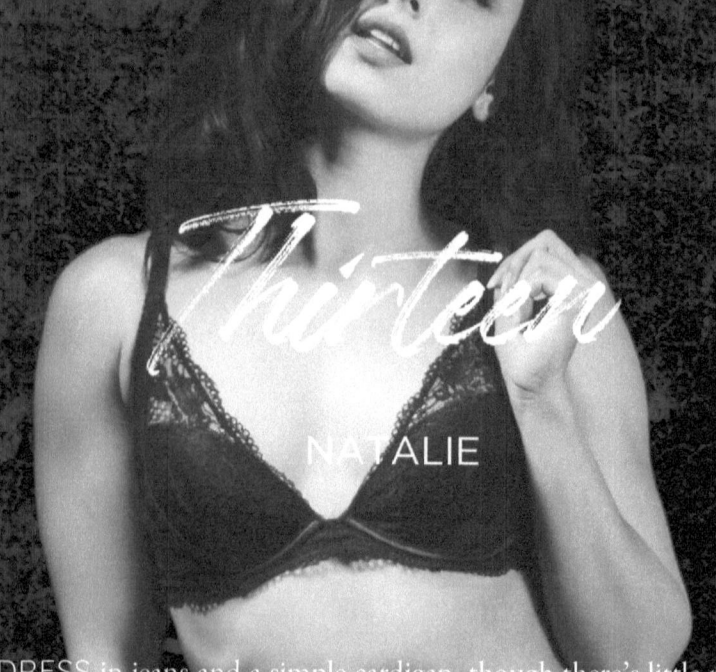

Thirteen

NATALIE

I DRESS in jeans and a simple cardigan, though there's little need for clothing to warm my body. Shame heats me all over when I leave my room the next morning, acutely aware that I'll have to face Tristan in mere moments.

A cop who's bound to see right through me. See that it's only been eight hours since I came on a stranger's face. The very stranger he's been up all night protecting me from. The irony isn't lost on me, and the guilt has my hands curling and uncurling over and over.

Sighing, I lift the message I woke up to find on my pillow, staring at the written words.

I'M OBSESSED WITH YOU, LITTLE BIRD. IF YOU THINK YOU'RE WINNING THIS GAME, YOU COULDN'T BE MORE WRONG. NOT ONLY WILL WE MAKE IT TO THE END TOGETHER, BUT WE'LL GET THERE AFTER I'M BURIED IN YOUR SWEET, TIGHT CUNT.

The words burn in my brain while I debate whether or not I should show this to Tristan. I mean, it's another message and he should be aware of it, but those words reveal something much more depraved.

82

Conflict rages through my stomach. This is all so messed up, and I do want him gone, but when my midnight visitor gets caught, it means my life returns to normal and I lose him. I lose the way he makes me feel, the slim excitement he brings to my nights—just *him*. For now, I fold the paper up into the tiniest square possible and tuck it inside my nightstand drawer, right beside the vibrator he once used with me.

Let's go, Natalie. Deep breath.

I swing open my door, coming face-to-face with a sight I could *definitely* get used to: Tristan, bare-chested, with nothing but a pair of sports shorts on, walking by on his way to the bathroom. He stops in front of my door, his eyes scanning me up and down. I pull my cardigan tighter around me, hoping it acts as a barrier against my guilt.

"Morning," I murmur.

"Good morning." His voice, soft and gooey, has me shivering, and I lift my eyes from the ground to lock on his chest.

His chest that, I swear, has been sculpted by the gods. It's the only explanation for how perfect it seems—not a hair in sight on his chiseled abs and broad chest. My mouth goes dry and I swallow through the lump, willing my brain to say something intelligible.

"Last night go okay?" I ask, feigning interest.

"Yep. No one came near the house."

Lying and I don't go well together. I can do it, sure, but I hate it. I throw my eyes to the ground, hiding the truth from him and mutter, "That's good. Want breakfast?"

"No thanks. Just heading to the bathroom." He gestures down the hall again.

"R-right. Go ahead. I'll be leaving for class soon."

But he doesn't move. Instead, he continues to study me, and the longer he does, the more my skin prickles and I feel like he somehow knows what happened last night.

"You look very pretty today," he says, his expression a mask. "Give me twenty and I'll be ready."

"O-okay."

Only when he walks away, do I release the long breath I was holding onto. *Natalie, get a grip.* Eight hours ago, I was with my shadowy stranger and now I'm getting flustered over another almost-stranger. I'm not a guy-hungry girl; I never been one. Five partners, which I realize may be sad, and maybe a bit pathetic, but it's me.

Or maybe I am sluttier than I believe. It's the only explanation for why I'm salivating over my bodyguard one moment and happily engaging in salacious behaviour with my stalker the next.

I shake my head and finish getting ready for class.

Class.

Where Tristan will be following me around, because, somehow, night-time messages result in a daytime guard. I may need to have a chat with Alex.

For now, I'll bite my tongue and continue on. Tuesdays, I have lunch with Elena and that'll be something different and welcoming.

ELENA

Sorry, can't make lunch today.

DAMN IT. I haven't seen her since she was warning me off Tristan, but that was also the time she had a meeting. The last time we actually spoke was when we met at the coffee shop. That was a pleasant day, and unlike something we typically do, but enjoyable, nonetheless.

Even then, she seemed off. I left to go to the washroom, and when I returned, she was staring at a retreating form—a guy from high school, she had said—like she saw a ghost from her past. From the back, I didn't recognize him as anyone I know. It's obvious something's been bothering her, but I'm also not one to overly prod.

I glance up from my phone and across the table where Tristan is scanning the campus. His eyes bounce from student to student, building to building, reminding me of a child. He's taking everything in with an awed expression.

"What's your university experience?" I ask, pulling his attention back to me.

"You know your class we attended this morning?"

"Yeah."

"That was my experience. By the time I graduated high school, I was already accepted into the police academy, so I jumped right into my training."

"Impressive," I tell him honestly. "Usually by now, I'm meeting with Elena, but she texted and said she's unavailable, so it's only you and me today." Probably for the best, if Tristan and Elena don't have good history. I straighten and rest my phone face down on the picnic table before asking, "Do you like being a cop?"

For a moment, I think he hasn't heard me. His expression remains flat and his eyes continue to scan the campus as though he's searching for something. After a long five seconds—I count—he speaks: "Yes. It's quite thrilling."

"But you've only been on the force for a few years," I comment, mentally calculating his time since graduation. "Unless I'm *way* off on your age, how did you end up with this personal bodyguard position? Shouldn't you be, like, a beat cop or something?"

He smirks, and the way the sun catches on his lighter strands has him looking like Apollo relaxing in the clouds. "I am a beat cop, but I'm also good at my job and one of the youngest on the force." He waves his hand to the space around us. "It's not a smart move to stick a fifty-year-old in school with you."

"True." Someone that age would stand out, versus Tristan, who fits right into the life here.

Professors had a head's up as to who he is, but we received a lot of curious looks from others. A new arrival did *not* go unnoticed, based on the salivating and ogling from other girls.

"Disappointed it's me?"

"Not at all. Simply curious."

"I've answered something, so it's your turn. Why English Lit? I've never seen you with a book in your hand."

Not even Jolene knows this truth. Beneath the safety of the picnic table, my knees pull together, hating the embarrassment I'll be forced to embrace. "Between you and me—it's 'cause I don't know what I want to do with my life. English Literature seemed like an easy degree."

His head tilts, curiosity deepening. His lack of judgement—so far —unlocks my legs. "Is it?"

"No." I laugh, the sound an almost sputtering instead. "Not at all. I'm insane. Should have done something else instead. Drama or Art, something I can at least pretend to fake and earn points for attempting."

His face cracks into a smile, momentarily making me forget why I was worried at all about telling him. "That's funny, Natalie. It surprises me though. Seems like you have everything figured out."

I shrug, letting seriousness back in the conversation. "Life isn't as easy as they make it seem. Still, I'm aiming to do well in the degree because, who knows, maybe I'll end up using it after all."

"Are you enjoying it at least?"

"Yeah." My mind drifts to the various topics I never thought I'd ever sit through. "I think people misconstrue it for simply reading books and writing about them, but there's a lot more going on than one would think. Like, did you know there's an entire meaning behind print and the effects it had on society at the time? It was quite chaotic, to have a new form of communication. Or how *Frankenstein* even came to be created, and what Mary Shelley had to do to get her book out there? Or how poetry was once the most popular form of literature?"

His lips twitch, making my shoulders sag. Maybe he did know all that and I'm the slow one here.

"What?" I bite.

"Nothing. Just, for someone who claims to not know what they'd like to do with their life, you seem quite smitten with literature. Maybe you should stick with it."

"Huh," I say, having nothing else to comment. Sometimes it's an outsider's perspective you need, and Tristan is giving me exactly that. I do enjoy it; have never skipped a class simply to avoid going. I don't know what an English degree would allow me to do in life, but perhaps, he's correct. Maybe I should start looking to determine what options are out there.

"Huh, what?"

"Nothing."

Tristan's eyes bore into me for long moment, searching my face. After another minute, he glances down at the phone in his hand. "Oh, Chief is calling. I should answer this. One moment." He stands, taking the phone, and walks down the path, disappearing from view.

A bit far for a simple phone call, but okay. Perhaps police business is too secretive for the likes of a busy campus location.

I breathe in the spring air, relieved to allow the scent of mud and wet grass to fill my senses, but after the freezing winter and the insane amount of snow we got, I'll take anything that isn't white and cold and makes me hate life. The campus is fairly quiet at this time, with most people in classes, which is why I love my break. It's easy find a table to sit at no matter where I am—the library, outdoors, or another location since the campus isn't overcrowded.

My phone rings, the ongoing vibrations sliding it across the wood. I snatch it up, placing it to my ear instantly, without reading the call display. "Hello?"

"Little Bird."

Fourteen

NATALIE

HIS PURR JOLTS itself straight to my spine, straightening it. My hand tightens around the delicate metal device against my face, and I lean, working through different angles to see if I can spot anyone staring at me, but there's no one. Then I check for Tristan.

"H-how did you get my number?" I whisper, despite the fact that the nearest person to me is at least twenty feet away at another table.

"You have no faith in me if you think I can't get something as simple as a phone number. Natalie, aren't you happy to hear from me?"

Am I? My body sure is, considering my hands instantly go damp. My knees press together, attempting to hold my nerves in. But this is next level, and perhaps the wake-up to make me realize how dangerous it is for me to be hiding truths from Tristan and Alex, the people trying to help me.

"I-I don't know."

He tsks. "Not the response I was wanting, considering I haven't been able to stop thinking about you. Your cries, your moans... your taste. Each night, I take a bit more of you."

"Yes," I breathe, nearly soundless. I want him to take all of me—because I'm a stupid person.

"It wasn't supposed to be like this," he continues, his voice heavy with regret. "I was never supposed to touch you, but then I saw you and couldn't help myself. And now, I'm slowly making you mine. How do you feel about that, Little Bird? Can I keep you in a cage all for myself?"

Mr. Darcy has nothing on my stranger in the night. "I think I'd like that," I whisper, my body feeling weighted down by my truth.

It's so fucked up, especially with Tristan protecting me from this guy. Hell, *I'm* the one who asked Alex for help, adding another level to how truly messed-up this is, but I never imagined I would come to *want* what's being dished out.

"Good girl," he murmurs. "As your reward, and before your bodyguard comes back, I want you to get up and slowly walk toward the left. There's a space between the library building and another one. Go there."

My head whips up instead, scanning the campus, specifically the small patch of grass between the buildings he speaks of. If he's describing it with so much detail, it means he must have seen it for himself. Which means he's *here*...

I stand, almost dazed with shock. "Will I be finding you there?"

"Maybe."

Maybe isn't a yes. I gather my things and walk toward the library, continuing to search the area around me for both my stranger and Tristan. I linger, doing a last check to ensure no one is watching me before I slip into the shadows between the buildings, finding it, unfortunately, empty of anyone else.

"Good. Continue into the shadows. Keep yourself away from sight of anyone walking by."

I do, scooting deeper into the darkness.

"Natalie, do you remember what my mouth feels like on your

pretty pussy? Do you recall how my tongue consumed your insides, how you fell apart in bed last night?"

It only kept me up half the night. "Of course."

"Picture me there, doing it again. Touch yourself until you come."

"What?" I still, gaze whipping back to the opening between the buildings. Here? Out in public like this? He's crazy. "No. Thought you said I can't make myself come."

"*You* won't be, because I'll be right here with you. When it's your fingers touching yourself, it'll be mine entering your body. Mine playing with that clit I know to be swollen and begging for attention already. It won't be you touching yourself because it'll be the memory of me making you orgasm. My words right here in your ear. Now, unclasp your jeans and touch your clit."

"No," I say weakly, breathless after his rant. "I'm in public."

"No one's watching," he counters. He's likely right. With my position, someone would have to come to the opening between the buildings to even see me.

But for him to be making that bold statement... "How do you know that?"

"Maybe I'm closer than you think. Stop stalling. We can't have that guard of yours coming to look for you. Put your hand down your pants. Now."

It's insane and reckless, but his command makes my head go light —makes me want to respond in the way he's demanding I do. It's why I'm waiting for him each night, and leaving my window open tonight.

It's awkward to maneuver and keep the phone to my ear, but I manage to undo my pants and squeeze my hand in between the tight denim.

"Touch your clit, Little Bird. Squeeze it. Stroke it. Pretend it's my hand."

I lean against the brick wall, using it to keep me upright and steady as my mind travels to the past—to last night when it was his fingers touching me.

I moan.

He groans. "Tell me, are you wet?"

"Yes," I respond. The moment I took his call, I was wet.

"You're wet with the same flavour I was gifted with last night, aren't you? Put your finger inside that tight cunt."

I do, flushing with his dirty orders. "Done."

"And now another."

My core stretches to accommodate two fingers and I bite down on my lip, keeping my noises low as not to cry out and risk calling attention to myself.

"One day, it'll just be you and me, and you'll be able to make all the noise you want, I promise. No bodyguard. No school."

"We're only doing this right now because you started it."

"And I'll finish it." Based on the deep promise in his tone, I think he means it. "Pump your fingers. Imagine my tongue circling your swollen clit while I thrust my fingers inside you."

"Hard to when I have no idea what you look like." But I do regardless, moving my fingers in and out, allowing the tingle to grow in the base of my stomach as I, indeed, picture his tongue playing with me.

He laughs quietly. "One day you will."

My fingers freeze, pleasure taking second chair to what he's saying. "Do you mean that?" My pulse picks up speed, but I'm not sure if it's from excitement or fear.

"Most likely."

It's the closest I'll get to a yes, so I take it.

"You've stopped."

"You're watching?" Again, I scan the little bit I can see, even tilting my head to check above me, to the tops of the buildings.

"I can tell by your breathing you've stopped. It's as if you don't want to come. If that's the case, I may not come over tonight..." His threat hangs in his drifting silence.

"No." My fingers move inside me again, continuing where we left off.

"Good girl," he murmurs in my ear.

I've never been the girl turned on by someone calling me names, but then, I've also never been turned on by stalkers in the night. My few hookups have been quick, casual, and a lot less exciting than this.

"You're squeezing your fingers. I can't wait until I can replace them with my cock and feel you tighten around me the same way."

My muscles constrict around my fingers in anticipation. "Me neither," I say, thumb flicking my clit.

I imagine it. Me facing the brick wall as he takes me like an animal from behind, just a few feet away from where people can see us. My nails breaking as they try to grip the stone wall while I beg for him to let me come. His hand holding my hips, keeping me steady as he rocks me to my very core, hitting places no man has ever found before.

A whimper breaks my lips, kind of loud and wanting. The imaginary feeling of him inside me, consuming me, taking me for himself brings me to the edge.

"I'm going to come," I tell him, forcing air into my words.

"Do it."

I tumble off the edge, my teeth sinking into my bottom lip as I wildly ride my hand, imagining it's my nameless guy. Slowly, as I return to reality, I bring my fingers out from my core, wipe them on my jeans and button my pants up, again glancing to ensure no one is watching me.

He groans in my ear, reinforcing everything I did. "Little Bird, you have no idea how much I wish I was with you right now."

"I imagined you," I say boldly.

"What did you picture?"

"You. Inside me. Here." My fragmented words are laced with embarrassment, but I'm sure he can piece them together.

He hums in pleasure. "My beautiful girl. I need to go now, but I'll be seeing you tonight." He hangs up, not giving me a chance to reply.

I tuck my phone in the back pocket of my jeans and remain there against the brick wall until my heart pounds at a normal speed and my breathing isn't so laboured. Tristan is bound to be back now and wondering where I've gone. He hasn't texted yet, but I'm sure it's just a matter of time.

Once I've collected myself, I leave the space between the buildings and walk back to the picnic table I was last sitting. Tristan is standing beside it, his body facing away, head twisting as he scans the area.

"Hey," I say as I approach.

He spins instantly, capturing me with those soulful eyes I've come to enjoy, but before the truth appears on my face, I lower my gaze, hoping I'm less obvious. "Where did you go?"

"Bathroom," I respond. "Sorry, should have let you know. Your phone call went on for a while."

"Yeah, Chief had a lot to say." But his words are guarded, his eyes shielded as if he knows something is up. "You okay, Natalie? Your skin is flushed."

"Yeah." I cough, changing the subject to get his attention focused elsewhere. "My next class is soon. Coming?"

And with that, I walk away, leaving him to follow me.

Fifteen

TRISTAN

THAT WORKED BETTER than I could have ever dreamed.

It was a shot in the dark, one I hoped she wouldn't piece together with my obvious and sudden absence to speak with "Chief," but damn, it worked.

Since I've been at this campus so many times, I've already surveyed it. Between the library and another building, the sun is at a position above that results in most of the area being shadowed. The time of day means likely less students out and about, giving maximum privacy for when I dragged Natalie out of her shell.

She surpassed my expectations.

She's surpassed all my expectations. Being by her side, chatting with her like two normal people is amazing. The last time I enjoyed simply talking with a woman was... never. Women see me, they take me for a ride, and that's it. It's never more—something I've never cared about until now, when comparing quick moments with them to spending quality time with Natalie.

And then at nighttime, when both our other personas come out to play... Fuck. Me.

Is it possible to be this in-like with a person—this *obsessed* with a person already?

She's fucking addictive.

My leg bounces and I shift in these damn wooden, uncomfortable chairs. Easily the worst part about attending her classes. Thankfully, the stupidly small table is able to hide the erection that continues to pop up each time I think about our phone call.

That was way too fun.

Her breathy moans, the excitement of it all... it didn't take her long. She thinks it was for her; when in reality, it was for me. Because after last night, waiting until tonight feels damn hellish, especially when I'm stuck sitting by her side all day.

The call was an appetizer before the main meal, if you must.

I glance sideways, noting how her skin is still flushed pink. I'd die to know where her mind is because as she continues to take notes from whatever her professor is speaking about, she appears focused, but I recognize the small divot between her eyes, telling me her mind is elsewhere.

She thinks she hid the truth from me well, but she didn't. When she returned to the picnic table, guilt was there in her eyes and in the way she moved. Her jerky movements, her avoidance of eye contact— cute, but obvious.

I continue to watch her. How when she's not writing, the tip of her pen slips between her plump lips—lips, I've become engrossed with staring at all day. Kissing them last night was as good as kissing her other lips. Nearly as flavourful and just as powerful. Her eyes dull when she's listening, but when the prof says something she feels the need to jot down, they grow bright again and she sits up, scribbles her notes, almost eager, before adopting her blasé body position again.

It's fascinating to watch. *She's* fascinating... and I have no idea why.

She's a seemingly normal girl. Other than being a sister to a psycho, she attends school and stays home in the evening.

And has secret rendezvous with a total stranger, but that's beside the point.

So why, as every moment passes, am I becoming more and more obsessed with her?

Sixteen

NATALIE

"TOMORROW AFTER CLASS, I want to go see my aunt." A sudden choice, but one I decided on during the walk home. She represents my old norm—before Tristan, stalkers, and the moment I lost my mind. Not that I plan on telling her everything, but maybe a simple conversation will help settle my sanity.

"Sure." Tristan peeks up from his phone. "You're the boss. You lead the way and I'll keep anyone from touching you."

The heat in his words burns in the air between us, and I glance over, noting his hooded eyes and turned-away expression. Of course, he only means it as his job, but the weight behind his words seem to go past why he's here and—

I shake the insanity from my mind. My trysts with my stalker have done more than remove rationality from my mind; they've made me think even Tristan is interested in me. I mean, there's the flirty comments and heated looks, but based on my knowledge of guys, I'm suspecting it's simply Tristan's personality. *I* do not look like a girl who would ever be found attached to someone like Tristan. I'm not tall, skinny, or have flawless skin.

So, before I end up making a fool of myself, I refocus on TV show episode we're in the middle of. Of course, my mind continues to drift away to places—to a person—it shouldn't be daring go to though.

This is dangerous. I still have no idea what this guy wants from me. Maybe I'm literally falling into his trap. There was an episode I once saw where the girl fell in love with her captor, only for him to turn around and brutally murder her.

The only saving grace is when I don't leave my room by a certain time in the morning, Tristan is bound to come hunting for me.

"Another one?"

"Hm?" I blink, realizing the episode is over. I've missed over half of it and will need to re-watch it some other time.

"Another episode?"

"Sure." In the same second, my stomach grumbles, alerting me to its own mood. "I'm also thinking a snack. Chips?"

"Please." Tristan stands, towering over me in basic sports shorts and a T-shirt, and I focus on a loose string attached to my shirt to avoid drooling at him like a moron. "I'm going to the bathroom real quick. I'll be back."

He's gone for a few moments and I use the opportunity to gather us snacks and get comfortable on the couch again, setting up another episode.

When he's back, he plops on the couch beside me, his hand immediately going for the bowl of chips I've placed between us.

I wish I could say having Tristan here is still awkward but truthfully, it's not. He's oddly pleasant to be around—funny, polite, and quiet. When I'm near him, there's a different feeling I also get. Like I *know* him. I don't—obviously—but there's a small flip in my stomach when he's close. He's comfortable, as though we've been friends for a while.

"You know, I can feel you staring, right?" His eyes cut over, a grin overtaking his expression before he pops another chip in his mouth.

"So what if I am?" My nose wrinkles, going for playful. "I'm allowed to look. It's my house."

"I'm the guest, so don't the same rules apply and I'm allowed to look at you?"

My face heats. He may be playing around, but his expression sure as hell isn't. It's pure sex and I want—

God, I'm a whore. Hours ago, another man made me come, and in a few more hours, he should be returning. So *why* is it when I'm with Tristan, it's easy to forget my midnight obsession? I should confess everything to Tristan right now and allow him to catch the guy and end my unhealthy habits.

But that's the problem with bad habits—there's a reason they're bad in the first place. I know he's dangerous. He claims he won't hurt me, but how much of anything he says is a lie? Still, I find myself swallowing the pill, shooting back the shot, and gorging on the snack—habits all equivalent to the toxicity mine is.

I shake the thoughts from my mind and lift the remote again, readying to un-pause the show, when Tristan speaks, "Tell me more about yourself."

Doing a double take in surprise, I lower the remote again. "We've already played this game."

"You can't tell me after one conversation, I know everything about Natalie Miller."

My shoulders lift in a shrug. "I'm a boring person."

"Favourite song?"

I shrug.

"Favourite food?"

"Too many to choose."

He sighs. "Favourite colour?"

"Red."

"Finally, a real response! White or red wine?"

"White." My nose wrinkles again. "Red makes me gag."

Tristan sits forward, twisting to face me head-on. "See, there're still things I can learn about you."

The question being why he wants to know these things.

"Favourite hard liquor?"

"Gin."

"Gin?" he repeats, brows lifting. "That's unique."

"Unique bad or unique good?"

"Just unique." He grins. "Not too many gin drinkers around here."

"I like how it hits me differently than other alcohol."

Tristan's chocolate eyes glint in the light. "Another interesting fact."

I giggle, loving how freely we're talking and I lean back, tucking my feet underneath me, the TV now forgotten. "What about you? Favourite liquor?"

"Bourbon."

"What a guy answer." I roll my eyes, grinning regardless. "Favourite colour?"

"Don't have one."

I snatch the bowl away, tucking it on the other side of me. "For that, you don't get any more. Making fun of me for not knowing all my preferences and yet, you don't know all yours."

"Blue."

"You're only saying that to get the food back."

His mouth stretches into an easy grin before he scoots across the couch, and I realize how close we've gotten. His hand reaches over my lap, but I quickly position myself in front of the bowl, protecting it from him.

"If you don't share, I'll have to take it from you."

"I'd like to see you try."

He growls—*fucking growls*—and the sound shoots itself straight into my core. A sound only discussed in literature, but now I see why women are such a fan. My head goes momentarily light. He could take the chip bowl if he wanted, so long as he does that again.

He lifts himself onto one knee, so his form overshadows mine. His arms come around me, one on the back of the couch and one at the armrest at my back, caging me in. I inhale his sweet minty scent, letting it flood my senses.

I've smelled this before. Where have I smelled this before?

But his nearness continues to wipe away any thoughts in my head, causing me to focus on his proximity. His eyes study my face, landing on my lips. Mine part in response, aiming to get any bit of air I can into my lungs before I accidentally pass out. His pupils narrow, making his eyes a larger pot of coffee. One I'll drown in if I'm not careful.

"If you don't give me the bowl, I may just have to convince you."

I still, my heart unwilling to take another beat and ruin the chance of this moment.

"H-how?" I dampen my lips while mentally cursing myself for stuttering.

Tristan's mouth curls, pulling my attention to how attractive his lips are. Attractive lips are not a thing I ever imagined thinking about, but they're perfectly symmetrical and just plump enough, making them extremely kissable.

"I'm sure we could come up with a few ways."

"Yeah?"

"Yeah," he murmurs, his lips barely moving.

Oh my God, what is happening right now? This isn't me. I'm the quiet girl. The unsocial one. Not the one who strings two guys along. Is this what loneliness does to a person? Any attention is good attention and my soul is drinking it all up.

Similar contemplations must go through his head because the pool of his eyes hardens into dark ice, a wall pushing me away from him. He clears his throat and leans back, reclaiming his seat again. His hands find his lap and rest loosely there, but from the way the tendons in his arms pop, he's not at ease.

"I'm sorry, Natalie. That wasn't... it wasn't right or professional. I shouldn't—not while I'm here to—"

"I get it." I do. Rejection burns my chest, and I bring the chip bowl back to its spot, placing a barrier between us once more. His dismissal hurts, but I truly do get his point.

I angle my body in a way that'll avoid being facing in his direction. I press play on the episode we were about to begin and say nothing more as it begins, colours flashing rapidly over the screen.

A few minutes into the episode, Tristan speaks again, but they're words I nearly wonder if I've dreamt up.

"Natalie, you have no idea how much I wish things were different."

I glance over, but he shows no sign of ever talking at all. *If* he truly said those words, he obviously doesn't care enough to show me.

For the rest of the episode, it's not his words I focus on. It's how he said them. With deep-seated desire, masked by something else—something secretive. Something that chills my spine and makes the couch feel as if I'm sitting on spikes.

When the show is over, I scurry to bed, barely throwing a, "Goodnight," over my shoulder before I lock myself inside my bedroom and ready for bed. Before I do, I unlock my window, all the while wondering if my emotions can handle a visit.

Whoever he is makes me feel free and wanted. He doesn't reject me. But when I'm with him, I'm lying to Tristan, whose entire purpose in my life is to help me. Then when I flirt with Tristan, it feels like I'm cheating on my stalker.

I leave the window unlocked and the ultimate decision up to him. If he comes, I could lose myself in my second life and forget all about Tristan downstairs.

But he never does. Midnight passes and not a blip.

I fall asleep, dreaming of Tristan's sweet scent and a faceless man bringing me to orgasm.

Seventeen

NATALIE

"NATTIE, WHO'S YOUR FRIEND?" Jolene's brows spike, her attention locked on where Tristan sits a few tables away, scanning the closed compound.

He insisted on coming inside, even though I told him the centre is privatized and guarded. The only reason he got through the front doors at all, in fact, is due to the badge he whipped out of his jacket. It was kinda hot.

"Just a friend."

Jolene narrows her eyes. "Nattie, what's happening to you?"

Guilt rumbles beneath my skin. My hands tighten around the bench seat, leg bouncing under the safety of the table. I've never been a good secret-keeper.

"Nothing."

"Natalie," she looks sternly at me, "I know you. You've arrived with a cop in tow. What is happening?"

"And you won't believe me if I say nothing? We're friends." I shrug, hoping it's a half-truth anyway. "My friend, Elena, introduced me to him." Not a complete lie.

"Then why's he way over there?"

"He wanted to give us time alone," I counter.

"Then why come at all?"

I huff, hating how inquisitive she is. "Because." I give her a non-answer. "Jolene, I'm here for you. Forget about him."

The wrinkles around her eyes crinkle even more as they narrow. "I'll leave it alone for now, but I can tell you're lying to me, Natalie. You have the same guilty expression you always have when you try to lie. Eventually, you'll crack. Besides," her expression smooths out, "he's impossible to forget about looking like that."

"Jolene!" I playfully exclaim, unclamping my hand from the bench to swat at her, thankful she's off the previous topic for now. "He's, like, a fraction of your age."

"Doesn't mean I can't look." She laughs, and when it tapers off, her head tilts, studying me. "There's a light inside you, Nattie. It wasn't there the other day. You're obviously hiding something, but you're happy. It's good. You need to be happier."

Happy. Is this what I am? It doesn't feel like I'm happy.

Not when I woke up miserable this morning, with only a message to show for it.

By the time I arrived, you were sleeping and looked way too peaceful for me to wake. I'm selfish enough to claim you but not selfish enough to keep you up all night when you clearly need the sleep.

He came and it did cause me to smile throughout my morning routine, providing me with the energy I needed to face Tristan.

Which was awkward. He barely spared me a glance, shooting me a quick nod on his way to the bathroom. A freaking *nod* is what I get from him.

Since my stranger's note didn't indicate anything other than being a watchful creep, this one I gave to Tristan, but I wonder why. Without any threat from my stalker, Tristan will have to leave me—which will allow me to live uninterrupted with my stalker. On the other hand, despite the lust-clouds consuming me each time he comes to my room,

I do still need Tristan to take care of this before he finds my body in a dumpster in a few weeks.

Plus, I don't want Tristan to leave. Not yet. So, I handed it over to him, mentioning it was in my room when I awoke.

Tristan took it, read it, and stuffed it inside his pocket. Other than his nod, that was the only form of communication I managed to yank from him. Even our walk to Jolene's centre was silent until he had to speak with the front desk.

Last night ruined us.

Us? I scoff. *What us?* There isn't an us. There's an awkward, lonely girl and a guy who's paid to sit inside her house and search for a stalker who she's stopped being afraid of. The only *us* there could have even been was rejected on the couch last night.

"Natalie?"

Right. Jolene was complimenting my "happiness."

"Yeah, thanks," I say weakly. "How has your week been?"

"Quick, considering it's Wednesday and not Sunday. They surprised me right out of my knitting chair when they told me you were here to see me." Her withered smile stretches her face. "Not that I'm displeased to see you. Just curious."

I shrug, wishing I had more to say but opt for the truth. "A niece can't some see her favourite aunt out of the blue? I wanted familiarity for a moment. How was your poker game last night?"

Every Tuesday is poker night here, though what they gamble away, I've always been scared to ask.

My question lights her expression, and she straightens. "Oh, that Bob. I swear, one day I'm catching him on cheating..."

I lose myself in her story, laughing at her amusing antics and impressions of her fellow community here. And through it, I don't think about the chaos waiting a couple picnic tables away.

"YOUR AUNT IS AMUSING," Tristan says as the guard closes the gate behind us. "She reminds me of you in some ways. Like, I see where some of your attitude is learned from."

"Attitude?" I whip my attention to where he walks beside me, his hands stuffed in the front pocket of his faded jeans. His usual leather jacket is tight on his form and with his flop of hair over his forehead, he looks less like a police officer and more like an actual bodyguard. He's commenting on my attitude when he's the one who's refused to speak to me all day.

"Demeanour would be the better word," he interjects. "Sorry. I meant, the way you speak and laugh and such, it reminds me of her. She's funny."

Of course he feels that way. After Aunt Jolene went on and on about the poker game, she circled back to me—my classes, what I've been eating for dinner, and Tristan again. When I didn't give her the answers she was so clearly hoping for, she invited him over.

I couldn't be angry. Jolene's social circle got a lot smaller upon her admittance to the centre. Besides me, the nurses, and her fellow residents, she never meets anyone new, since I've never had anyone to bring around.

Tristan was lovely with her. Polite and answering nearly everything she wanted to know, coming up with answers even I couldn't think up. When she asked him why he's with me, his response was simple.

"Because I want to be." A lie, but one that not only worked on her, but me as well.

"I think she enjoyed talking to someone new," I comment. "Thank you for being nice to her, by the way."

He tilts his head in my direction. "My pleasure. Do you mind me asking what happened to her? You mentioned a medical condition once."

"It was random. She was driving when the first blackout occurred, and she smashed her car into a pole. The doctors ran their tests and came back with some condition."

"Do the blackouts happen often?"

"Often enough she shouldn't be alone. If she was cooking or something, and I wasn't with her..." I trail off, leaving Tristan to fill in the gaps.

Based on his, "I see," he does. "It's a very fancy place."

The underlying question is obvious. "Yeah, my brother's paying for it."

I keep my attention focused on the sidewalk in front of us, watching my feet as we stride down the darkened side roads back home. Given my classes run late into the afternoon, we didn't get to Jolene's until early evening.

Nonetheless, I feel his eyes bore into my side. "You never mention your brother."

"Not much to tell. He is..." I trail off, genuinely not knowing how to describe Alex. Instead, I circle back to Jolene. "I was paying for a place, but it wasn't as good as I wanted for her. Then my brother offered to get her into a better facility. I haven't known *of* him until recently, but his help is appreciated. This place, as you saw, is beautiful and generous. Clean, which is important." I shiver, remembering the last place. Small, thin mattresses, dead gardens, and few group activities. It was more a jail than anything, but it had people to assist Jolene, and that's what I needed and could afford. "This place is perfect. She enjoys cooking, and they allow her to continue that, under supervision."

"It's very generous of your brother," Tristan rumbles, his voice sounding far away.

I glance over, using the overhead street lamp as a spotlight to examine him, but I can't tell what's on his face.

"It is," I agree finally.

We turn the corner onto another street. I'm so lost staring at my feet against the dark cement, I don't see the body until it's too late. Until it bumps into me and I feel my purse straps sliding from my arms.

"Hey!" My grip tightens around the strap, but it's too late, the person already having too firm a grasp.

In the same instance, Tristan spins on his heel, throwing his body past mine. He's quick and has the guy's shirt in his grip. His arm cocks back and a sickening crack echoes through the air around me as he throws his fist in the guy's face.

"You thought it was wise to fucking steal from her, motherfucker?"

Without waiting for a response, Tristan sends another punch his way. Blood spurts, the guy's body going slack. Mine goes weak at the same time, my eyes falling to the ground to look anywhere but at the guy's blood. My bag drops to the ground between their feet and Tristan kicks it toward me.

"Tristan, leave him. We have the bag."

I'm unsure if he hears me though, because instead of following my instructions, his hand whips into the guy's face again.

"The moment you decided to steal from her was the moment you sealed your fate, you fucker."

Oh, God, I hope he doesn't mean death.

"Tristan," I call again.

He releases the guy. Having been hit in the face so many times, the man merely slumps to the ground, groaning. His hand scrapes at the cement by his side once, before going lax and giving up his attempt to move.

Tristan yanks his cell from his pocket, throwing it toward his ear. He speaks so fast I don't catch all the words, but after a few seconds, he hangs up, commenting, "I have some of the guys on their way here." He kicks at the seemingly-lifeless body on the ground. "Think about the charges for theft before you do it next time, bastard."

I step away, putting my back to the nearest building as my hands latch onto my purse, and I stare at the guy on the ground, forcing air through my lungs. With the adrenaline and shock of the moment gone, my throat tightens.

I've never seen something like that—the violence. My life isn't interesting enough to typically have a hot guy protecting me. I've never seen a real fight break out, and now that I have... I don't like it.

Tristan remains guard over the guy's form until bright red and blue lights brighten the immediate area. The pierce of sirens cut off as the police cruiser pulls up. Two guys jump out, one stopping by Tristan and one heading straight for the thief. He hoists him up, clamps handcuffs on his wrists and throws him in the back of the car. The guy remains slumped over in the back seat, not seeming to realize what just happened.

The officers talk with Tristan a few more moments before hopping in the car and driving off, and with them, the excitement of the moment vanishes, leaving the area as silent as before.

"I guess we should continue on," I murmur, hoisting my purse higher on my shoulder and tightening my grip on the strap with some sense of being able to protect it from that occurring again. I manage a step before being blocked by Tristan's form pushing me back against the wall.

His head hangs over mine, his normally bright eyes darkening. "Are you okay, Natalie? I'm so fucking sorry."

His deep tone sends comforting shivers down my spine. "For? It wasn't your fault."

"I'm not a very good guard."

My hand waves through the nighttime air, hoping to brush away his negative thoughts. "He came out of nowhere, it's fine. I'm fine."

"When I'm given a task, I see it through." Tristan crowds me with his delicious scent. His arms rest on the brick by my head and he cages me in with his body. His expression is deadly but nonetheless, butterflies take off in my stomach, flying toward my throat.

"I'm a task then?" I whisper, hurt seeping into my tone again. His comment isn't surprising after last night, but it still stings. He only saved me because Alex and his boss would flip their shit to know I was robbed with him right beside me.

"You know I wish you weren't."

"I don't usually feel like this with guys." The admittance slips out and it's too late to take back.

"Like what?"

"Like we... we just work. I feel something between us, but I have no idea what. It's crazy, right?" I huff, masking my humour.

"Not at all, because I feel it too." One hand pushes off the wall and he strokes a finger down the length of my face, his eyes melting. "I'm sorry if he scared you. Or if I scared you. When I saw him, I reacted without thinking." Though his touch stays soft, I spot the veins in his arm tightening.

"It's fine," I say mutely, eyes drifting to the hand by my face. More noticeably, the red streaked across his fist. "Are *you* okay?" I pull my face away, reaching for his clearly injured hand. "Tristan..."

He tucks his hand away, wiping it against the leather of his coat. "It's not my first scuffle and it won't be my last." He steps back, breaking the spell between us. "Come. We should probably get home before I have to hit anyone else who dares come near you."

I sense he's slightly joking, but as I fall into step beside him, noting his hands fisted at his sides, ready to attack if he needs to, I realize he's not.

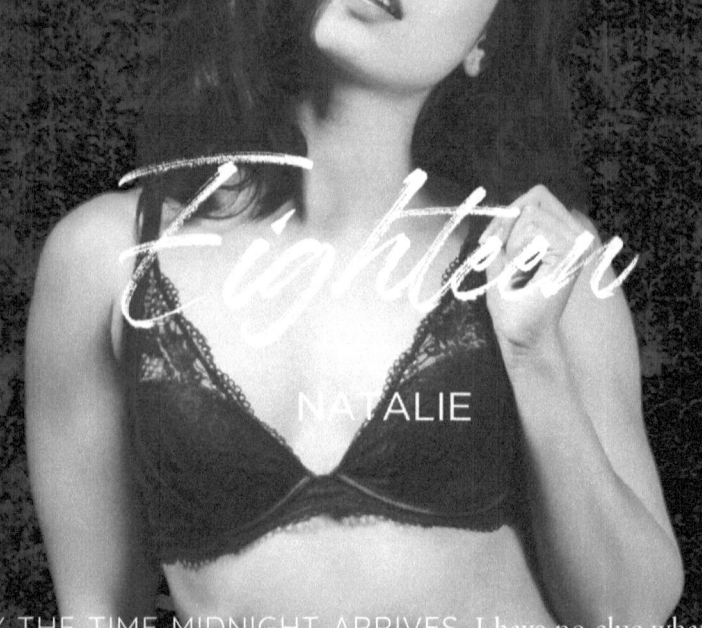

Eighteen

NATALIE

BY THE TIME MIDNIGHT ARRIVES, I have no clue what to feel. My stalker is exciting and lights my desire in all sorts of ways, but Tristan is sweet and protective and *here*.

But he's unavailable, at least that's what he said.

Wait—why am I choosing between them as though I'm picking a boyfriend?

The window slides open, capturing my attention, and as he climbs inside my room, shutting the window behind him, all thoughts of Tristan dissipate in the air, like they were never there in the first place.

"Hi."

"Close your eyes," he demands. His tone is a few degrees colder than usual, and again, my body jerks with unknown feelings.

"I missed you," I say, attempting to thaw his heart.

"I don't believe you." He pauses and I hear a slight noise. "I want to see you tonight. Lights on, so I've brought a blindfold. I'm going to put it on you now."

It's a demand not a question. An instruction. Still, I murmur, "Okay."

I hear his steps—hear him approach. His skin brushes mine as he slips a blindfold over my hair and behind my head. Before his touch goes away, his thumb brushes over my lips. I part my mouth.

Behind the protection of the blindfold, I open my eyes in time to hear him switch on my bedside lamp.

"Fucking Christ," he curses. "The moonlight doesn't do your body any justice. Even clothed, you're perfect, and I can't wait to unwrap you."

The fact he thinks my imperfect body is perfect for him is another reason this feels right, even if it's *so* wrong. "Now?"

"Soon," he promises, his hand stroking the length of my arm. "I've missed you, my Little Bird. It was agony not to wake you last night with my tongue between your legs."

My stomach heats. I *feel* the memory of what he's describing, and I want it. "I wouldn't have minded."

"I know," he says, a smile in his tone. "I figured by giving you the night off, you'd be reenergized for tonight."

My teeth dig into my bottom lip, holding in my grin. "That sounds right."

"But," his voice drops lower, "then I saw your fucking guard holding you."

I still. "You were watching us." It's not a question. He had to have been. It's the only way he'd know.

"I'm always watching you. And I'm watching him get close to what's *mine*."

"I'm sorry," I rush to say, having nothing else to respond with.

His grip tightens on my wrist. Not painfully, but enough to tell me he's there. He climbs over my body and then his lips smash roughly against mine.

The blindfold stealing my sight increases my other senses, and I hear his ragged breathing by my ear, feel the annoyance coursing through his body, and smell and taste the musk of anger making the room stuffy.

His lips pull away. "You gave yourself to me the other day, Little Bird, or have you already forgotten about that? I'm gone one night and you move on. Giving yourself to another man." His irate tone slashes my senses, but he's not wrong. Without his touch, my lonely body did latch onto the next available guy. "Do you even realize how difficult it was to watch tonight and not intervene?"

While I may not be a believer of God, I send a silent thank you to the sky and whatever or whoever is up there that he didn't approach Tristan and me. I'm not sure who would have made it out alive.

"Who owns you, Natalie?" Without waiting for an answer, his lips smash against mine, once more, pulling a kiss that's full of malice, full of hate but still, I part my lips, welcoming in his wrath.

"You do," I manage when he pulls back. My heart races, breaths catching up to the moment.

"Fucking right." His hands tear at my tank, pushing it down my body. My nipples pucker instantly with the cool air in my room. He attacks my panties next, ripping them in two until they fall away. "Who's the only one to make this pretty pussy come?"

He touches me there, his finger lightly tracing my core.

"You do," I whisper, heart rate picking up.

"Your bodyguard won't be coming near here."

"No."

"Good girl." His voice drops softer, back to the tone I'm used to him using. His finger continues to circle my clit. "Did that fucker hurt you? The thief?"

He truly did see everything. It should make me fear him more, but somehow, knowing he's always watching me is right. "No."

"Good," he rumbles. "I can't have a murder on my conscious too. Attacking what's mine like that..." He trails off, leaving the threat unsaid.

I sit up, while blind, using my hands to feel the blanket around us, moving it until I find the roughness of his jeans. "Are you going to touch me at some point tonight? My last orgasm was between the buildings, and I've..."

"You've what?"

"Missed you," I whisper, hoping I didn't accidentally give him more than he wants from me.

"Me too, Little Bird, me too. I planned on fucking you tonight, but I think I'm still a bit too worked up and don't want to hurt you."

Surprise flickers from behind the blindfold. He never gives much emotion away, leaving me to question if he even has a heart. But then my mind registers his words, on what he almost gave me tonight. I should be terrified he's wanting to take that step, but I'm not, because I do too.

"You're still mad because Tristan got too close?"

"Yes, but that's not it."

My hand continues up the path of his jeans, feeling his hard body beneath my palm. I find his belt, and past it, his flat stomach covered by a tight shirt. "Then what is it?"

"I'm annoyed at myself. Angry, because I've taken you for myself and it was a stupid thing for me to do."

"Oh." For what feels like the millionth time this week, I'm rejected, but this is worse than Tristan's. At least with Tristan, nothing happened between us and now nothing will. But that's not the case with my midnight visitor.

"I can hear your thoughts, my beautiful girl. It's not because I don't want you. It's because you and I are not done playing this game. We need to make it to the finish line, and by the time we do, you'll hate me."

I stop breathing, knowing this is the most "why" I've gotten out of him yet. "And if I don't?" I counter. "You're assuming I'll hate you, but there's no guarantee."

He chuckles, but it's not a sound of amusement. Rather, it turns the air frosty. "We'll see, Natalie."

"When's the game over?" I find myself asking.

"Soon, I think."

"And then?"

"And then, I throw away the key to your birdcage, and you either come to love it or hate me."

But he's keeping me. And if the game is over, I'll know who he is and perhaps why he's chosen to play this messed-up game at all. Maybe, once I see him, there will be a reason for my fucked-up choices. For my obvious obsession with a psycho who speaks of claiming me when he won't even tell me his name.

Still doesn't answer why I'm enjoying this so much. Why him speaking about keeping me isn't scaring me away.

I drag my hand up his shirt, over his chest, finding the skin of his neck. It's warm, and he allows my hand to trace his face, noting its smooth skin, the soft cheekbones, and the short hair.

"What colour is your hair?" I ask, hoping he'll give me even just a small piece of him.

"You'll see," he answers instead.

"Your eyes?"

"You'll see."

"I'm starting to see a pattern with these responses," I say wryly. My hand lowers back between us, slowly gliding down his chest. "I still want you, even if it is a bit crazy." I brush the crotch of his jeans, feeling him below the material.

The beast wakes then, breaking from his chains, and I'm thrown back on the bed, his fingers knotting in my hair as his mouth opens mine. I return his kiss, revelling in the roughness between us—the knowledge I managed to spark his actions with a few simple words.

There's never been softness between us, and while his words may be pretty sometimes, I prefer this version of him. This is the one I've spread my legs for, letting him touch me in places typically only reserved for people whose names I know.

"You know how hard it is to deny you anything, Natalie? Even when I'm *trying* to be a better person here."

"Maybe I don't want a hero. I want you to be my villain."

He groans, taking my mouth again at the same time his hands find my hips, his fingers sinking into the soft skin. From beneath him, my thighs fall open for him, and he nestles his body in the space.

"Believe me, I can smell how much you want it." He groans, grinding his jean-clad cock against my bare centre. It's rough against my soft skin, but he rubs me in the perfect place, igniting the fire inside my body.

My legs circle his waist, forcing him to remain on top of me, ensuring he won't leave when he's about to take me to that delicious place called heaven. I buck my hips, using my own leverage to continue the sensation.

His hands find my breasts, taking one in each palm and squeezing them to a point that should be painful but only intensifies the experience, the pleasure.

"You're a whore, Natalie. You're rubbing yourself on the jeans of man you don't even know."

"Yes," I gasp, shoving my face in his neck. His scent assaults my senses, reminding me a bit of my bodyguard downstairs. As if they use the same brand of cologne. "But I'm *your* whore."

His fingers tighten, pinching my nipple until I cry out in his mouth, and I know he approves of my statement. He uses the opportunity to reach in with his tongue, controlling mine against his own.

It's with that touch, I come, rubbing myself against his jeans while my mouth remains fused to his. I ride the wave, lifting my hips into his body, moaning until it passes.

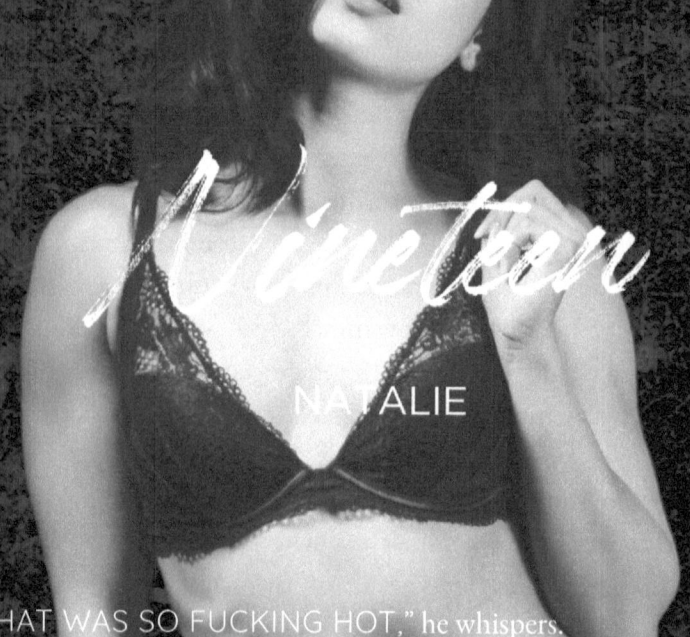

Nineteen

NATALIE

"THAT WAS SO FUCKING HOT," he whispers.

He scarcely gives me time to come back down before he's shuffling lower in bed, lifting one of my legs over his shoulder.

"I've been dreaming of this since last time, Little Bird," he says, before putting his mouth on me.

With my eyesight gone—not even able to see shadows—everything's intensified. Every inch of his tongue as it swoops over my centre, capturing my clit. He bites my clit lightly, enough to make white stars decorate the inside of my blindfold.

"You taste like mine," he growls against my inner thigh. "Fucking *mine*, Natalie, you understand?"

"Yes." I'll understand anything so long as his mouth continues its claiming.

He grants my silent request, a finger sinking into me this time as well. He pumps me slowly, then faster, enticing my orgasm to the brim, before slowing down again, making me groan in annoyance. My hands tighten in the sheets by my side.

"You're so damn tight, my Little Bird. I love that. Love how unused you are."

His fingers curl, hitting that delicious spot only one other guy has ever found, and I cry out.

"How many men have seen *my* pussy, Natalie?"

"Five."

"Have they all given you what you wanted?"

"No." Maybe it's my shy demeanour, but when I hook up with guys, they go for gentle. Even when I ask for it rougher, they don't do it. Perhaps I'm picking incorrectly, maybe it's me... Either way, I think it's why my nighttime trysts thrill me. He's not gentle. He's possessive, domineering, and everything I crave.

"That's a shame." His tongue flicks me again, reawakening the fire in my belly. "A pussy like this deserves to be revered. But I'm also not that upset about it."

"No?"

"No," he reaffirms. "Because it means your mind is mine as well. You'll never be thinking of them again."

Oh. Well, he's not wrong.

Then I learn the definition of being "eaten out," because it's exactly what he does to me. His mouth covers my entire core, his finger still wreaking a delicious havoc on my insides. I jerk my hips into his mouth and tighten my grip on the sheets beside me, allowing him to take me to an enticing dark place.

His mouth moves on me, sucking up anything I have to give him before pulling back. What I wouldn't give to see him right now. Not to know what he looks like, but to witness the expression on his face.

Though he gives me a fairly good idea, leaning forward again and putting his mouth on mine. Our kiss is sour and different, his lips coated with the taste of me.

His weight disappears after that and my skin cools from where he was last touching me. My mouth opens, ready to call him back, but the welcome cling of a belt reaches my ear and I settle back down, waiting almost patiently.

After a few more seconds, he rejoins me. His bare body slides against mine and, on its own accord, my nails drag up the side of his stomach, revelling in touching him. Obvious muscles form beneath my hand, adding hills in my path to his face.

"Your hands feel really good touching me." His tone is wondrous, marvelled, as though surprised by this fact.

"You feel good in general," I tell him. My hand slips between us, finding the heated piece of skin that rests hard against my stomach. His cock twitches in my hand, my thumb stroking its head. I do this for a few seconds, my mind getting stuck in the past, in the other times I've done this. "I'm sorry."

"For?"

"I might not be very good." Heat blossoms on my cheeks and I'm almost positive I'm acting like a moron right now. "Um, lack of experience and all that. I guess I'm not as worldly as some."

"Listen to me." His hand comes up, folding around my chin and keeping my face straight—presumably so he can get a better look. "I'm on the verge of coming with just having your delicious body under me, your taste imprinting itself in my soul, your scent finding its home in my mind. Natalie, I don't need worldly. I only need you."

Maybe I'm dreaming. It's the only possible explanation for this—a midnight visitor who I've come to crave more than what's sanely normal. Someone who claims me, treats me like a queen, despite the danger he poses. Guys like this don't exist.

"Natalie, I've lost you."

"Sorry, I just... Thank you," I tell him instead. "I..." I suck in a breath, readying to release the entire truth. "You've noticed from watching me, I'm sure, I'm not exactly a people-person. I don't go out. I don't have friends. I stay home and study or watch movies. When I need sex, I have my vibrator. When I want something more, I swallow up my discomfort and use an app to find a guy. But the guys I choose, I guess they see me and only see the plump introvert. They go gentle and soft. When I ask for faster, harder, or simply different—different positions, different anything really, they never do it. So, your question about them satisfying me. No, and this is why. But in the midst of that, I never got very skilled. So... yeah..." I trail off, my hand loosening its grip around him.

There's no way I haven't killed the mood. Maybe it's him, maybe it's having my senses taken from me—whatever it is has me opening up like a damn book and I suspect this whole fantasy life I'm so clearly leading is about to come crashing down.

Instead, he kisses me gently. His lips softer than ever and he pulls back, murmuring, "That'll be the only gentle touch you get from me, unless you command otherwise. I'm sorry sex before now hasn't been good, but I'm also not sorry no man satisfied you, as I've already said, because it means your mind, body, and soul are only mine. Thank you for sharing that, but I'll admit, it makes me feel a tiny bit guilty."

Panic bubbles beneath me. I'm right; I'm ruining everything by talking too much. I reach out, gripping his cock once more. "Don't be. I want this."

"And I can't deny you. I love that you're exactly like me. Little Bird —baby, you were fucking made for me and we're going to burn this house down now, okay?"

"Okay," I say weakly, my previous fears dissipating. Desire swoops into its place and my hold tightens on his cock as he gets into position between my legs.

"You better be on the pill or something."

"I'm on the shot."

"Perfect, because I need to feel you bare."

Normally, I'd still demand a condom, but I also crave the feel of him without a barrier.

"One day, I promise I'll be looking at your gorgeous brown eyes when I fuck you. I want to see them when you orgasm, see myself in them, knowing I'm your entire world."

From the safety of my blindfold, I shut my eyes, preparing for the sensations about to wrack my body as I lock his last words inside my heart.

Then he enters me.

And my world is complete.

"Fuck, you feel good."

He pulls back out an inch before sliding the rest of the way in. We fit, I realize. He's the perfect size to stretch me but without pain. My legs fall open wider, bringing him as close to me as I possibly can. My feet hook around his legs, ensuring he remains inside me.

And then he moves. His hand wraps around the strands of my hair, tilting my head back, as his face descends into the curve of my neck. He clamps down on the skin there, at the same time my core clenches on his cock, willing him to live out the rest of his life right here in this bed with me.

I bite down on the groan working itself through my throat. "I don't know if I can be quiet." Alerting Tristan would be so unwise right now.

His hand slips over my mouth. "When you're going to come, bite me."

When someone has wanted something for so long and then finally gets it, it doesn't take much for their body to reach that ultimate high.

So when his hips jerk quicker and his hand comes up under my leg, pushing it over his shoulder, the new angle tightens my core at the same time the orgasm ripples through me. Stars take over my vision and a scream rips through my throat. Before my noise can project, my teeth clamp on his hand.

His own groan mingles with mine, and he moves once, twice more before warmth fills my insides. The sound of his own pleasure extends mine, as we continue falling into the abyss together.

Once the sensation subsides, my lungs work overtime to breathe normal once more. My teeth unhook from his skin and he pulls his hand away from my face.

"Little Bird, you've injured me," he murmurs.

"Sorry."

"Don't be." The smile is clear in his voice, and I'd kill to have this blindfold off to see the real thing. "It means you've marked me in the same why I marked you."

When my breath catches, I manage to ask, "How've you marked me?"

"As mine."

His lips press into mine and I lock my arms around his neck, trying to tug him back on top of me for a second round. Instead, he pulls away, and my body instantly cries for his touch. I sit up, reaching toward him, but I hear the rustle of clothing and the window sliding open.

"You can't stay?"

"I can't," he says, regret strong in his tone. "Soon I will, but for now, I must go." He pauses before adding, in a much more serious tone, "If I don't return tomorrow, it's because I was held up, okay? Nothing you did."

Still, my body folds into itself, my knees tucking up under my arms. He's not rejecting me, but I hate the feeling—the loneliness—at the knowledge he's leaving and not staying, despite what we shared.

But then I shake my head of the dreamy thoughts. He always leaves after concluding his visit, and having sex doesn't change anything, other than making me stupider because I allowed myself to be taken *there* with this unknown person.

"Okay," I finally say, recalling he's waiting on an answer.

"Have fun at your brother's party."

He leaves, shutting the window firmly behind him, and I lie back down, tugging the blanket over my body. I'll need a shower first thing tomorrow to ensure Tristan doesn't smell the scent of sex on my skin, because at this point, I won't know how to respond to his questions.

It's long after my midnight visitor leaves, his parting words repeating in my mind. Before I pass out, they finally hit differently.

"Have fun at your brother's party."

I never told him about this Friday night with Alex.

Twenty

TRISTAN

I'VE BECOME VERY proficient at slipping out of her window, navigating down the side of the house, and entering back through the front door, all without making a sound that she'll hear from upstairs.

This time when I leave her room, I feel victorious.

And guilty. Having sex with her was a momentary lapse in judgement. She's fucking mine and now even my dick has the stains of her.

On Friday, this will all be over—or it better be. Tomorrow, I'm "checking in" with Chief and snatching a tracker from the precinct. In some way or the other, I'll ensure it remains on her in case Alex has me stay behind.

Which, I have a feeling is exactly what will happen.

From what we know about the guy, I don't see him allowing me into his house, especially with me being a cop. Doesn't matter if I'm on his payroll; he won't take the risk. Not if he's smart anyway.

Because that's exactly what allowing me into his home will be. A motherfucking risk.

For now, I'll play it smart. If all goes well, this will end Friday. From the texts they've been sending me, Ryker is thrilled and Brent relieved.

And then what? My original idea was to simply disappear in the night, never seeing my Little Bird again. But that was also before I touched her. All my plans disintegrated into thin air, leaving me with a blank spot on my planner.

If I disappear and stop the visits, my real self has no reason to remain here either. If I tell her what I've done, she'll hate me. She'll think this is messed up—that I'm sick and the villain of her story.

She has no clue who the real villain is but maybe when she discovers that, she'll understand why I've done all this. Why I *had* to do all this. Then she'll hate me all over for taking her brother away. An impossible cycle that'll never stop moving.

Too bad for her, I'll chain her to my bed if I need to. When I told her, she's mine, I wasn't kidding. She's my obsession, and you know why obsessions are even referred to being that in the first place?

Because she occupies—no, consumes—every fibre of my body, mind, and soul.

That's why.

Next, she'll occupy my bed forever.

Twenty-One

NATALIE

THURSDAY PASSES and I'm thrown back into my old life. To where I go to class, return home, study, and then go to bed. Tristan continues to follow me, but from his perspective, I wonder why he's bothering.

And why I haven't sent him away yet.

Perhaps it's the minor spark of logic buried deep underneath my lust-riddled brain having me know, regardless of what my body and mind say—that my stranger is filling my every thought and desire—I still don't know *who* he is.

His comment about Alex's party resonates in my head. He obviously knows Alex, or at least about him, begging my original consideration of his visits having something to do with Alex being my brother.

A debate that has kept my mind busy most of the day, so when I go to bed, I'm still thinking about it and not how he may not be coming tonight. I go to bed disappointed, but sleep well, waking up on Friday to two texts.

ALEX

I'll have my dresser there by 6. Billy will pick you up at 7. Leave the cop. He won't be needed here.

Makes sense. At least Tristan will have a night off and away from me and can go back to whatever he normally does in his evenings since I truly have no idea what he does in his spare time. Whatever it is must be better than watching me though.

ME

Okay.

The next message is from a name I'm pleased to see on my screen.

ELENA

I am SO sorry I've been so flaky lately. I hope all is well. For a while, I was going through some stuff, but it's all fixed now and I have news. Talk soon!

I shoot her back a quick reply, telling her I look forward to her news and I'm glad all is well before getting on with my morning and finding Tristan already in the kitchen.

"No messages?" he asks, as per his usual morning routine.

"Nothing," I respond, prepping the coffee machine to make me my cup of energy. Even though I only have two classes today, they're easily the most boring. The history of literature—do people care that much? —and Shakespearean Literature. Enough said there.

"I'm thinking my presence may have scared him away for good. You may not need me soon."

Facing the cupboard, I ensure he can't see my expression—see the clear and heavy disappointment. He's right. I know he is. I simply don't wish to believe it because I've gotten used to his presence. Even when we're not talking and only watching TV, he's been another person to feel a human connection with. It's nice not to be so alone.

"You agree?" he prods.

If I have no choice. I swallow over the lump in my throat and turn around to murmur, "Yeah." But before he has a chance to ask me anything else, I brush by him, leaving the kitchen to get ready for my class.

BEFORE LONG, it's nearing six in the evening and the person Alex is sending over should arrive any moment. Tristan hovers in the living room, leaning against a wall, his arms crossed over his chest.

He's been in an off-mood since lunch—when I told him he doesn't have to come tonight.

The bell rings and he changes into my doorman, swinging open my front door, examining the person on the other side. The woman is tall, blonde, and willowy—everything I'm not, and most definitely looks out of place in my small home. She's dressed impeccable in a pantsuit, her arm held above her head to keep the garment bags in her perfectly manicured hands up in the air and off the ground. In her other hand, she grips a large makeup tote, but based on the size of it, I'm sure there's more than only makeup in there.

"Hello, hello," she chimes—there's no other way to describe her speech—and enters, shouldering past Tristan's hulking form. "Name's Melody."

The bags in her hand hit him on the way in, and he jumps back. A silent laugh pulls at my mouth.

"Where's your room?" she continues.

I indicate up the stairs. "I'll lead you." I start up two steps, glancing back at Tristan, who's shutting the door. "See you later."

Tristan says nothing, but his silent gaze tracks me up the stairs until I'm gone from sight.

Only then, do I release the breath I was holding onto. Why, I'm not even sure.

Melody whistles. "*That's* your bodyguard? Geez, next time I need a guard, I'm having your brother pick for me."

I lead her to my bedroom, stepping aside to let her through. I never hear much about Alex's life, but this woman obviously knows him well.

"How long have you worked for Alex?"

"Hm, two years." She drops the dress bags on my bed, her hands going to her hips while she considers my words. "I'm his personal shopper-slash-dresser. Basically, I buy the clothes and tell him which items to pair with what. Tonight, he's sent me over here, so I can only hope he's managed on his own without me." She rolls her eyes, chuckling at her own wit before indicating the pile she's brought up. "I've picked out a few dresses I think would match the occasion nicely."

A personal shopper? And here I hesitated about him paying my tuition balance. Jeez. Our father left him a great life, if he's able to afford someone to do his shopping for him.

"O-okay," I stutter, hands wringing together. This is the part I despise about parties. Melody no doubt found me something ostentatious and flawless—everything that isn't me. "I'm kinda a simple person. I don't do parties typically."

Her eyes scan my body, but it doesn't feel probing or rude. Then she smiles, and it's a completely gentle, polite one. Melody in no way appears to be someone I would *ever* get along with, but her gracious demeanour is relieving to the anxiety tonight is spiking.

"Alex mentioned," she says after a moment. "I chose dresses that will make you stand out but also don't seem too showy. Want to see?"

Her words ease my bouncing nerves and I unclasp my hands a bit, feeling slightly better. "Sure."

THE NEXT HOUR consists of a shower and more hair products than I ever believed I'd see in my life, resulting in a cute partial up-do thing involving sparkles I know will be a nightmare to wash out later; makeup Melody artfully applied, leaving my face light and not cakey; and a dress that will stand out without being "too much," as she put it.

Melody claps her hands together, smiling. "Believe me when I say dressing you is much more fun than your brother. If you ever need someone to work for you, please have him call me."

"Erm, sure. Thanks." That'll be a no. The day Alex pays for my own dresser is the day I donate everything to charity because that's taking things a bit too far.

"I'll let myself out. Have fun at the party." Melody blows me a kiss, shutting my door behind her, as if we're the best of friends.

My cell shows it's just past seven, which means Billy should already be here. A simple check out the window could tell me, but my attention remains glued to the stranger reflecting back in the mirror across from me.

All I know is it's not me. It can't be. Beauty and I, we don't get along too well. But somehow, Melody made it work.

Strands of my bangs fall on either side of my face in soft curls, leading the path toward my bare chest. The dress remains high and modest, while still leaving the top of my chest and shoulders bare. The simple dress skirts the side of my curves, hugging me, before stopping mid-thigh in a small flare. It's tight, while still keeping my flabby parts covered up, removing any worry of being self-conscious or uncomfortable. Plain, black heels extend my legs to an impossible length.

Simple and yet beautiful, exactly as she planned.

Gathering my wits, I grab the small silver clutch she gave me to keep my essentials close, before making my way down the stairs.

It's the same staircase, the same path I always take, yet this time it feels different. Maybe because I'm Cinderella, all dressed-up and ready for the ball, while knowing tomorrow will be normal life and I'll revert back into a pumpkin.

By the time I make it down the stairs, my arms already feel damp and all I want to do is strip the dress off and hide in bed. I'm a fraud and everyone at Alex's party will be able to snuff me out, right through this façade, and uncover my insecurities.

I'm not even a nail biter, and yet, my nerves ache to clench down on them.

By the living room's front window, Tristan turns at the sound of my entrance, his passive expression falling into utter awe. His mouth parts, his eyes sparking up an inner fire. He stops walking mid-step, faltering in his spot.

"Natalie... wow."

I twirl, my dress swinging around my legs. "An hour of work and that's all you have to say?"

He takes another step before stopping again and shakes his head, his dazed gaze still locked on the dress. "It's all you'll want me to say, believe me. If I actually admitted what's in my head, you won't be leaving this house."

His words light a fire in the space between us. It ignites at the ground by my feet, shooting up my legs and straight to my core. I flush, my cheeks no doubt reddening beneath the makeup.

The desire to hide, to clench my hands, and bite my nails is gone, leaving in their place a rich power I want to embrace. Tristan's never hid the fact he's appreciated my appearance, but right now, it seems like he more than appreciates it.

My nighttime visitor wouldn't hold back. He'd drag me back upstairs and tie me to my bed and show me how beautiful he thinks I am.

Again, I'm comparing them, and I shake my head free of those thoughts while I lift my phone from where I left it charging by the couch and slip it inside my purse.

"Your driver is here." His thumb hikes to the side, his tone almost regretful.

"Thanks." My hands tighten around the clutch and I bring it closer to my body, using it as a barrier between him and me as I turn away, heading for the door. I open it, stopping only when I hear Tristan call my name.

"Natalie." Heat builds behind me, his body towering over me in a similar position he was the night on the couch. His face hangs over mine, his sweet scent making my mind momentarily blank. "Be safe, okay?"

Strange words, and I tilt my head, a question in my eyes. "Of course. It's only my brother's party."

"I know," he says softly, his lips moving in perfect tandem. "Still."

I smile, telling him it'll be fine with my expression. "Thanks, Tristan. And have fun on your night off. Sleep, or whatever. Lock the door if you go, please."

I leave then, carefully navigating my three-inch heels down the stone steps and across the sidewalk to the waiting town car. Tristan's gaze burns into my back, a heat so strong it makes me want to strip the clothes from my body.

"Evening, Miss Miller." Billy tips his head in my direction as he opens the back door to allow me entrance.

"Good evening." I stop, hand resting on the door before I climb into the dark interior. "Will Alex be allowing phones tonight or no?"

"As usual, no, ma'am. Why do you ask?"

"I'll be leaving mine in the car, if you don't mind." No point in the clutch getting weighed down with it for no reason when I must carry it.

"Very good." Billy nods. "That's fine, Miss Miller."

I finish climbing in the vehicle, adjusting the dress on the seat and settling into the soft leather in time for Billy to pull away from my townhouse. At the last second, I turn, peeking out the back window, and find Tristan watching us drive away. I'm too far away to see what he's thinking, but surely, it's unresolved longing.

The same, I'm positive, I have for him.

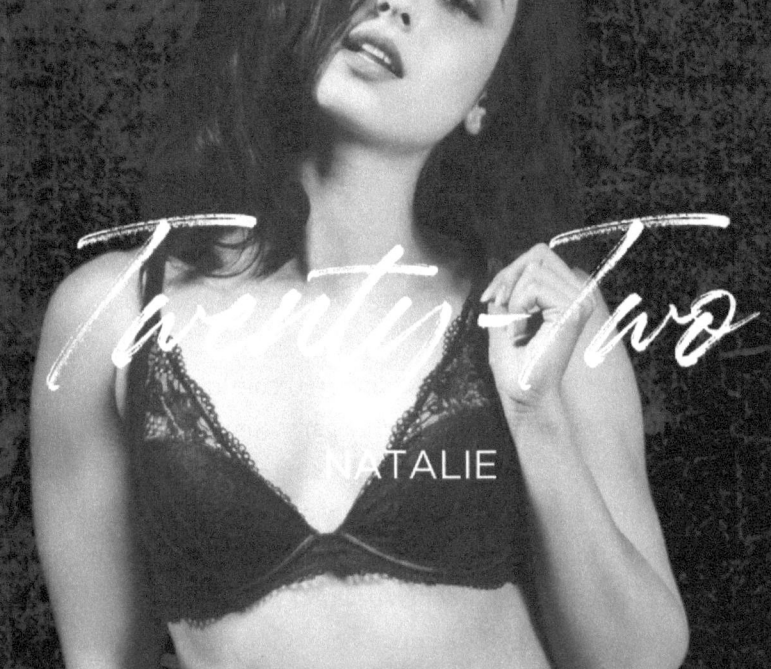

Twenty-Two

NATALIE

ALEX'S TASTES ARE... strange. There's no other way to put it.

When Alex brought me inside, I was blown away by the glittering colour scheme of silver, gold, and black. The walls draped in silver and gold curtains and the chandelier strung with thin chains. Even the partygoers seemed to follow the theme in their refined clothing choices. Men in tuxes and women in dresses I'm sure cost as much as one semester of my tuition. Beside them, I appear plain.

What I first believed to be an elegant engagement soon shifted. Because when Alex leaves my side to go find his girlfriend, I'm able to properly examine the guests. Mixed in with the well-dressed men and women, are other women.

Less dressed. In fact, their dresses are shorter than mine, and way more revealing.

With collars around their necks, and chains coming from them.

The other end? Held by the men they stand near.

What the fuck am I doing here? Hair stands on my neck and I look wildly around for my brother.

Alex chooses that moment to reappear by my side, a woman on his arm. I pay her no heed, even if her extremely bold red hair tempts my attention, instead focusing on Alex.

Voice low, so no one else can hear, I ask, "Alex, what the hell is going on here? Women, with collars around their necks?" My arms fold over my chest, stretching in a painful way due to the tension in my shoulders.

He breaks out into a laugh, his hand even coming up to rest on his chest. "Nat, you're amusing. It's merely a game for them."

"A game?" I peer behind me, eyes locking on the nearest woman with a chain around her neck. She's young, definitely no older than me. A small smile tilts her mouth, but her eyes are locked on the ground past the circle of people her holder is speaking with.

"They enjoy it, Nat. I don't judge here. Couples often find other thrills and pleasures in their marriage, and for some, it's another woman to share."

"And they have to be on a chain?" I bit my lip, doubt still heavy on my mind.

I suppose, it is a thing. I'm not worldly enough to experience anything like it, but I've read about certain sexual preferences. To see it outside one's house though and so publicized is surprising.

"Again, it's a game. In fact, Teagan, you tell her." Alex gestures to the woman on his arm, using our conversation as a segue into introductions. "Natalie, my girlfriend, Teagan. Teagan, my newly-found sister, Natalie."

"It's a pleasure to meet you." She—Teagan—holds out a perfectly manicured hand toward me, and I give her my less manicured hand to hold in return.

Figures, Alex's girlfriend would be as perfect as the rest of his lifestyle.

I step back, examining them together. Although her deep red hair stands a bit out in the sea of blonde, black, and brunette the other women seem to only have, it highlights the small spattering of freckles on her cheeks. In a silver floor-length gown, she's flawlessly beautiful, and matches Alex's neatly-pressed tuxedo.

"Nice to meet you." I smile, taking my own hand back. "Alex only recently mentioned you."

Her eyes flash, but with what, I can't place. Her lips stretch into a smile, but it's one that doesn't quite meet her eyes. *Trouble in paradise?* "Yes, Alex likes to keep me hidden."

His arm shoots out, pulling her closer to him. His nose buries in her hair as he says, "Maybe I'm a bit possessive, that's all. It's because I care."

I glance away from their happiness, focusing on the table of champagne glasses across the room instead. Alex can snuggle with his girlfriend in public because he's lucky like that.

Mine is my stalker, who I only see at night and will never admit that to anyone.

The guy I'm lusting over is my bodyguard, who refuses to cross the line.

And when I'm with either, I forget about the other.

That's not fucked up *at all*.

"I'm getting a drink," I mutter, though they're so lost in their own conversation and pay me no attention.

I stride off, head down, and purposely avoid any stray looks until I make it to the safety of the drinks table. A server smiles politely and hands me one, which I down instantly.

"Another," I demand.

The server's glance implies I'm crazy, but I don't care. I down another one, making it my third in the half-hour it's been since I arrived. Alcohol and I don't have a deep history, so no doubt I'll feel this in the morning, but thinking about my own damn love life and seeing Alex's so clear as day... sucks.

Add the fact that I'm surrounded by men and women, single,

married, and married with their own girlfriends, I really am a sorry sack of—

"Natalie." Alex's arrival interrupts the train of negative thoughts I'm working on driving off the railway. "You ran off. I wanted to introduce you to people. That's what tonight's all about, right? Networking. Getting out of your comfort zone."

And that's why I gesture to the server for another champagne flute before Alex tugs me away to socialize.

With strangers.

With classy people.

I'm not classy. Or rich, despite Alex's gifts.

Still, I swallow the lump of nerves in my throat and keep pace with Alex as he leads us to a group of guys, not standing too far away.

"Gentlemen," Alex tilts his head, "might I introduce my sister, Natalie."

More than ever, I need a drink of alcohol, as five strangers concurrently bore their gazes into me, scanning me like they're considering moving on or not.

"H-hi," I push out, clamping my fingers around the glass's stem, rather than fiddling with my hair or dress like my hands crave to do.

One steps forward, his blond hair trimmed neatly to his head. He stands tall, his smile blindingly natural. If perfection had a human form, this is what it'd look like—flawless, beautiful, and rich.

"Charmed," he says, lowering his shoulders in a half-bow, as if we're characters from an Austen novel. "I'm happy to be meeting the sister I've heard so much about. I'm Ryan. I work with your brother."

"Hi," I say again, firmer this time. I manage to lift the flute to my lips and take a sip, pushing more alcohol down my throat.

"What do you do?"

Clearly Alex hasn't told them all that much. "I'm a student. University."

Ryan smiles appreciatively. "A smart girl. I like those."

He asks something else, but I tune him out, focusing on the group behind him. Now that I see them as one, they all look like typical business types. No doubt, everyone works with Alex in some capacity.

Some appear bored, their attention drifting to the side, and I can tell they're merely being polite. The others keep their attention firm on me, their eyes continuing to scan me up and down, and I take a step back, wishing I chose the floor-length gown Melody offered me. I declined the dress, opting for something I could see my feet in instead and wouldn't risk tripping on, but now I wonder if I made the incorrect decision.

"Natalie?" Ryan prods, reminding me he is still speaking.

Luckily, Alex slips in at that moment, lifting my arm to loop inside his. "Thanks, Ryan. You know the drill though. She has to do the rounds."

Has to? If speaking to Ryan for the rest of the night gets me out of socializing, I can't deny I wouldn't mind it all that much. At least he seems less daunting than the others who continue to stare at me.

Instead, he leads me away. "Ryan likes you," he comments. "He never talks to people more than a few moments when he has to. He and you are a lot alike, actually."

My heels dig into the ground, free hand reaching out to grasp at his suit. "Alex, is this a set-up?"

Truth fills his eyes, making them soft and emotional. His arms open in a way meant to be inviting. "Nat, do you blame me? All you ever do is stay home. Your outings consist of school and visiting me."

"And Jolene," I counter, face warming, though I know he's correct. "Besides, I like it like that. Nothing wrong with being a homebody."

Based on his expression, he disagrees.

"Nat, just try." His voice lowers, pleading. "Let me introduce you to some friends, maybe you'll find someone you like. Who knows?" He shrugs. "And if no one interests you by the end of the night, so be it."

He gave Jolene a better life. He gave me a better life. And now he's using this party to ensure I remain happy. Can I really be mad at my newly-found sibling trying to do the best by me?

No.

I sigh, lowering my fight with my easing breath. "Okay. Sorry. Sounds good. Can I slip away to the bathroom for a moment?" All the champagne is finally starting to make itself known to my bladder.

Alex gestures to the wide doorway at the opposite end of the room.

Wasting no time, I find the nearest table, resting the flute upon it and escape from the room as quickly as I can, passing anyone who dares to glance over at me as I rush out.

The ballroom—because *that's* apparently a thing this mansion comes equipped with—acts like a gilded cage. Its four walls contain all their birds, chaining them inside and forcing them to socialize with one another. But once I pass the entranceway—the cage's door—fresh air assaults me, as if I entered another world. I breathe it in, holding it in my lungs while walking the length of the corridor, toward the nearest bathroom.

I enter, noting the bathroom is the size of my living room. Ornate countertop, glass sink, and even a velvet, red chair. Why Alex thinks anyone needs a chair inside the bathroom is beyond me, but regardless, I toss my clutch on it.

Maybe it'll become my new throne and I'll wait here until Alex comes looking for me or sends someone. I suspect, it won't be long before he chases me down.

I'm taking my time, washing my hands, and slowly—at a snail's pace—preparing to leave.

I can do this. Be social. It won't be horrible. By now, the night *must* be half over, right?

The door opens and the water splashes from the sink with how quickly I jerk my hands away. I could have sworn I locked it behind me, but maybe I didn't. I back away from the sink to get a clear sight of the door, expecting another regal-looking woman, but instead finding a man.

A man with beautiful, dark and light hair and a haunting smile. Eyes that light me on fire, drench me in desire, and dehydrate my senses all at the same time.

Tristan.

"What the hell are you doing here?" I exclaim.

His hands come up in the same instance, shushing me with the universal signal as he crosses the room. His hands clench my upper arms and he faces me head-on, his gaze becoming manic as he scans me over and over. From beneath his tight grip, I'm able to feel the slight quiver.

"Fuck, Natalie, tell me you're okay."

Should I not be? I pull from his grip, more confused than ever. "I'm fine." I suppose not *fine*, but fine in all the ways that matter to him. Again, I ask, "What are you doing here? How did you even know where I was?"

But he doesn't appear to be listening. Instead, he crosses the room and tosses me my clutch. "If that's important to you, hang onto it. We're running."

Oh, are we now? My hands fly up. "Whoa, no, I'm not going anywhere with you. Tristan, answer my fucking questions. What are you doing here, and how did you find Alex's house?"

His gaze whips to the door, his hands clenching at his sides. He's anxious. More reason for his answers.

Finally, he glances back at me, his gaze softening for a moment. "I put a tracker in your phone earlier. It's tucked inside your phone's case."

So many more questions arise, the main one being, *"Why?"*

Tristan's teeth clench together—a sound I hear from where I stand a few feet away. "I wish I could tell you everything right now, Natalie, but we *really* need to go." He reaches for me, grasping my hand, and tugs me to his side. His strength causes my heels to stumble, and I crash into him. His arm comes around my waist, holding me to him, searing a band of heat over my body.

"Tristan, no." I push against his form, locking my heels into the shiny, slippery tiled bathroom floor—a futile attempt to say the least. "Why do we need to go?"

Exasperation finally wins out and his face lowers, eyes lining up and locking with mine. "Natalie, your brother is trying to fucking sell you. Those men out there—they're buyers. They're looking at you like you're a piece of meat. The women on chains... How did Alex explain that one to you?"

Nothing he says makes sense, and I stumble back, putting more distance between us. His arm drops and he releases me. Still, I answer his question. "Sexual preferences."

He scoffs, a rough sound echoing over the small room. "What a damn joke. They're not there by choice, Natalie. The lost look in their eyes is damn real. *That's* what Alex is hoping to do to you."

"No." I shake my head. Tristan is—he's crazy. I'm sure there's a technical, more political term for what he is, but crazy is what I'm going with. He's been by my side for days, being paid by the very man he's making ridiculous claims against. "You have no proof."

"I do," he sighs, "but not here. Come with me, and I'll show you."

"No." The motions from my constantly shaking head loosen some of my curls. "I'm leaving, and so are you, before I get Alex to throw you out of here. If you plan on making such horrible claims against my brother, then get out of my life right now." I stride to the door, my heels making an extra loud sound against the tile with my stomping. "Goodbye, Tristan."

Hopefully, the bathroom door hits his ass on the way out. I stride away, feeling more than ever revitalized to go spend time with my brother—with the guy who's done *nothing* but make my life better.

"Natalie," Tristan whisper-yells from behind me, also exiting the bathroom.

I continue to walk. If I'm lucky, I'll run into someone who will be able to kick him out.

As if the gods responded to me, Billy turns the corner that very second. While still halfway down the hallway, I quicken my pace, my heels echoing down the corridor.

"Bill—"

My body jerks roughly to the side, my partially spoken word remaining unfinished and hovering in the air, waiting for me to complete it. Through the haze of my vision catching up to the quick movements, I feel a tight grip holding my wrist.

And then a wall meeting my back.

A body against me.

And a mouth taking mine in a domineering kiss, his tongue slashing through my senses, clearing away the rest of the fog only to add more.

Because I know these lips. The feel of these hands gripping my waist. The taste of his tongue, and the sensation it shoots through my body at the knowledge this very mouth knows every inch of my body better than I do.

Tristan yanks his mouth away, keeping his head in the crook of my neck. He peeks down the hall to where Billy was, but is now gone, and when finding it clear, steps back, cursing.

Whatever crazy he's about to throw my way no longer matters. Not his accusations. Not his arrival. Not his determination to get me to run away with him.

"Y-you're..." How can one's heart beat so rapidly and yet be dead at the same time? My throat constricts, preventing me from saying the words.

You're him. You're my midnight visitor.

Tristan is my stalker.

"You—" Again, I stop, the lack of air in my lungs choking me up.

Tristan—my unnamed stalker—or whoever the fuck he is meets my eyes again. His own bounce over my face, no doubt picking through the anger, shock, and disbelief I'm stacking up there.

"I'm so fucking sorry, Little Bird. For everything. For today. And for what's about to come."

"What's about—"

In a flash, his arm wraps around my neck, pulling tight on my throat. My arms fly up, my feet kicking out at him as survival takes over above everything else. My foot barely makes contact before black coats my eyes.

And I sleep.

Twenty-Three

TRISTAN

FUCK. Dealing with Natalie's passed-out body and trying to get out of this mansion with as much security as there is right now is not how I planned on doing this. Being inside Alex Miller's mansion, also wasn't the plan. When I tracked her, it was only to find Alex's house, to determine where all the doors and windows would be, so when I return with the guys, we can get in easily.

But then I saw the guests lingering on the front step and noticed the girl with a chain strapped to her neck. And then the next car, a very similar group exited, only this one spoke words that will forever haunt me.

"His own sister. I bet she's worth every penny."

I didn't think logically, didn't think how getting us both out of here would work.

Alex is a dangerous bastard, but when Natalie left tonight, I was sure she would come back in one piece—and not be sold to whatever other fucker he's connected to.

Finding an unlocked window was easy, so was scaling it to get inside. Then it was a matter of finding her, and avoiding her brother and his driver, because, no doubt, they know what I look like.

Fucking sexual slavery.

This shouldn't be a surprise, though. The man who rapes and murders women on his off-time clearly has no qualms about selling his sister.

My Little Bird is under the impression Alex is the newest light in her life. Someone to take care of her, to fund her life, but all he's been doing is primping her up, earning her trust, so he can turn around and stab her in the back.

My arms tighten around her form, and I drag her back into the women's bathroom before someone stumbles upon us in the hallway.

I'll always protect what's mine, and regardless of her newest revelation, she's still mine. She wanted me during the day; she gave herself to me during the night. It's now only a matter of her realizing both versions of me are one and the same.

I brush the hair away from her face, readjusting her in my arms. In the time I've known her, I've noticed how she hides herself away from the world, but it's a shame. She's damn gorgeous and the world needs to know that, and how she's dressed tonight, she's practically shouting it from the rooftops.

I need to get us out of here.

Kissing her wasn't in the books either. But her driver hadn't noticed us, and before she could call any attention to us, I needed a way to make us blend with the event. By the time he noticed us, we were nothing more than a passionate couple who snuck away from the party for some action.

I knew the moment she figured it out. Betrayal soured the kiss, her muscles going stiff and unresponsive. When I pulled away from her, a different version of my Little Bird stared back at me.

Knocking her out was the best way I could get us both out of here, because there's no way in hell I would be leaving her here, and she was refusing to come with me.

After peeking out of the bathroom and scanning the empty hallway, I exit, lifting her in my arms bridal-style as I lightly jog down the length of the hallway, toward the sitting room I earlier entered through. With every step, the party's music fades.

By now, she's been gone for a while and, no doubt, Alex will be looking for her soon. I knew it was only a matter of time before she needed the bathroom, and it'd be my only shot to grab her.

With my shoulder, I nudge open the sitting room's door—an entire room to do nothing but sit in seems excessive, but I'm not rich, so what do I know? After a brief scan to ensure no one's come in during the time I've been gone, I enter, eyes locked on my exit.

Opening the window and climbing through is a lot more challenging with an extra body, but my damn training literally prepared me for fucked-up scenarios like this one, and after a bit of a struggle, I manage to make the three-foot jump, landing on the balls of my feet and clenching my Little Bird tighter to me.

The benefit of Alex's mansion being outside of the city is the large land it occupies. Land, they'll never search through when realizing she's gone. Land, I left Hawke's car nearby.

Almost home free.

ADRENALINE PUMPING, I realize I never texted anyone about the outcome of tonight, so when I push through Hawke's front door, tightening my grip on Natalie until the door shuts behind me, Elena throws herself in my path.

"What the fuck is wrong with you, Tristan? When I said to not hurt her, *this* is what I'm talking about."

I hurt her? Elena still doesn't understand the monster we're dealing with here. I push by her, taking the stairs two at a time, but, of course, she scurries behind me. More feet pound behind her and I know

Ryker, Brent, and Hawke are all following as well. Questions trail them, demanding answers only I have.

"Shut up, Elena. I'll explain when I get her settled."

I find Hawke's bedroom—the only room in the house—and lay Natalie on it, pulling the unmade bedspread over her. Once I adjust her neck on the pillow and brush the stray strands of hair away from her face, I leave her, ushering everyone else with me.

The only thing I want is to hold her. To bring her to my own bed and care for her there, but my tiny apartment is barely large enough for me, and with tonight's news, they all need to hear it.

"Tristan, I thought you were tracking her," Ryker states the moment my feet touch the bottom step.

I ignore him, striding into the living room instead, and drop on the chair nearest to the door as everyone else gets settled. But the need to move is still too strong, and I jump to my feet, pacing by the doorway.

"I did."

Of course, Elena doesn't give up. "What the hell did you do to her, Tristan?" She stomps toward me, seemingly heading for the stairs, but I hop in front of her, growling over her head to Ryker.

"Get her in check, man, or I will."

He gives me a responding glower but yanks her back to his chest.

Her arms fly out, body pushing away from him. "Ryker, let me go. Tristan, why is she asleep?"

I ignore the direct question, opting for the explanation. "I found Alex Miller's house. He's on the edge of Cortville." Brent shifts in his seat, but it's Hawke who curses, fisting his arms on his legs. My veins chill with my next words. "He was going to motherfucking sell her off. It was a damned slave party. Alex is in deeper shit than we ever assumed."

Three "What's?" echo through the space.

"You got her out," Brent finishes.

"She was freaking the fuck out at me, siding with her brother, and I had to get out of there without her calling attention to us."

"Wow." Elena blows out a breath, her arms relaxing after her fight. "That's... fucked. I should be by her side. When she wakes, no doubt she'll be confused."

"No," I growl, intercepting her path again. "No one's fucking going near her until I do."

"Bro..." Ryker steps between his woman and me, his hand tentatively lifting as if to control me like a damned wild animal. "It's over. You've done what you needed to with her. We have his mansion's location. Elena will talk with her and she can go home."

And leave me? "No." I bare my teeth. "Her and I are far from over."

He moves in front of me, his face getting into mine. "Tristan, what did you do? You... care for her?"

Of course, I fucking care what happens to my Little Bird. She'll only be set free when I choose to unlock her cage.

My jaw only ticks in response.

"Tristan," he repeats, boring his gaze into me.

Agitation has my neck tightening. Since high school, Ryker and I have been inseparable. I helped him with any trick he played on Elena, both in the present and the past. I was there when he went to prison. I fucking looked into Alex Miller, even when I said we should leave it alone—when I didn't want to drag up my own shadowy memories. He owes me.

"Back off," I snarl. "It's none of your damned business. She's fucking mine, and that's all there is to it."

He must see how serious I am because he backs up a step, arms lowering to his side. He doesn't check with the others, doesn't glance at Elena; he merely nods and lowers his chin.

I turn away, knowing Elena's correct about one thing. When she wakes up, she'll be confused.

But she'll also despise me.

Twenty-Four

NATALIE

I'M WARM. I'm in a bed, snuggled under what's easily the comfiest blanket ever. A sweet scent fills my nose, but it's one I don't recognize. No matter, I roll deeper into my heaven, enjoying the peace sleep is providing for me.

As I turn over, the heel of my shoes gets caught in the blanket, tangling in it.

Heels.

Why am I wearing heels?

Because they match my dress.

Why am I in a dress?

Because of Alex's party.

The party involving women in chains and men staring at me.

Alex leading me around.

Tristan.

Warm skin brushes my hand, and I stiffen, vowing not to let him know I'm awake.

Tristan is my fucking stalker. I let him *touch* me in the night, while he followed me around in the daytime. He attended my classes with me, spent evenings protecting me, sat outside during lunch—and conveniently took a phone call right before my call came through. That's why he didn't come looking for me; he knew where I was the entire time.

How in the hell did I never see it before? It's obvious now, looking back.

Why he could never catch the guy. Why he never saw him around the house. Because he was upstairs with me.

Holy hell, I'm a moron. It was always there in front of me, I was simply too dumb to pick up on the clues. Worse, I even *knew* Tristan's scent smelled familiar—I simply didn't focus hard enough on it.

Same cologne. I scoff. I brushed it off as both men using similar brands.

"I know you're awake," he says lightly, amusement tinging his tone.

Amusement, because for him, everything he's done has been a damned joke. A game.

A game. He even called it such, but, yet again, I ignored the signs. I've been a game to him, while he's been realer than anything I've experienced so far.

What a damn joke. He won, that's for certain. I was so bound up in my secret happiness, I didn't dare look closer and study the clues he left.

"Natalie, I know you're angry."

Anger is only the icing of what I feel. It's the cold, hard sensation of betrayal that has my nerves igniting.

I open my eyes, readying to face him, hating how the mere sight of him already has my blood heating. He's sitting in a chair pulled close to the bed, his hands resting lightly where mine recently were.

The very hands having studied every inch of my body. The very hands that made me come undone with a few simple strokes. The very hands I *wanted* to touch me, when he was merely the forbidden guard.

I get it now. He couldn't because I'd recognize him.

The blanket gets tangled in my legs when I push into a sitting position, swinging my legs off the bed in the same instance. The entanglement slows me down from my goal of making it to the door of this unknown room—probably his.

Tristan leaps in front of the door, blocking my path, his hands reaching for me. "Natalie, stop freaking out. I won't hurt you."

"You've already hurt me," I snarl. Hate, anger… something hot burns through my chest and I force deep, staggered breaths through my body, using them to fuel my next words. "You *lied* to me. Which version of you is even real?"

"A person has many sides of themselves, and I showed you a piece of both."

"No." My head shakes, a smile gracing my expression. Not a real smile, of course. The one a person has when they're betrayed, but trying to make sense of it.

"I never lied," he continues. "Omitted the truth, but never lied to your face."

"Omitting *is* lying." Beneath the heat, a question arises, and I breathe deeply, allowing logic to borrow my senses. "Why? Tell me why and we'll be done with this."

He can explain himself—I'll give him that much—and then I'm walking away from this place, from him, and never looking back. I'll go back to my quiet life, where I happily sit home alone each night, and I'll never think about my midnight visitor again.

Tristan glances at his hands and back before responding. "I wrote the first message to scare you. I first visited you to increase your fear. I needed you to report me to the police, so when I stepped in, you saw how I wasn't the guy Elena described me as. You did one better and contacted your brother, who went to my boss and made me your bodyguard. A freak accident, yes, in which it could have gone so many other ways. I had to get close to you to learn what you knew about your brother. Tonight provided one better and I stuck a tracker in your phone."

Which is currently still inside Alex's car.

"But why?"

"Little Bird—" I flinch with how easy the nickname flows from him—and how obviously similar it sounds from his lips compared to the other times I've heard it in the dark, "—Alex is not a good man."

Memories spark in my mind, of at the party when he told me this very thing. I scoff, shaking my head again and take a step toward the door. "All right, Tristan. I'm done listening. You hold your grudges. You got what you wanted. I'm done here."

In the next flash, my back is against the far wall, Tristan's body pinning me there. I feel everything—all of him—and when I close my eyes, I *see* my midnight visitor. His sweet scents floats around me, clouding my senses. He bends, lining his face up with mine and he looks *pissed*. Like a beast I accidentally set loose.

"I did get what I needed, yes, and what I wanted—*you*—even if I didn't realize it at the time. Natalie, listen to me. Your brother hurts people. Women. He was planning on *selling* you." Tristan shudders. "He won't fucking touch you. I promise you that."

I jerk against his hold, only stopping at the grim appearance of death in his gaze. He means it. But that's not the Alex I know. Since he's come into my life, all he's done is save me, time and time again. Making my life better one dollar at a time. He's not the villain here.

But how well do you truly know him?

"I was never supposed to go as far as we did, Little Bird. I was only supposed to scare you, but I touched you that first night, and you imprinted yourself on me. I became fucking obsessed." He laughs humourlessly, his breath blowing his addictive smell over my face. "You have no idea how hard it was to hold back during the day. To be the man —the bodyguard—I had to pretend to be. Tasting you and then ignoring you the next day, like it wasn't my tongue claiming your pussy only hours before. Like it wasn't my tongue you rode into oblivion." His eyes flicker unabashed. "Listen to me, Natalie. None of this was supposed to happen, but I am *not* sorry. You hear me? I. Am. Not. Sorry." With every word, his grip around my waist tightens. "Because I got you out of it."

I stop fighting, with only the speed of our racing hearts separating our souls before they merge, becoming one. Everything he says is all I've ever wanted from him— from both versions of him.

But it changes nothing. Pretty words are not an effective mask for betrayal.

"Tristan," I pull at my wrists again, "let me go. I... can't." Fire ignites down my throat, burning it to the point of pain, but it's still less than what his actions have done. No matter how he spins it, he still lied to me. He pretended to be someone else.

But you let him.

Lost in my thoughts, I don't see Tristan swoop down until it's too late. Until my mouth is fused to his own, his tongue slashing away any logic deeming this a horrible idea. With my eyes shut, I'm taken back to all the nights he's come into my room. His mouth, his hands all over my body, his claim. When he was a nameless stranger who I allowed to consume me.

So what's the difference in me knowing him now? How does it make it any less fucked-up?

It doesn't.

I moan into his mouth, losing myself in the sensations he wrenches from my body. Before I know it, my arms are wrapping around his neck, fingers weaving in his hair to hold him still.

Tristan smiles against my mouth, and I know he thinks he's winning, but he's not. His hands follow the line of my body, finding the edge of my dress before hoisting me up. My legs wind around his waist and he pulls his mouth from mine, dropping it to the skin of my neck.

"Remember," he murmurs, "what you said about the documentary I told you about? That it's not the meeting that matters, but the outcome."

This isn't the same. Except it is...

Of its own accord, my neck falls to the side, while I press my core into his waist, feeling the edge of his pants against my thin panties. His lips bite and nibble on the skin at my neck while his hands get to work on my panties.

The delicate cloth rips, and suddenly, I'm bare to him, realizing how fast this is going. We haven't said anything; our actions hurried and messy.

But for the second, I also don't care.

His mouth merges with my own again. His kiss continues to steal any leftover logic as my hands lower, tugging on his shirt.

The only other time he was naked in front of me, I was blindfolded. I need this. I need to see the lie in all its glory.

Tristan yanks his shirt over his head, throwing it to the side before kissing me again. My hands rove, finding tight muscles and a smooth chest. His own work at his belt, and a second later, I hear the telltale sound of his belt flying across the room.

He takes his cock out, already thick and ready. I nod my head, not moving his mouth from mine, while my heels lock behind his back, pulling him toward me.

"My pretty Little Bird," he whispers against my mouth as he lines himself up. When he enters me, he murmurs, "I fucking told you you're mine." As he rocks inside me, claiming me in more ways than he already has, he kisses me. This time, he kisses my soul. My very life, reclaiming it for himself. "Whose are you?"

"Yours," I gasp.

Someway, somehow, as messed-up as this is, he's done exactly that. This doesn't change the fact he's slandering my brother; it doesn't change the fact he kept secrets from me. But it does mean I can't leave him.

That I don't *want* to leave him.

That both versions of him have made me feel something. I felt like I was cheating on the other, but really, I was in a threesome with his two halves. Both claimed a part of me for themselves. Tristan took me, my past, my likes and dislikes, where I go, and what I do. My midnight visitor took my breath, my heart, and my soul, locking it up in a bird-cage only he has the key to open.

With the wall as leverage, he continues pounding roughly into me, proving to me, or to himself, the true meaning behind his words until I come, screaming his name into the air. My fingers clamp down on his shoulders, nails digging holes into the skin there as I ride out the beautiful wave he's dunked me in.

"You're not fucking leaving me, Little Bird," he promises. "In the dark, you gave yourself to me and now it's time for you to keep your promise."

He speaks of promises when all he's ever done is falsify truths.

The fog surrounding us hovers, remaining thick and dark until he lowers me back to my feet. My panties rest on the ground, torn, stark evidence of what we've done. He snatches them up, tucking them into his front pocket and with a smirk, says, "We can't have Hawke seeing these."

"Hawke?" *Oh, God, this isn't his house.* My eyes bounce through the space, landing on the bed I slept in, the shut closet, and the night-stand, holding a single book. I'm too far away to determine the title though. All not Tristan's...

Tristan's eyes lock with mine, his hands resting lightly on my arms. "Do you believe me yet? About Alex."

"It's not him," I murmur, shaking my head. "He's been good to me." No matter what Tristan and I still need to battle through, I won't believe the stories he's spouting about Alex.

Tristan's jaw flexes and I know he dislikes my response. "Will you let me prove it to you then?"

"Do I have a choice?" My breath hikes. In fear at what proof he'll show me—that he may be telling the truth. And in nervousness he'll show me something I'd rather keep buried deep beneath my happiness.

"No." His fingers interlock with mine, and he pulls me along like we're some normal couple, out of the room and down the stairs, a speed so quick I catch nothing identifiable of the house.

"So this isn't your house?"

"It's a friend's."

We pass the living room—plain with an old couch and TV. No décor. "Your friend isn't much of a decorator."

Tristan makes no comment, leading me to a door under the stairs. He opens it, flicking on the light and disappears inside.

"It's only the basement," he comments. "Follow."

"To the truth or my death?" I ask wryly, following him regardless down the wooden steps. The light downstairs gets brighter as we approach, and finally, when I get down the stairs, a body throws itself at me, causing me to stumble backward into Tristan.

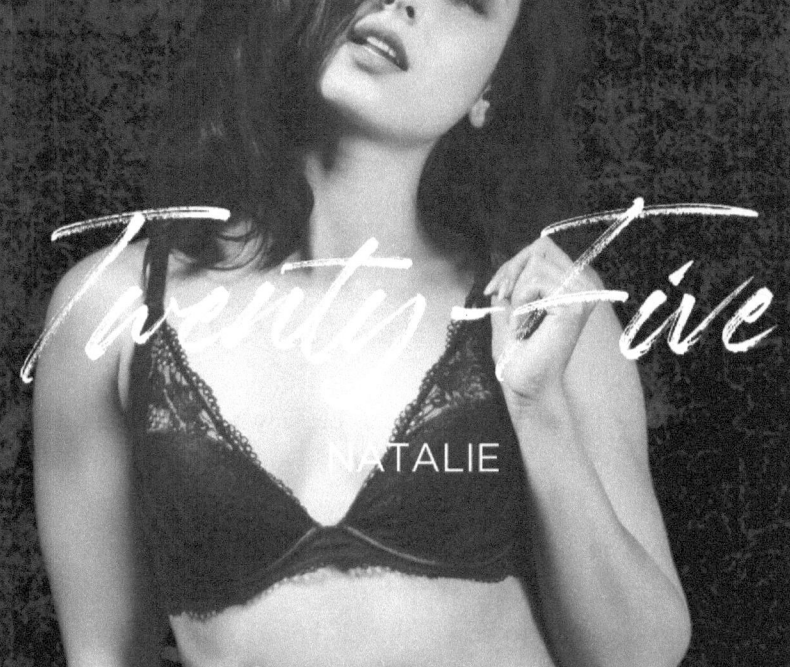

Twenty-Five

NATALIE

"GIRL, I am so sorry for what's happening right now." The comforting voice of Elena has me blinking twice and stepping away, confusion overtaking any thought in my head. Her glare goes over my shoulder to Tristan behind me. "I asked them not to rope you in."

Finally, my throat clears. "Elena. What are..."

Guilt has her lips pursing. "This is why I've been busy." She gestures behind her. "Meet Ryker."

I follow her gesture, not only finding one guy, but three. They couldn't be any different from each other. The one she indicated, Ryker, is big. Like, huge. Beside him, she looks puny.

Beside him, another guy, one with tattoos stretching up his neck and coating his crossed arms. Piercings decorate his lips and nose and shaggy midnight black hair falls over his forehead. Seriously, he looks like the emo kids I went to high school with. He catches my eye and winks.

Finally, I glance at the third guy. He reminds me of the perfect-looking man Alex introduced me to last night—Ryan. Blond hair trimmed neatly to his head, while blue eyes reflect back at me, a small smile pulling on his mouth. He stands at ease, a slight slump to his shoulders.

Oh. I see the theme here. The muscle, the troubled one, the good one, and—I glance over my shoulder—the pretty boy. Like a damned high school movie, they all have their role.

"Hawke," Elena points to the tattooed one, "and Brent." She shifts her hand to the right.

Brent? Wait— I jerk my gaze back to Elena, who's already nodding. I never met her boyfriend—ex-boyfriend, I suppose—but sure have heard about him.

Red blooms on her cheeks. "Yeah... it's a long story. We're not together anymore, which is the short form."

Ryker chooses then to make himself known, shouldering to the front. "Enough with the intros, Dolly, they came down for a reason."

"By the way," Hawke speaks up from where he's leaning on the wall, "I don't appreciate you two banging on my bed.

I cut my gaze to Tristan, whose grin is huge. So this is the "friend" who owns the house.

"It wasn't on the bed," Tristan counters.

Hawke shudders, unfolding his arms and taking a seat at the table in the centre of the room. "Still. Ew. Thanks for that, by the way. We all had to hide down here till you were done with how much noise you were making."

"Oh shush." Tristan makes a motion in the air with his hands.

Brent, Elena, and Ryker take their seats around the table, leaving only Tristan and me standing. Am I supposed to sit too? I go to take a step, when Tristan cuts to the side, grabs something off a shelf against the far wall and returns, laying down a sealed folder on the table.

Coming down and being thrown into introductions hadn't given me any time to study the room, but I realize now, I'm in a crime documentary. It's the only excuse for why I'm in a sketchy basement, with cork boards and whiteboards all over the walls, with notes, I can't make out, written and tacked to them.

A particular image catches my attention, and I focus on it, narrowing my eyes until the picture becomes clearer from this distance. It's of a girl I recognize. A girl wearing a plain black sweatshirt and jeans as she's leaving her house on a particularly chilly day, only a few weeks back.

Me.

"Natalie." Tristan's voice pulls my attention toward him. His gaze follows the line mine last left, and his eyes harden, his mouth flattening into an unamused expression. "This is real. You wanted proof, but I need you to keep an open mind. The man inside this folder," his finger stabs the cream cardboard, "is not the man you've come to know. I'm sorry." His tone is low, and I think he actually means it.

"Show me," I murmur. My lips go cold, unable to form any other words.

His chest expands with the breath he takes and he reaches into the folder, pulling from it a single sheet. "Read what's at the top of the paper."

"Miller, Inc. Alex's company."

"And the rest?"

I scan the sheet. Lines of names. "Women's names?" Skin furrows low between my eyes. "Who are they?"

"These," he plucks the sheet from my fingertips, placing it back inside the folder and returns with more papers, "are names of Alex's old secretaries."

Ice freezes my veins. "Why do you have those? Hell, *how* did you get them?"

"Through a long time of following the news," he responds, laying the papers down in front of me. He hesitates, his hand remaining overtop and covering whatever's under them. Curiosity climbs my throat, leaving a sour trail behind. "Just..." Whatever he wants to say goes unfinished and he moves his hands away.

Red.

Blood.

Bodies.

I spin, giving my back to the group of onlookers. My hands go over my eyes, willing to rid my memory of what I saw.

"Who are you guys?" I whisper, horror and fear replacing the insanity my eyes took in. They lock on the basement stairs, mentally counting how many steps it'll take for me to get away before they murder me too.

Tristan comes around and his hands grab my wrists, pulling my hands away from my face. "I told you to keep an open mind."

My hair rubs across my back as I shake my head. "Who the hell are you people?" I glance over my shoulder at the one person I would remotely call a friend. "Elena, what did you get yourself into?"

"We didn't do it," Tristan says, pulling my attention back to him. "Every secretary Alex had has ended up murdered. Brutally raped. Tortured."

"No." My whisper slashes the air, louder than I meant it to be. "You're lying."

"And you're in denial." Anger makes his tone hard, but he softens it to add, "Little Bird, why would I lie? For years, we've been following his trail, trying to come up with some pattern, rhyme, or reason. It wasn't until recently we learned of you, and you became our ace in the hole." His hand rests on my cheek, two fingers pinching my chin to keep me steady.

I rip from his touch. He can speak calmly about this all he wants, but I refuse to. "So, you *used* me." It's not a question.

Maybe my anger is irrational, considering he's basically told me as much already. But hearing it again, so blatant, about how I was a mere convenience hits home harder. This is worse than rejection. Hell, this is worse than being lied to about his dual personalities. This is being used, plain and simple.

"Yes."

His single-worded admission also hits differently. This time, it rips my heart open, stomps on it, and leaves it behind for the animals to eat for dinner.

All a motherfucking game. Here I was, believing I *liked* the guy—both versions of him—and he's been laughing behind my back at how he was able to get the shy, heavy girl to spread her legs, unsuspecting of the giant trap he laid.

"Little Bird, there was an alternate outcome." Tristan's body comes closer, his scent overwhelming my senses and making my head go light. His pupils narrow, keeping me in his gaze. "You know when I used you for information, something else happened between us. I've shown you how I felt upstairs, but if you need another round for you to understand—"

"Ugh!" Hawke's obnoxious voice pushes between us. "Not another fucking one. Ryker and Elena are enough as it is."

Brent laughs, but there's nothing humorous about this situation. I throw my arm out to the side, pointing to the folder on the table. "None of it changes the fact that you're making accusations about Alex without the proof."

I don't know which part of my speech did it, but he explodes then. His body puffing up, chest expanding as his face flushes red. "*That's* the proof, Natalie! Pictures. Police reports. Hospital reports. All of his secretaries end up dead within a year of working for him. You don't think *that's* a coincidence?"

"Is there DNA that links him to them?" My arms fold over my chest, cockiness entering my bones. Crime dramas taught me one thing—always use DNA for proof, so no one is falsely convicted.

Like a Greek god about to shoot lightning down upon the world, Tristan straightens, his mouth parting to no doubt give me the contradiction of a lifetime until a body pushes between us, her arms coming up to Tristan's chest, creating a barrier between him and me.

"All of you get out," Elena orders, scanning the group.

Tristan drops his eyes downwards, momentarily making her the source of his anger. "Elena, we talked about this. Ryker, get her to back the fuck off."

Instead, she whips her gaze to her new boyfriend. Couples do that thing where they silently communicate with one another—not that I ever had that experience—and it's exactly what they do. Whatever battle they're both in, she obviously wins because Ryker sighs, striding over to us.

"C'mon, man. Let's take a breather before you freak her the fuck out more than you have already. Let Elena talk with her."

"But—" His eyes fall to mine, anger still making his pupils small. Whatever expression he finds on me, though, has his expression falling, dejection lowering his fight. "Fine, Little Bird. You win."

And then he stalks away, his stomps sounding as though they could break through the wooden steps.

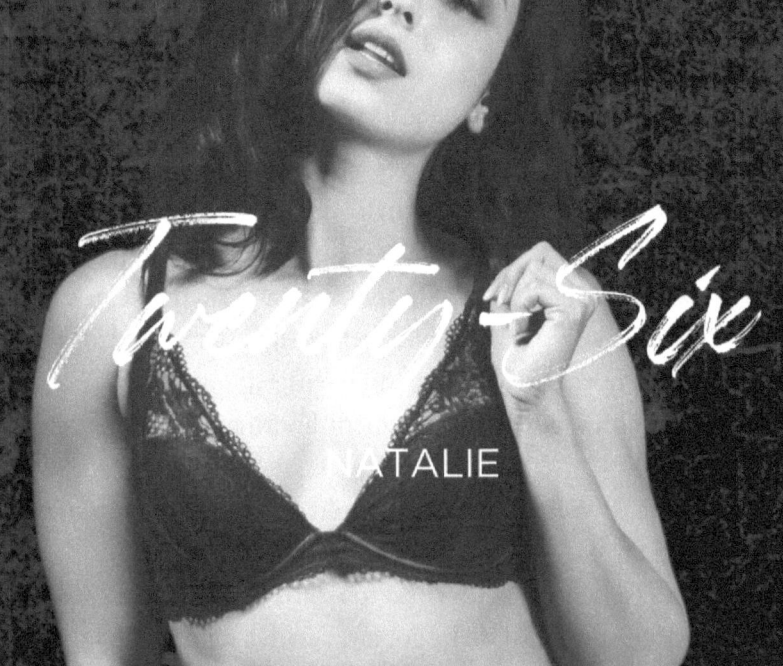

Twenty-Six

NATALIE

RYKER SHARES another look with Elena before disappearing after his friend, while Hawke and Brent follow, both granting me small smiles on their way past. Only when the basement door shuts behind them does she speak.

"Men and their testosterone." She rolls her eyes and leads me to the side of the table, gesturing to the chair Ryker had recently vacated, far away from the folder of lies Tristan left out. She frowns, her lips pursed and shifting side to side, as if debating her thoughts. "I'm really sorry, Natalie," she says after a while. "I was only recently brought into this and when I learned you were next on their list, I did try to get you out of it but in the end, they had no leads and you were it."

She agrees with them. "What Tristan is saying... it's true?"

Elena smiles sadly. Having never lied to me before, she's at least more reputable than Tristan. "I suppose I don't have concrete proof of it either, but I do believe their claims." She glances at her hands and back. "I'm not sure if Tristan ever mentioned, but he and I used to go to school together."

"He did. Said you had a thing with his best friend—Oh." Now, it all makes sense.

Sorta. But Brent is also a friend...

"Yeah. You figured it out. Ryker was my high school bully. He tormented me back then. Tristan helped him when he needed two people. Brent was also their friend, but he looked a lot different back then." She waves her hand. "I'll skip that drama though and leave it for another time. Anyway, a few months before high school ended, Ryker went to prison. He recently got out and re-entered my life."

She stops, staring down at the cement flooring, her lips pursing in contemplation.

"What is it?" I whisper, wishing I could get rid of the numbness in my veins. Even my body knows the worst is yet to come.

"We went to school with Alex too. His father—your father, I suppose—was the principal, so he got away with a lot of stuff."

"He did mention our father running his school, yes. I never put much thought in it though."

"One day, he said some things in front of Ryker... about me. About raping me."

Alex wouldn't—would he? How much do I truly know him? Still, my head shakes, though with less conviction than when Tristan was explaining.

"He said it clear as day, apparently. Both Tristan and Ryker were there. It's why Ryker went to jail. It's why when they showed me that exact folder, I believed them. Not at first." She snickers softly, her eyes drifting into a memory. "I thought Ryker was bringing me into some cult where *they* were the ones doing it." Her smile fades back into solemnnness. "But with everything I know about Alex from high school, and from his comment to make Ryker go off on him... I do believe them."

"I just—I..."

"I know." Elena clasps my one hand into both of hers. "It's why I sent them away. I'm not here to stronghold you into believing it. I understand it's a lot, to think of your own family like this. All Tristan and the rest are doing is trying to send him to jail and get those poor women the vengeance they deserve."

"How do you know I won't tattle to Alex?"

She shrugs one shoulder. "We don't. We're hoping you'll come to see. Natalie," she swallows before starting again, her eyes shadowed with sadness, "Tristan told us about your brother's party. Those women with chains around their neck are sex slaves."

Every word she speaks breaks something inside me. Some long-buried piece of denial I've felt since meeting Alex. Hell, every time I'm there for dinner, I *know* there's something more he's involved in, but I pretend the wrenching in my stomach is nothing and I move on. So, when he told me it's all about play and sexual preferences, why wouldn't I believe him? Believing his lie is easier than surviving the truth.

And that's when I no longer pretend. No longer *believe* Alex isn't up to sketchy shit. It's there, written in the walls every time I come.

Why he never picks me up himself.

Why my phone must remain off when at the mansion.

Why asking the police chief to send someone over to be my body-guard was no issue. Because he's paying them.

Why the women at the party seemed *off*. Why their smiles never reached their eyes.

Why Alex was parading me around the ballroom.

Oh God.

The vision of Elena seated in front of me goes blurry, and I soon feel it. Cool tears drip from my chin, hitting my fists in my lap.

Alex has made my life so much easier. For once, Jolene and I weren't struggling. I was being taken care of by the very family who once discarded me. I was *wanted*. I wasn't alone.

"I'm sorry, Natalie."

My head shakes, willing the depression to fly from me as easily as my tears drip. "I've been denying the truth for so long, Elena. Once he came into my life and started to make things better, I stopped ignoring the churning in my stomach that said something didn't feel right."

Her hand rests on my knee as she leans forward. "Natalie, do you know something that could help us?"

"No." My useless whisper is one more crack in my foundation and tremors have my arms vibrating. I wrap them around myself, hoping to keep myself together a bit longer. "No, sorry. It was just the feeling I got every time I went there. Alex said he merely ran our father's multi-million-dollar company. Mentally, I questioned if there was more to it. He was always so secretive about everything, but I was happy to remain blissfully unaware. Which is why, when he mentioned the party—bringing other people in the house—I was really surprised." *The party...* Memories of earlier flood my mind, and a fresh wave of torture bursts to the top.

At some point, Elena comes closer, wrapping her arms around me.

"Elena, he was going to *sell* me. Dispose of me, after everything." He's no different than our parents, literally cut from the same cloth.

We sit like that for a long moment, her holding me as I travel through mental hell. If everything's true, then it's Alex who's been the villain in my life this entire time. I should be raging mad. I should allow his betrayal to fuel me forward and move past this, but I'm not—I can't be. Being mad requires my muscles to have strength and react, rather than be lifeless and limp how they are.

Literature studies texts from the great writers of the past—Shakespeare, Bronte, Bryon, Hobbes, to name a few—and they all discuss how love is the driving force amongst people. How love is what most often leads to heartbreak, anger, despair, and even happiness.

Every single one of them is correct.

Because it's my growing affections for my newly discovered brother that had allowed me to fall into this trap of his.

And it's heartbreak that'll get me out of it.

"I need to talk with him. I need to ask him this."

"Natalie." Her rough tone implies she doesn't think it's wise.

"Not now. When we catch him in the act—however you plan on doing that. Before anything, I want to hear those words from his mouth. Have him tell me what he planned on doing to me."

Resignation has her brows lowering and she nods once, standing, and taking me with her. "Do you want to come upstairs with me, or send Tristan down here?"

Tristan. In all my mental discovery, I forgot about the one constant still remaining.

"You know," she continues, "in all the time I knew him in high school, I never saw him with a woman. And in the short time I've gotten to know him again, he's never mentioned anyone. What I saw earlier... well, he cares for you."

"He lied to me," I whisper.

Two new people in my life. Two new liars.

What makes Tristan any different than Alex? Both deceived me for their own gains.

Elena must agree because her gaze drops to her feet. "I know. I'm not sure what fully went on between you two, but I need you to be aware, he truly does care about you and no doubt," her eyes lift to the ceiling, a smirk tugging at the corner of her mouth, "the guys have him tied down to prevent him from coming down here. And," her gaze locks back onto me, awareness filling her bright eyes, "from what I heard earlier, you care about him too."

I fall back into the chair behind me, my hand sliding from hers. "Is it fucked that I do? That even when he was stalking me, climbing through my window at night, he became my obsession?"

Her brows lift, arms falling to her side, and I realize I gave a piece of the truth away. In the end, it hardly matters. I'm pleased Elena found her happy ending with Ryker because it means she's here right now, helping me through these moments.

She sits again, elbows sinking into the skin of her knees as she focuses on me. "Natalie, you and I will be starting a club soon then. Because Ryker used to bully me and all I wanted was to be his girl-friend." She snorts, shaking her head softly. "And when he got out of prison, he picked up where he left off all over again, and that's how I fell in love with him. You think you're fucked-up for falling for your stalker?" Her eyes roll. "You're not. Ryker lied to me in the worst way possible, by convincing Brent to date me, to hold onto me until he was released from prison. But I got over it."

Despite the whole shitty, odd situation, I chuckle, and damn, it feels good to. "That's horrible."

"It is. And I know Tristan's lies hurt, and for good reason. But those boys up there? This has been their goal for years now, and they're finally making headway with Ryker being free. In the end, they have their strange methods, but they're good guys."

I watch her stand again. She slowly walks toward the basement stairs, leaving me in my chair. "Why are they doing all this? Seems quite elaborate, no?"

Elena doesn't answer for a long moment, but when she does, it's with a sad smile that doesn't quite meet her eyes. "That's definitely a conversation you need to have with Tristan. It's not my story to tell."

She leaves then, her quiet steps echoing through the basement. With every stride she takes away from me, it's another realization how truly alone I am. Jolene isn't home with me anymore, though soon, I suspect I may need to take her in, since it's the only way I'll be able to afford to help her when I lose Alex's support.

And Tristan... He's brought me more company than ever, while also making me feel more alone.

I nearly hate him more for that than for lying to me.

Twenty-Seven

NATALIE

AS IF SIMPLY THINKING HIS name called him, he appears in front of me. His steps were so quiet, they never reached my ears as he descended the basement stairs.

"I believe you," I murmur, continuing my staring contest with the concrete floor beneath foot. "I-I think I've always known something was off about Alex. Every time I'm there, he's so secretive, and it never sat right with me. But he's been good to me, and Jolene, and I suppose I didn't want to admit it."

Tristan bends on one knee, kneeling at my feet. His eyes, shadowed beneath long lashes, lock on mine, but his walls remain up, and I can't determine what he's feeling.

Instead, his jaw moves, his soft words release between barely moving lips. "Little Bird, it's nearly midnight. We should go to bed."

Bed. Home. No doubt when Alex determined I was no longer in the house, home is the first place he'll look. Rising panic bubbles inside me, forcing my mouth open, words ready to speak—

"Hawke said we can have his room tonight. He'll take the couch."

And just like that, I'm relaxed again.

His hand reaches for mine, not giving me a choice when I stand. He begins to lead me toward the stairs.

I dig my heels into the cement. "You don't want to talk?"

For some reason his responding, "No," sends pangs of disappointment to my heart. Perhaps, considering how he acted when Elena kicked him out of the basement, I was expecting a bit of a fight.

We make it to the top of the stairs and he adds, "Tomorrow. Right now, you need sleep."

He continues pulling me along, past the empty living room and up the stairs.

"Where is everyone?"

"Hawke's driving them home. He'll be back later."

In Hawke's room again, my gaze falls to the wall where he fucked me earlier. A weird feeling courses through my body. Like, I'd be open to doing it again, but also scared he'll be expecting it, and I'm not sure my heart can handle being used any more tonight.

Tristan flies around the room, ripping open the closet door until finding what he wants, and he returns with a shirt, handing it to me.

"I hate to imagine you wearing another man's clothing, but well, we're pretty stuck on options. I figure it's better than your dress."

I grasp it, pulling it to my chest. Hawke's scent most definitely isn't Tristan's, and while it doesn't stink by any means, it's undeniably not what my senses prefer. "Thanks." With the clothing in hand, I place distance between us.

Anger drops the skin between his eyes, making him appear vengeful. "Don't hide from me, Natalie. Don't run because you have no idea how far I'm willing to chase you."

His words are a trap—tempting, inviting, and one I want to willingly fall into—but before I allow this to get any further than it already has, I need to know I won't lose myself in the process.

More than I already have.

"Why?" I ask, muted.

"Why not?"

"That doesn't answer my question. Why me?" My grip tightens on the shirt, using it as a barrier to keep distance between us.

"Because."

He plucks the shirt from me, and I have no fight in me to stop him, or to prevent him from reaching behind me and unzipping my dress. My breasts are the only thing stopping it from sliding off my body, but just when I believe he'll push it down, he doesn't. Rather, he throws the shirt over my body first, letting it fall into place.

When the cotton settles, his hands grasp the dress and pulls it from my body, disposing it on the floor next to us. He straightens, his eyes not looking at my face at all. He's completely fixated on me undoing the clips in my hair, letting it fall in waves over my shoulder.

"You have no idea how hard it was to let you go earlier, looking how you did." His warm breath coasts over my shoulder and I shiver, letting it become the blanket—the hug—I need.

"You told me that."

His eyes flicker, warily. "You assumed it was merely because of how you looked, when really I fought to let you go into the devil's lair. Mind you, I never imagined Alex would be parading you around how he did." His hand weaves its way into the strands of my hair, holding me tightly by the back of the neck. "*That's* how I know this is real for me."

My heart stops beating; my mind stops thinking. "But you barely know me."

Tristan backs me up to the wall, using it as leverage for the kiss I'm nearly sure he's about to grant me.

"I know you better than you think I do. I'm so attuned to the sounds you make when you orgasm. Your smile when you're happy, and the smile you use when you're trying to fake happiness. How determined you are in class. How much you care for your aunt. How much you want to believe in the best in everyone."

Him included.

"Do you feel any guilt for lying to me?" My breath rattles in my chest, the beating of my heart increasing as it waits for the response I need.

"I already told you, no, because it got me you. Question is, do you want me as well?"

I lower my eyes to the ground, fingers picking at the edge of a stranger's shirt. So much has happened, in even the past twelve hours, and I don't know how to wrap my head around it all. If I listen to Elena, and be with Tristan—*is it even that easy?* —would it be the same as forgiving him? Forgiving him seems like such a messed-up thing to do.

But he's become my obsession. I was falling for both versions of him, even if I hadn't known they were both him. So, maybe, as Elena indicated, I merely embrace the person I am and accept him. She did with Ryker, making it seem so easy.

My entire life, it's been Jolene and me. Mom saved me, I see that now. Even without knowing everything, my father was a dangerous man. Only a dangerous man would have raised a dangerous son. It's why our mother kidnapped me away. She knew I would merely be a tool for the family—sold to the highest bidder as soon as I became of age.

From this whole situation, I found someone new. Someone who made me feel less lonely, and who gave me something in return. Who made me fall for both parts of him. So maybe, I am my father's daughter too. I'm dangerous, only in a different way. I love danger-ously, and if that means loving my stalker...

Instead of responding, I stand on my toes, initiating the kiss to solidify everything existing between Tristan and me, between my name-less midnight visitor and me.

He kisses me back, tentative for a moment, letting me keep control until his alpha personality wins out. In a flash, his hand, still laced in my hair, has my head tipped back, my neck bared to his mouth as he walks us backward to the bed.

"I wasn't going to do this with you tonight," he mumbles against my skin. His lips may form the word *wasn't* but I only feel *will*.

"I want you," I tell him simply and tug at his shirt, pulling it up over his chest. My hands find his smooth skin, recalling the feel of him that night in my room and all the wonderful things he did for me. "This time as you and me. I want to see you."

"You'll see me." He smiles against my skin. "From now on, you'll see *only* me. Want to know why?"

Electricity courses over my skin, my heart feeling like it'll explode with every lick of his tongue. "Because I'm yours."

"And I'm yours."

My back meets the bed as he pulls Hawke's shirt over my head, tossing it in the same corner my dress is currently lying. My nipples bud instantly. My hands reach for his belt, sliding it from his pants belt loops.

"No." He takes my hands, placing them up by my head. "Let me enjoy you."

His words would normally please me, but every other time has been about me. He wants me to show him I care for him too, then how better to than this?

"No," I counter, pushing myself back into a sitting position. "You've enjoyed me plenty. It's my turn."

"Little Bird," he purrs. "You better learn really quick I'll never take no for an answer. My entire concentration is ensuring you are treated like a fucking queen. *My* queen. You'll be guarded, cared for, and cherished."

His hands fall to his waist and in a flash, he's shoving his pants off. His cock springs free, hard, waiting, and bounces against his flat stomach.

My hands crave to touch him. Seeing him is everything compared to our last experience. I lock my eyes on his thick member, noting the delicious looking veins running up the side of him, waiting to be touched. My mouth goes dry, imagining all the ways I can please him.

I sit up, reaching for him, but again, he evades my touch and nudges me back to the bed. I huff. "Tristan, maybe I want to show you how much I care as well."

He climbs over me, his arms braced by my head. "I know you care. The fact that you let me fucking touch you at all—that you're panting for me right now says you care. It's all I need."

I narrow my eyes, hands lifting to touch the base of his stomach regardless, a mere inch away from where I want to be.

"Thought you said I'd be your queen. A queen needs to show her king how loyal she is."

Our breaths mingle, his eyes studying my face until he smirks. "Fine. I concede, Little Bird. But—"

He stops talking and grasps my hips, rolling us over until I'm on top of him. The room barely goes still before he's flipping me over again and my new line of sight puts me staring at his cock. I have to lower my head only a fraction before I can take him in my mouth.

Then he speaks, his breath entering me, seizing me in an entirely new way.

"I concede to a tie. Not to allow you to win."

And then he kisses me on my pussy, his lips lingering, tongue flicking just past his lips to barely touch me. I jerk my hips, demanding more as I focus on his cock by my face. I grasp him, noting how my hand does not fit around his girth. The same time his tongue flicks against my clit, I wrap my lips around his cock, swallowing his head.

Our mutual groans fill the room, mine vibrating down his length and eliciting a secondary groan.

"Your mouth..."

He trails off, seemingly lost in the wonder of my tongue working his head, circling it while my hand pumps him. His tongue dances around my clit, back and forth, up and down until my hips move of their own accord, urging his tongue to go harder, deeper, and faster.

His hands grasp my ass, pulling the cheeks apart as his fingers slip in between, one stopping at my other hole.

"Has anyone fucked you here before?"

I moan my no around his cock, adding a small shake to my head in case he doesn't understand the sound.

"I will," he promises, giving me no choice. "Not today. One day, when you're ready, Little Bird. No part of you will be hidden from me, understand?"

He speaks pretty words, but I roll my hips again, urging him to finish what he started. My core tightens in anticipation, his words bringing me to close to the edge again, and it won't be long before I fall off.

I lower my mouth and swallow as much of him as I can. His hips rock and his cock hits the back of my throat, but I don't gag, instead, tightening my mouth for harder suction.

He makes a sound partway between a groan and a moan as he attacks my pussy, giving everything I'm doing to him back to me, and it's like that, with me wantonly riding his face and Tristan jerking his cock into my throat, I come.

I cry out my orgasm around him. The need to shout it to the ceiling is strong, but I focus on Tristan, wanting him to feel the same pleasure he's given me countless times. My nails scratch up the sides of his legs as he comes too. Warm liquid shoots to the back of my throat and I swallow it down, keeping my mouth around him until he's spent and softening.

After an awkward shuffle, I climb off him, kneeling beside him, grinning.

He sits up, his thumb going for the side of my mouth. My eyes want to shut instinctively, but I keep them open and on him, watching as he brushes the skin there once before pulling it away, a bead of cum on his skin.

"That's fucking sexy, Little Bird. Seeing your mouth literally dripping with my semen... it does something to the possessive fucker inside me."

"Next time you can make it my entire body."

He smashes his lips to mine, yanking me on top of his body. Our skin slides together as I move over him, shifting my hips until they're lined up with his.

"You can't say things like that and not expect a man to respond, Natalie."

"Maybe that's the point."

His partially-thick cock waits between us and I slide myself along his length, my slick folds bringing him back to full attention.

"There we go." I grin, heat blooming in my chest as I take charge, lowering myself onto him.

I don't know when it was. Perhaps sometime in the middle of the night with my stranger, I found myself. The quiet, shy bird I was spread its wings. Tristan believes he put me in a cage, when really, he unlocked my existing entrapment. Made me feel desired, wanted, and most importantly, understood. Our story may have had an odd, unconventional twist, but it's ours and why would I deny myself the happiness I get from it? The way my heart expands with simply breathing in the same air he does.

"I gotta admit," he starts, eyes lifting from my bouncing breasts, and toward my face. "This whole having the bedroom light on thing is working for me. You're much easier to see."

My laughter tightens my core around him.

"Ride me how you wanted to ride that damn vibrator of yours."

I do, rolling my hips as he meets me move for move, slamming himself in deeper until I lose myself in the sensations, silently thinking about the vibrator in my bedside table that helped start this.

Another orgasm wracks my body and just as my breaths return to normal, my body falling slack and weightless, he clamps down on my hips again, picking up his pace until I'm coming again on him.

And again.

And by the final time, I'm a useless form he's pounding into from below. My body is slack, unable to so much as even climb off him properly. Not that he seems to care, pulling me to the side and wrapping his arm around me.

"We dirtied your friend's bed," I murmur, my mind already drifting away into the sweet oblivion post-orgasmic sleep is.

"I'll buy him a new one. It was worth it." His face nuzzles into my neck, lips grazing my skin.

I snuggle in deeper, letting my mind forget about the insane day it just endured—classes, a party, Alex, and now Tristan. But before darkness consumes me, there's still a flicker of light, something that has me saying, "Tristan?"

"Hm?"

"Tell me this is real. That I won't lose you too. I don't want to be alone anymore." From my loneliness after Jolene's hospitalization, and to when Alex has come into my life, bringing his lies and darkness, I won't handle another loss.

"As long as I'm breathing, you'll never be alone."

For the first time in years, I go to bed, feeling more okay than I've ever been.

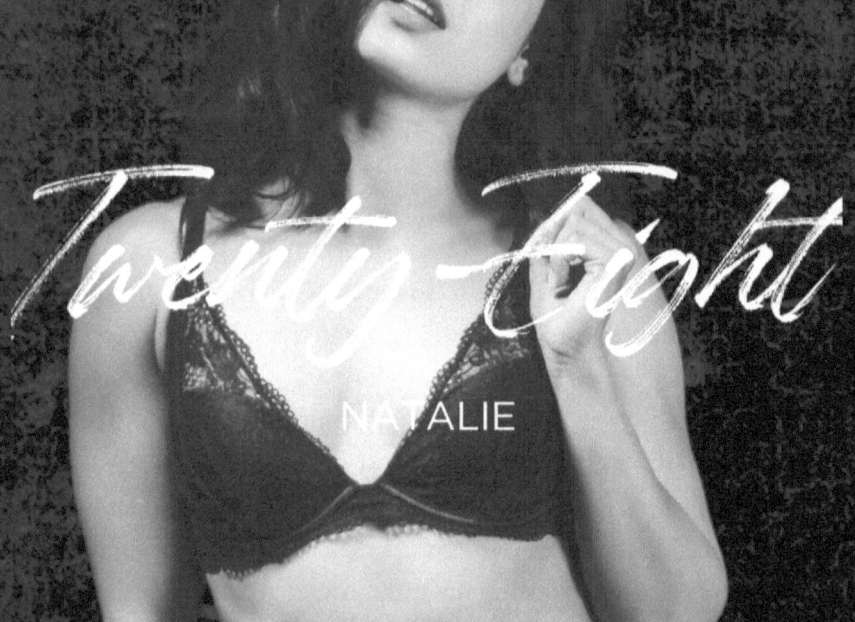

Twenty-Eight

NATALIE

FOR A MOMENT, everything seems normal. Even if normal now means waking up in someone else's bed, beside Tristan who's... whatever title he wants to give himself, with the shadow of the previous day over us.

We dress silently, me getting back into my dress from last night and wondering when I'll be able to go home. After all, regardless of what Alex is doing in his personal time, it doesn't change the fact that I have only two more months until graduation, and exams don't ace themselves.

We make it downstairs, Tristan's hand wrapped tightly around mine, and find Hawke already seated in the living room. He raises a mug in a toast, indicating to the back of the hallway. "Coffee's ready if you want any, Natalie."

Him remembering my name is a bit of a surprise, considering he's only ever met me once, last night, but it does beg the question of how long Tristan and the others have been planning all this.

Tristan leads me to the kitchen, pours my coffee, putting the right amount of cream in it and hands it to me. His mouth opens, readying him to speak, when the shrill sound of his cell interrupts him. He glances at it before answering, his expression a mask.

"Hello," he says, phone to his ear. Whoever speaks on the other end makes his mouth tilt downward, while his spine straightens from his slouch. "Morning, sir. Yes... yes, I have her with me." His eyes shoot to mine, silently telling me something. "Sure. I'll let her know. Bye now."

"That didn't sound good." The addition of Hawke's voice in the room makes me flinch. He slides into the doorway past me, his strangely opalescent blue eyes bright beneath his dark bangs.

"No," Tristan agrees, his mouth flattened. He tosses his phone on the table in front of us, taking no care for its delicate nature and clenches the back of the chair in front of him, his knuckles going white from his grip. "Alex obviously eventually noticed you were gone. Called the station. That was Chief wondering if I knew where you were."

"Oh." My shoulders deflate, feeling slightly less concerned now. "Well, that's good, I suppose." Means he's not out looking for me, nor is it at my house. Which means I can go home. "What are you supposed to tell me?"

"To call your brother. He's worried."

"Is that a good idea?" Hawke interjects.

The telltale slamming of a door interrupts Tristan, and a horde barges down the hallway until the kitchen crowds with Elena, Ryker, and Brent.

"You guys are early," Hawke says, falling into the chair at the head of the small circular table. He slouches, his shoulders nearly level with the table, his legs cocked lazily to the side, taking up more space than he should.

Elena navigates the maze he's left her, claiming the seat beside me. "How are you?" she asks, keeping her voice low.

I smile, my attention drifting toward Tristan, who's still glaring down at his phone, as if waiting for it to catch on fire. "I'm good."

Elena glances between us, a knowing smile lighting up her dark eyes.

Ryker steps forward, taking up a position behind Elena's chair. "We have shit to do, so obviously, we're not going to wait around."

Tristan finally pauses on his quest to destroy his helpless technology. "Chief called. Alex is looking for Natalie. Wants her to call him."

"Is that a good idea?" Hawke asks again.

They all look to Ryker, the obvious leader. I glance up too, curious what his decision will be.

"It's a good idea. As of now, we have no reason to bring attention to ourselves. He knows nothing is amiss and we need to leave it like that." His unique green eyes glower at me. "Do you know his number?"

"Y-yes."

He jerks his chin toward Tristan's phone between us. "Call him. Put it on speaker."

I lift it, more nervous than ever to hold a phone. What do I say to him? How do I keep my voice steady, knowing what I now know? Seeing the photos of those women and being ninety percent sure it was Alex's doing.

Once again, Tristan is aware of where my thoughts are and he says, "Tell him you were overwhelmed and got me to come pick you up."

My lips twitch, wanting to show my gratefulness but the overwhelming sensation of dread still weighs my body down, making it difficult to feel anything else. I dial the number I've only barely memorized, putting it on speaker as I lower it to the table.

It takes one ring before Alex's voice comes through. "Hello. Alex Miller speaking."

"It's me," I say weakly.

"Natalie." Elation is obvious in his voice, before he switches to an anxious, caring tone. "What happened to you last night? I sent everyone home and had people searching my home and the nearby area."

I scratch at my arm, feeling like absolute shit. He's done nothing but be good to me and here I am doubting him. "I'm sorry," I whisper, meaning it more than one way. Emotions were elevated last night—it's the only thing that makes sense. "I suppose I got overwhelmed with everyone there. I called for a ride home. Stayed at a friend's house."

"Is the cop with you?"

"Yes, he stayed with us. This is his phone I'm using, since mine is in your car."

"Right." He pauses. "Well, Natalie, running off like that was an impolite thing to do. You should have said something. Instead, I had people scouring for you all night. When Billy said your phone was still in the car, I couldn't be certain what happened because I had no way of reaching out."

He's scolding me like a child, and like one, my shoulders lower on their own accord. "Sorry," I mutter. "I'm used to doing things on my own."

Seemingly the correct words, since his next ones are, "I understand Natalie. Next time, think first, okay?" He blows out a breath on the other end. "Now then, there is something I wanted to speak to you about. Would you be willing to come tonight? I promise, no fanfare. Just drinks in my office."

An office he's never shown me before. I raise my head, glancing at Tristan's firm expression telling me no. His widened eyes and shaking head totally contradict that of Ryker's firm nod.

Leaving the decision up to me.

Too bad I'm so fucking indecisive. I'm basing the feeling I have about Alex on exactly that—a feeling and nothing more. The pictures they have down below aren't proof the guy who's been nothing but good to me did all that shit. Even if my body tells me otherwise. Even if

I told both Elena and Tristan yesterday, I accept what they've shown me.

As I scan the room of waiting faces and varied expressions, I know it's a debate I'll keep to myself. Maybe it is true. Everything I felt last night in the basement hasn't gone away, but today, with the new day, I want more. I want clarity.

I want one hundred percent certainty before I throw away my family—my chance at a future of happiness and not loneliness.

"Nat?"

"S-sure. I'd love that," I reply, keeping my attention locked on the phone—and not Tristan.

"Wonderful. Billy will be by your place at four. Have a good day." He hangs up, leaving me to face the wrath of my decision.

The second Alex's voice is gone from the room, Tristan slams his hand on the table, causing his phone to leap. "You are *not* going there tonight. I don't care if I have to tie you to a damn bed. It's not happening."

"If I don't, he'll know something is wrong, Tristan." I stand, resolute in my decision. Firm, like how my jaw juts. "He won't do anything to me."

His knuckles form a vise around the chair again. From across the table, I hear the grinding of his teeth. "It seems I fucked common sense out of you last night, Little Bird."

Hawke whistles, cutting into the stagnant air. "I'm trying to debate whose possessiveness is more amusing—yours or Ryker's."

No one pays him any attention.

Ryker approaches the table, bumping it with his large form. "No, this is a good thing. Natalie, if you can get inside, you'll be able to look around. Find anything that would indicate where he's leaving these women, whether it's inside the house or not, and let us know. He won't be as guarded around you."

I nod, because it's essentially my plan as well, only a lump forms in my throat, preventing me from speaking. This is something from a crime drama. I'm investigating my own brother to determine if he's a murderer or not. This isn't right.

"Ryker—" Tristan starts, but Ryker holds up his hand, ending Tristan's speech.

"He won't hurt her. If he was working on selling her last night, or giving her away, or whatever the fuck he was doing, he needs her. He'll send her home tonight because he knows if she doesn't show up to school for a while, her profs will question it. If she doesn't return tonight, *you'll* question it." Ryker pauses, leaning on clenched fists as he swings his head around in an arc to focus on me. "He's been doing this for years, so he won't make an error now. Natalie, you do need to be careful and not let anything slip, though. Do not be obvious with your questioning and lead him to wonder if there's more to your visit than he believes. Act normal, but curious about his business in a way greater than you have before. Understand? You'll be fine." His attention whips to Tristan. "Dude, you've helped me in more ways than I can recall, but you need to let her go. This is *me* helping *you*. She'll be okay."

"Besides," Brent rumbles from the corner, where he's been so far silent. "If he hurts her, it'll give us more reason to react ourselves."

"Brent!" Elena leans forward until he's in her eyesight. Her eyes go wide in a way meant to be urging and disciplinary. "Your 'if' certainly isn't helping."

But it no longer matters because Tristan is already stalking by us, down the hall, and throwing himself out the front door. It smashes behind him, causing Hawke to frown from behind his mug. In his leave, the deep scent of rage hovers, cruel, sticky, and uncomfortable.

Ryker sighs, his gaze trailing after his friend. "I'll go find him. Hawke, get her home." His hand briefly touches Elena's head in a goodbye before he follows Tristan outside.

Hawke slurps his coffee in response, his brows lifting above his mug and he speaks to Ryker's retreating back. "Only if you make sure he doesn't break my house again. Or fuck in my bed." His eyes glint, amused, as he smiles at me before finishing his coffee and taking me home, while I consider all the ways my life no longer makes any sense.

ABOUT AN HOUR after Hawke and Elena got me back home, Tristan arrived, and since then, he hasn't spoken a word, choosing to act like a giant baby. His obsessive behaviour is stifling, so after the first while of him sitting on my couch staring blankly at the news on TV, I hide away in my room to study. If I have the day free, I may as well take advantage of it.

Before four o'clock, I dress in clean leggings and a blouse. Going for pretty, but nothing over the top. Billy should be here soon, based on the timing Alex set forth.

At the top of the stairs, I suck in as much air as I can, hoping to release it slowly, to get me through the silent chaos at the bottom of these steps. Unhurriedly, I walk down, eyes locked on the living room across from the staircase, where he was last waiting for me. It's empty.

Maybe he's left. Or he's in the kitchen.

Either way, wherever he was put him at an advantage because suddenly, I'm pinned against the wall, my head squished between his large hands, his forehead pressing hard into mine.

"I swear to fucking God—and I'm not religious by any means, but I will be tonight—if you come back with a single hair out of place, I will slaughter him, Little Bird. It'll only be a small piece of the pain he'll experience at my hands."

I should be disturbed—should even back away and tell him to get away from me, but we've already determined that isn't me. That his brand of crazy is exactly the flavour I've come to crave, so instead of pushing him off me, my hands fist his plain black tee and I yank him closer, until his body is firmly against mine.

"I won't," I promise. "And you have no reason to hurt anyone."

One of his hands shifts to my neck, where he grips tightly, seizing control of my movements. He tilts my head to conquer my mouth with his own, kissing me in a way that has my head going light and requiring the wall to keep me upright.

When he pulls away, I ask, "Where is this coming from, Tristan? Last night you had no issues sending me off."

"Last night was before everything changed." His nostrils flare. "Before we learned how treacherous your brother truly is. Before you knew who I was. Before..." His eyes drop back to my lips, and instead of responding, he steals my breath once more, kissing me for long moments until Billy's telltale arrival honk sounds through the front door.

"I need to go."

But he doesn't step back. Doesn't give me the space to slip out from his clutches. Simply remains firm in his hold, his body a brick wall protecting me. Somehow, he grows larger. His chest expands, holding in the breath he'll no doubt keep trapped until I return later.

"You need to let me go," I repeat.

"Never."

Still, he eventually moves to the side, letting me pass. I can feel the force of his gaze on my back, but once I slip outside, I shut the door and block myself from his view.

Twenty-Nine

NATALIE

ALEX IS right outside when Billy stops the car in front of his mansion. He immediately grips the car door's handle and tosses it open before Billy even has the opportunity to put the vehicle in park. Alex's arms reach inside and latch onto me, helping me out. At the last moment, I grab my purse where my phone is, once again locked inside, safe and sound.

"Oh, my God, Natalie, why the hell would you not tell me you were overwhelmed?" Alex holds me at arm's length, his face a perfect mask of worry. If he was truly trying to hand me off last night, his poker face merely implies that of a caring brother.

I shrug, going for weak and helpless. "Dunno. You were really excited by the whole thing, and I suppose I didn't want to upset you."

"You'd never upset me."

He tucks my arm through his and leads me up the grand steps and into the even grander home. A grand home I now wonder how many ghosts it's held. How many girls' screams—how much bloodshed.

As Alex directs me down the long hallway toward his office, I glance at him through the low light. He doesn't appear to be what

Tristan claims he is, but why does my stomach knot and my nerves urge me to turn away?

It's the same feeling I've always gotten around him.

Stop it, Natalie. This is why you're here tonight.

Alex stops in front of a set of double doors, one being open, and gestures for me to go ahead. Immediately, I take in the depressing blank walls with a single bookshelf in the corner. An old-fashioned wooden desk hosting a fancy lamp that looks more expensive than my entire outfit, with two cushioned chairs are in front of it.

And nestled in one is that girl he introduced to me last night.

My feet pause in the doorway, shock holding me still, and I glance back as Alex shuts the door behind us.

"Hope you don't mind I brought Teagan here tonight."

Teagan. Right. I smile at her, taking the chair opposite. "Not at all. Hi."

She glances up beneath her red bangs to softly smile. Like the party, it doesn't meet her eyes.

Doesn't meet her eyes, giving her a sense of lifelessness and misery. Is this a hint?

"Good," Alex murmurs, moving to the left of the room. He pulls out two glasses and a glass of something amber, pouring them before handing one to me.

I flick my eyes between Teagan and my glass. "Do you want...?"

"She won't be drinking tonight," Alex states, like he makes these decisions for her often.

Maybe he does. Suddenly, my back tingles with discomfort. I shift, hoping he doesn't see my clear anxiety.

"Are you... pregnant?" I ask Teagan directly, hoping it's merely that. Her stomach is flat beneath a grey tank, but she could be very early in her first trimester. Teagan doesn't show any sign of even hearing me.

Again, Alex speaks for her. "She has to work later."

"Oh?" I lift my brows. "Do you bartend or something?" It's fairly late for someone to have a shift.

"Something like that," Alex interjects. He sits, his leather executive chair creaking as he swivels into place. "But pay Teagan no attention. She and I, we had something to talk about earlier before I realized it was nearly time for your visit."

"Oh, um." My hands tighten on the glass and I shoot my attention back to my right, momentarily hating how I've encroached on their night. Though, by the lack of attention she's showing me, I don't think she minds it too much. Still, for good measure, I add, "Sorry."

Alex waves his hand, readjusting himself in his chair. "Doesn't matter. Natalie, last night was more than just a party for me. It was an introduction."

To whom, I wonder. Small hairs lift on the back of my neck and my thighs clench as I wrap my ankles around each other, fighting the urge to remain looking demure and not concerned with his other meanings.

"You weren't raised in this life, and Father did you dirty, I know that."

According to Alex, once Mom ran away, our father never thought twice about me again, not even putting me in his will. Everything in our father's estate went to Alex, and it's only through Alex's generosity and his desire for a family that he's been finding ways to compensate for what he believes should also be mine.

"Upon your graduation, I would like to give you some of the fortune. You may keep the townhouse, and hell, I'll even buy you a car as a grad present, but you also need assets in your name. Stocks. Money."

My muscles can't unclench. They want to—want to open up to his inviting words, but goodness, the chill down my spine simply won't defrost enough to ease my trepidation. His unspoken *but* hangs in the air.

"But—"

And there it is.

"—you weren't raised in this lifestyle. I'm afraid you don't know what it's like to control so much wealth."

"Mhm." I plaster on a small smile and take a tiny sip of whatever it is he gave me. The burn comes back up in my throat, but I force it down. It's better than showing him how I truly feel about his insulting words, essentially implying being poor means I'm unaware of what it's like to have money and how to manage it.

Alex pauses his obviously well-thought-out speech and also takes a sip, his calculating eyes resting on me. He stands, wandering to the side of his desk where he positions his hip on the edge.

"What did you think of Ryan?"

"Um." *How am I supposed to answer this?* "He's... nice." It's obvious he's continuing his matchmaking scheme from last night.

"He's an old friend."

Alex doesn't add more to that, so to be polite, I ask, "From high school?"

"No. Our businesses have come into contact over the course of time, and I think they may again." He pushes himself off the edge of his desk, coming round to the front. I expect him to stop in front of me, but he continues walking, only stopping when he's standing behind Teagan. "I don't want to sound chauvinistic, Nat, but I think you two would be great together. He would help manage your money."

I tune him out, in favour of watching Teagan, because if there was a moment of doubt in my mind that Alex is truly the bad guy, the mystery is solved. Though subtle, her shoulders lift a fraction, her spine straightening. Alex's hand goes to her shoulder and brushes the strands of hair, baring her neck on one side. Teagan's eyes flash up, though by how fast she drops them back to her lap, it obviously was an accident.

Everything I've felt, everything Tristan and Elena told me, everything I *agreed* with them on... is true. Because fear can't be faked like that. The death in her vacant gaze, the way she flinches as he drags his fingers along her skin. The way her hands tighten on her lap, knuckles whitening.

But then she lifts them again. Slowly—cautiously. And her lips form words: *Run.*

I blink, nearly believing I've imagined her warning. Her eyes slide to the door and back, and she adds, *Now.*

My attention flashes up, checking that Alex, still standing behind her, didn't catch the silent communication passing between us, or notice how I'm suddenly itching to get up and do exactly as she suggests and leave here.

Oh my God. My hand goes weak around the expensive crystal, and it threatens to tumble from my fingers. I force air through my lungs, hoping it'll weigh me down, preventing me from running back to Tristan's arms.

The words are out before I bite down on them. "What are you doing to her, Alex? You're—"

I realize my mistake in the way his kind eyes freeze. In how his hand goes still on Teagan's neck. Her fragile neck he could very well squeeze the life out of if I don't back down.

He ignores me though, coming around to the front of her seat. "Whore, what fucking lies are you spewing to my sister?"

When his hands form fists by his side, I ignore all sense of self-preservation and leap to my feet, stepping between them. "Alex, what the hell? Don't speak to her like that. She's your damn girlfriend."

She's not, I now see. I know that, but I keep up the pretense of being a complete outsider to his evilness.

A different Alex emerges. One he's obviously taken care not to reveal before now. His hand snaps up in the air, quick as a flash, angled toward me, and as fast as I can react and get out of the way, he pauses, horror replacing anger.

But it's too late. I've seen what I need to.

Alex rebuilds his pretense of care, lowering his hand slowly by his side and stepping away from both Teagan and me. His hands brush once down his shirt, fixing any wrinkles his near-abuse created.

"I'm sorry, I seem to not be myself. I believe I'm simply tired. The company's been requiring extra attention of late, and Teagan's quite demanding in our relationship, you see."

I do, but more than you'd like me to.

He gives us his back as he stalks to his desk chair. It's in that quick moment that he's not looking at us, Teagan looks at me again, jerking her head to the side.

Go, her mouth says.

I shake my head. *Not yet.*

Alex drops back into his seat and focuses on me again, before sipping from his glass. "Now, where were we? Right—your engagement. You marry Ryan, and I'll ensure you'll get what Father should have given you years ago. A wedding present, we'll call it."

Everything that just happened no longer matters as he returns to his previous conversation where he's playing brother matchmaker. I recall the other women that were here yesterday. Is he aiming to make me a wife who controlled the chains or be a woman in those very chains?

I glance at Teagan again, sparing her a quick glance, sharing with her that I won't believe his lies in the swiftest look I can before giving Alex my attention once more.

My rough swallow does little to quell my nerves but still, I push out, "Would I be able to think about it, Alex?"

His head tilts, as if he can't possibly understand my request. Coupled with the strange emotion that passes through his eyes, it's a long moment before he agrees. "Fine. Graduate and we will talk about it again." He smiles, his shoulders relaxing back into the Alex I've come to know.

But it's too late. For a brief moment, he showed me who he truly is, and it's all the proof I need.

I WAVE goodbye to Billy and enter my front door, only to be greeted by a dark house. When leaving Alex's, I hadn't messaged Tristan I was on my way back. In the hours I've been gone, I'm sure Tristan went home.

My wonder is soon answered when I'm thrown against the same wall as last time. Normally, being that I live alone, my defences would go up. I'm not a good fighter, but I know where to kick and punch to do damage. But the hands that grasp me do more than simply push me against the far wall. They lift me up, one arm going around my hip and the other under my ass, nudging my legs apart to lock around his waist.

And then things move, and I open my eyes, glancing over his shoulder, finding we're getting farther and farther away from the front door and up my stairs.

"I missed you," Tristan mumbles into my hair.

"I wasn't gone long enough for you to miss me. Three hours or something."

"Two hours and fifty-nine minutes more than I wanted to wait."

I giggle, enjoying how the light feeling ricochets around my chest and wipes away the sinisterness left by Alex. "You're silly, but I love it."

We make it to the top of my stairs, but he doesn't release me, instead using the wall for leverage to kiss me.

"You seem to constantly underestimate how obsessed I truly am with you."

Words every girl loves to hear. My sigh blows over his face and I lift a hand from his shoulder to lightly touch his cheek, feeling rough stubble beneath my palm. "I think I'm getting an idea." Because I'm feeling it too, and while the words hover right there, available and ready to be said to him, my visit with Alex can't go ignored.

"Could you get everyone together?"

Everyone. Huh. A week ago, my circle consisted of Alex, Jolene, and occasionally, Elena. But now, I gained Tristan as well, and through him and this whole weird-ass scenario, I've gained a bunch of new strangers as... not friends, but something. Alex's horror is linking me with people I would have otherwise never met. In high school, I kept my head low and only spoke to a small handful of people, avoiding the cool, popular kids, but now it feels like I'm a part of them.

It's not a feeling I mind too much.

It's nice even.

"They already are," he smirks, "but I wanted to say hello first."

I glance past him, toward the staircase we're standing beside. "But I have news."

Tristan stops paying me any attention—my words that is—and drops his face to the curve of my breasts, barely hidden by my blouse. "News won't change anything whether we tell them now or in an hour. Now, shh." He snatches my skin between his teeth, nibbling lightly, eating away all worries about Teagan and Alex.

My head falls back, the wall keeping it attached to my body while Tristan goes for my neck again, my legs tightening around his waist.

While managing to keep me balanced, his hand works at my breasts until he's popping them free from my blouse, my nipples being exposed to the air and hardening instantly. By the time the chill registers, he robs it away, replacing it with the heat from his mouth and I groan, pushing my hips into him the best I can with the angle I'm stuck at.

As if answering my unspoken concerns, he tightens his hold and lifts me off the wall, continuing to move us toward my bedroom, where he lowers me on the bed, his hands stripping away the rest of my clothes. I reach for him, but he slides out of the way and removes his own clothes, tossing them in a pile with my own.

He'll try to take command again, as he most often does, but I slide forward on the bed, grasping his length before he has the chance to react. My hand pumps him a couple times, thumb swiping over his head, rubbing his precum around the head.

"Little Bird—"

I lean forward and swallow him whole, wrapping my mouth around his length and start sucking up and down on him.

"Little Bird," he repeats, only this time, it's a groan. His hand wraps in my hair, capturing it in a knot around his fist and he holds on tight.

My scalp burns, but I pull my lips, adding suction to my sucking as my free hand—the one not helping keep my balance—comes up and cups his balls. My hair pulls as male instinct consumes him and he controls my movements, pistoning himself in and out of my throat.

Although it's all for him, he still takes control of the situation, but this time, I don't mind. In fact, even though I'm sure my scalp will feel this for the rest of the day, I fucking love it. I'm handing him control in the hottest way possible, transforming myself into merely a mouth for him to use.

He thickens, twitching, and I know it's only a moment until he's—

He groans, jerking once more and releasing in my mouth. I keep my lips tight around him, draining him dry until he pulls away, his hand releasing my hair.

I grin up at him, tongue flicking out to lick at my lips. "Yum."

My single word sparks something inside him because, suddenly, I'm on my back, his mouth between my legs, tongue piercing my core. I cry out, hands going to his hair now, taking the position he was in a mere moment ago.

"This was... supposed to be just... for you," I manage between breaths.

"Believe me, *this*," he licks up my slit, "is for me."

Unlike him, I have no control in this. His hair is a mere handle for my grip, because in no way do I need to hold him there; he keeps himself between my legs, his control throwing my legs over his shoulder, ensuring I'm as close to him as I possibly can be.

I rock my hips, chasing the high he's leading me to, and it doesn't take much before I'm crying out to the ceiling, my hips locking tightly around his head as his mouth continues to eat at me until I have nothing left to give.

When I'm breathing normally again and my heart catches up with itself, my legs unlock, falling limply to the bed.

Tristan stands, looking more pleased with himself than ever. "I was planning on fucking you senseless, but there you went ahead with your sexy, little mouth and its alternate plans."

"Sorry." I flutter my lashes playfully and pull on my clothes again, knowing that while I only want to remain in bed with him the rest of the night, people are waiting to hear about tonight.

He dresses too, and on our way out of my bedroom, he catches my hand, swinging me back toward him and kissing me deeply.

"Let's get this bastard."

"*GOD*, you two were fucking again, weren't you?" is the greeting we get when Hawke opens his front door. "At least it wasn't my bed this time." His grumble leads us to the living room where Tristan immediately takes a seat on the couch and pulls me on his lap, wrapping an arm loosely around my waist.

Across from us, on a single-seater, Elena is in a similar position in Ryker's lap. She shoots me a soft smile. Beside Tristan is Brent, leaning back lazily on the couch. He only nods at me, remaining silent, per usual.

Hawke drops onto the edge of his coffee table and pulls his lip ring into his mouth. "Okay, so what's the news?"

Before I can respond, Ryker leans past Elena. "Give us every detail."

Tristan's thumb strokes a small patch of bare skin from where my blouse lifts up, urging me to tell them everything. "Well, I arrived like usual. Phone was off and in my purse. This time he brought me to his office. There's nothing there that indicated anything other than he's a boring decorator."

Brent snorts, and Ryker mutters, "Of course. It's not like what we're looking for will be left out freely."

"He obviously mentioned last night, and then asked me about the guy he introduced me to and began to go on about our father and how I hadn't gotten what I deserved."

Hawke leans forward. "What wasn't given to you?"

"Any money. My mother ran away with me when I was a baby, and our father apparently never wanted anything to do with me. So I was never in his will; therefore, I have no inheritance of my own."

"Says who?" Hawke again.

"Says Alex." The more questions about him I answer, the deeper I feel the crease between my brows going.

Ryker cuts his eyes to him. "Hawke, could you stop with the lawyer speak for a moment and focus on what matters?"

"Lawyer?" I squeak, eyes scanning his tattoo-sleeved arms and piercings.

But Hawke doesn't notice, his attention locked on Ryker. "When it's your future we're blowing up, then it won't matter. I know you want to take him down, but Ryker, have a damned heart. Alex helps her—uses the money that *should* be hers, if their father was a decent human being. When we put him in prison, that all goes away. So, yes, this is relevant because I want a copy of that will. I want to see if Alex is telling the truth."

My heart skips a beat. "You think he's lying? I don't see why he would. If our father wanted nothing to do with me, then..."

He's already shaking his head, making my speech trail off into nothingness. "Bad men do strange things, and I've seen weirder. Alex might be keeping money from you. Or we can contest the will."

"So weird to think that was our principal," Elena mutters.

What Hawke is saying could be vital for my future. It would mean I won't struggle to ensure Jolene remains where she is.

"You think?" The relieving possibility makes my skin tingle, Tristan's touch being second to everything else.

Hawke only nods, his next words interrupted by Brent's question. "But why would he reach out to Natalie at all then? Wouldn't he want to remain quiet and not risk her going for his money?"

Tristan shifts beneath me and moves my hair away from one side of my face, getting a better look. "All great questions, but Ryker is right. The money doesn't go away until we catch him. When we do, then we'll find the will. Go on, Little Bird."

My cheeks warm at the nickname he blatantly uses in front of everyone. "Anyway, he said he feels guilty and rather than simply paying for some things for me, after graduation, he wants to give me an inheritance." I take a breath, readying for the next part, but in my silence, Hawke speaks again.

"Why do I feel there's a 'but' coming on?"

"Because there is. In order to get the money, I need to marry—"

Tristan's growling rumble vibrates up my back.

"—but he didn't say those words. Only that Ryan and I would be a," I lift my fingers into double quotations, "'good fit.' Then the money would be a wedding present or something."

Tristan curses behind me, his hand stopping its gentle strokes and instead clutching my waist. His other hand wraps around my thigh possessively. Of course everyone notices, just like they notice my hand landing on his, caressing the skin there.

"Question is, is the money for you, or some sort of fucked-up deal between him and his friend?" Brent muses.

"It'll never happen," Tristan snaps, chilling the air around me with his tone.

I twist a few inches, keeping him in sight, so he can see my rolling eyes. "Relax there. Obviously. *Anyway,*" I face everyone else again, "that's really all that happened. I asked him to give me time till I graduate. It'll keep him off my back for now." Hopefully.

"So you didn't get to see the house in greater detail?" Ryker curses.

"No, but we weren't alone." When multiple eyes all crease with curiosity and Tristan stiffens beneath me, I add, "I assumed we would be, but when we got to his office, a woman was there. Apparently, she's his girlfriend. I first met her at the party."

Ryker jerks so hard, Elena slides from his lap and onto the couch beside him, though he doesn't remain long, lifting to his feet instead. "Fuck. His current victim, you think?"

"Or she's in on it," Tristan offers.

"No." I shake my head, this time turning my entire attention to Ryker. "She looked scared. Like, terrified. He didn't get her a drink. Mentioned she had to work later but didn't say where. She just stared at her lap the entire time we spoke, but when he got up, he touched her and—" I break off, my mind falling into the depression I felt *for her.* I'm scared for her.

"And?" Tristan probes.

"She flinched. I saw her eyes. Guys, it was cold, stark fear. I don't really know what to think because, at the party, she wasn't collared like the other women. But then, I've seen she is a victim too. She's terrified of him—tried to warn me about him even."

Ryker curses, turning away from the group to stalk up and down the open space of the living room. "This is helpful, Natalie. Truly. If this girl fears him, I bet it's because she knows what he can do to her." He stops pacing to ask, "Did you get her name? Describe her. Something."

"Teagan," I respond instantly. "That's her name."

A choking sound comes from my right, and I glance over at Brent in time to see him fly from his seat, his hand covering an open mouth.

"Brent," Elena murmurs to him. "It's not her. She left the area. You said so yourself, there's been no trace. You've been looking."

Her? As in, they *know* Teagan?

Brent faces Elena. "Then who the fuck else would be *with* Alex *and* goes by the name Teagan. That's entirely too much of a coincidence." His eyes cut to me, seemingly ending his conversation—if it can be referred to as that—with Elena. "The girl—Teagan—what colour was her hair? Describe her."

"Red," I whisper, eyes bouncing between him and Elena, seeking the punchline in his reaction. "Like a natural, deep red."

Brent chokes again, falling back a step, but his eyes are long gone from the room. "The fucking chances... She's still involved with him." He blinks and whips out his phone, scrolling through it for a moment.

There's a clear bated breath hovering above all of us. After another moment, Brent turns the screen toward me, showing me a picture of a girl, no older than a teenager—a younger version of Teagan.

"But that's—"

"Does your Teagan look like this?" he interrupts.

I nod, and Ryker cuts into my line of sight, his eyes going toward the screen. "Brent, Tristan, I thought you found no record of her in the area."

"There isn't," Tristan rumbles from beneath me.

Again, Brent's eyes, shadowed, wide, and scarred, stay pinned on me. His mouth remains open, seemingly unable to shut from shock.

"You know her?" Seems like most of them know her actually but weren't expecting her to be involved. I study Ryker's frustration and Elena's surprise.

Brent shakes his head slowly, though I assume it's meant to be a nod. Finally, he speaks, his astonishment ending enough for words to form. "I more than know her. I fucking *loved* her."

And then I see another Brent in front of me. Elena always portrayed him as the "good guy"—sweet, caring, and funny—but a new version of him arises. His lax body straightens, the muscles in his arms clenching so hard, that when he yanks his phone back and shoves it into his jeans, I think he might break it. His dark eyes harden, becoming rocks against whatever is going through his mind. His slack mouth forms a hard line, the skin between his brows dipping in determination.

And when he speaks, it's at the ground. "Natalie, you did well. We're not sneaking into his house. We won't be searching for anything because I have someone who will lead us straight to him. Whether she likes it the fuck or not." He backs toward the door. "Cherry-Girl will fucking pay for what she's done."

Pay?

"Wait!" I throw myself from Tristan's lap, flying across the room, stopping short of bumping into Brent. "Wait, no, Brent. She tried to help me. She was warning me off—mouthing words, encouraging me to run. We need to help *her*."

Brent glances down, but it's more like he's staring *through* me rather than at me. "Maybe. But until I know more—"

"No," I cut him off, disbelief growing by the second. "*No*, Brent."

I peek back at Tristan, almost wanting him to back me up, but I recognize the discomfort in his eyes as I argue with his best friend. He too believes Teagan's an enemy. I glance at Ryker and Elena, and Elena's staring at her hands.

No one's seen what I have.

"She couldn't have been faking that emotion," I whisper harshly, hoping an eased tone will make it through Brent's wrath. "Why would she tell me to run away then, if she wasn't trying to help me?"

"She still knows something though, Natalie," Hawke comments. "Either way, she has information we need. Whether or not she's on his side is irrelevant at this point."

"It's extremely relevant!" My hand slashes the air, gesturing to Brent. "It changes how he approaches her. Treat her like an enemy and she'll clam up in fear. If she knows we're trying to save her, she'll help us. She'll want to." I think. I'm assuming anyway.

"Why has she remained by his side all these years? Why has she never discreetly reached out to either of us?" Brent motions between him and Elena. "We were both her friends, and she never told either one of us when she took off. She *ran away* and yet found herself with Alex yet again." Brent's eyes harden and he backs another step toward the door. "Natalie, you might be right. She may have been trying to help you in the moment, but she still has a lot to answer for. And *that's* why I'll find her this time and get those answers."

And then he's gone, Hawke's door slamming shut behind him, leaving the rest of us to gape in his absence. Ryker is the first to break and he looks to Hawke, nudging his chin toward the door. "Go find him."

Hawke's gone within a minute.

"Holy. Fuck." Elena says what everyone else is thinking.

Holy fuck is right.

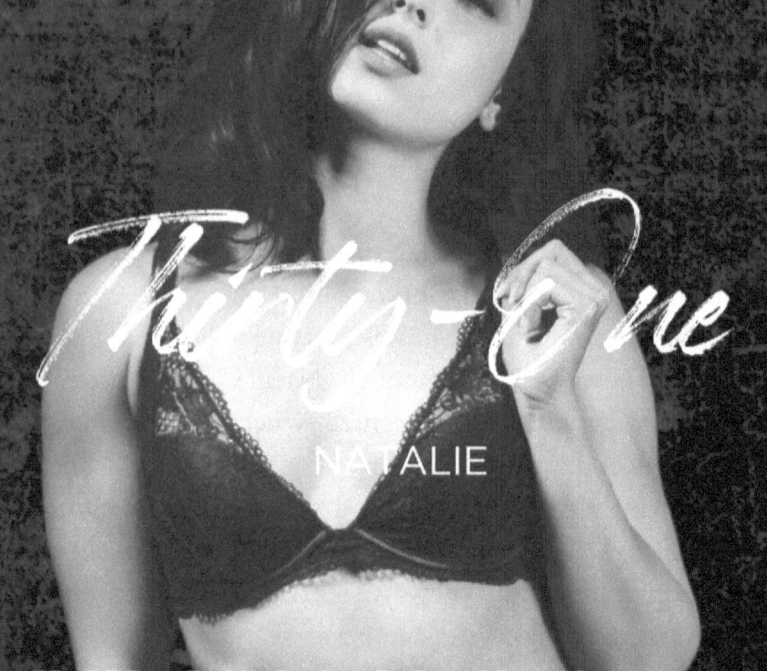

Thirty-One

NATALIE

OVER BREAKFAST THE NEXT MORNING, Tristan is on his phone, tapping rapidly while I quietly crunch on my cereal, thinking about how damn surreal life is.

Last night, Hawke did catch up to Brent, but he said Brent is determined to finish this thing. Ryker and Elena headed home, while Tristan and I came back to my place.

I gesture toward him with my spoon. "When's your boss going to question why you haven't caught the stalker yet?"

"Oh, I'm sure it'll be soon," he responds, not looking away from his phone. "I should probably mention he left you alone and go back to work." Finally, the phone lowers, and he looks up. "But going back to work means I don't get to spend every minute of the day with you."

"Probably smart, before we get tired of each other."

Cops must be trained to run fast because he's out of his seat, bending by my chair to steal my mouth in a single heated kiss faster than I can even register he moved.

"Little Bird, I could never get tired of you," he says, tone husky, after pulling back. He straightens, clearing our dishes and walks them to the small sink behind us. "Are you seeing your aunt today?"

"Every Sunday. In fact, I'm going to get ready now, and then we can head over there. I have things I need to ask her." Halfway to the door, I stop, a new idea forming in my mind. "Actually, would you like to meet her in a new way?"

His lips twitch into a grin that has my heart fluttering. Because despite all the bad shit right now, he's a new light I'll follow into the darkness, and do so, with a smile on my face.

"You mean, other than the creepy bodyguard who follows you around? I'd love to."

Whenever I prepare to see Jolene, I always feel cheery, but today, it's heightened.

Doesn't take a genius to know why.

"WELL, ISN'T THIS A SURPRISE?" Jolene's eyes twinkle as she takes her seat across from Tristan and me. Like the well-mannered woman she's always been, she stretches her arm out, reaching her hand toward him. "Tristan. My day is a whole lot better now that you're here."

"Likewise," he says smoothly, shaking her hand. "I hope you've been well."

"Why wouldn't I be?" She grins at me. "You didn't mention we'd be having a visitor again."

Tristan, the very guy who faked being two different people in my life, the cop who set out to avenge unknown women, the one who's never shown any fear, looks absolutely terrified in this moment, his face bleaching white and his grip on my knee going slack, and then disappearing altogether as he stands abruptly.

"I'm sorry. Natalie said it was fine. I can go."

Jolene sputters, waving her hand in the air. "My goodness, boy. You're too serious. Sit, sit." When Tristan does, she focuses her attention on me, a smirk pulling at her lips. "He's a worrier, but then, they're always the good ones."

I smile, but it doesn't last long. Because once I woke this morning and got thinking about this visit, there's topics I want to mention that we usually avoid.

"Jolene, my father—How much did you know about him?"

Her brows spike and she leans away, glancing once at Tristan before speaking, "Well, Nattie, this isn't what I expected from you. I didn't know him all that well, to be honest. Family gatherings, Christmas, that sort of thing. But I didn't go over often. *If* your mom and I hung out, it was typically out of the house, and honestly, we didn't see each other that much after they wed."

Tight knots form in my stomach. "Why's that?"

She shrugs, sadness coating her expression. "Your mother changed after marrying him. She wasn't the sister I grew up with. She became closed-in. Quiet."

My leg bounces slightly and I lean forward, eager and hungry for her answers. "You think it had something to do with my father?"

My question sparks something else in Jolene, and she whips her gaze sharply up, eyes narrowing. "Where are these questions coming from? Your entire life you've been content to block him and his entire cursed line from our lives. Ever since Alex came back into your life, I was scared this would happen."

"What would happen? Jolene, what do you know?"

She sighs, frowning, voice dropping back to its normal tone. "Your father was very powerful, very popular. He ran his company in the city, and then one day, decided to become a high school principal in Newton. I'm not entirely sure why. Your mother never said, but the suddenness was too strange. Right after that, the media was abuzz with some scandal involving the company. Staff were found murdered after hours. It was too coincidental, if you ask me. But I was smart enough to not ask questions and get involved."

I share a look with Tristan. It's clear by his tight jaw, he's fighting to rein in his thoughts.

"And your mother... I don't know. She was always scared of him. I was terrified he'd come for you one day, after she brought you to me, but he never did. I thank the stars every day you were left out of that life."

I lower my voice, ensuring no other visitors around us overhear. "Do you think she was killed by him?"

Jolene remains silent, but nods. "There was no proof, of course, but then, there never is with the Millers." Her head tilts as she studies me. "I don't know where this questioning is coming from, but for goodness' sake, Nattie, be safe and don't do anything stupid."

Tristan's hand clamps down on my knee and I can feel the pulsing anger beneath his skin. He leans forward, his bicep brushing mine, bringing him closer to my aunt. "I promise you with everything I have, Natalie will remain safe. I love your niece, and when I love something, I give my everything to it. I'll protect her until death takes me away from her side."

How can one's heart flutter and stop working all at the same time? No idea, but it's exactly what mine does. Breath whooshes out of me, my nerves igniting with every beat of my pulse.

Jolene looks taken aback but composes herself quickly, a sly smile stretching her mouth. "You do that, Tristan. Because if you don't, you're dealing with me." And then she gives the most menacing grimace she can manage through a face that appears to only be meant for smiling, and I laugh, interrupting my mind roving over the fact that he just said he loved me in front of my aunt.

"You got it." He winks, cocky, before glancing over at me. There's nothing cocky in the look he gives me then. He doesn't need to be, because he knows he already owns me; there's no need to prove it.

Jolene's eyes bounce between us, and I'm not sure what she finds, but whatever it is, has her frowning and rising to her feet. Her finger slashes the air as she says, "Stay. I'll be right back."

She wobbles off toward the entrance, not looking back, passing the attendant on the way in.

When she disappears, I murmur without taking my eyes off the door, "That was sudden, don't you think? Very strange."

"Very," Tristan agrees, matching my whispered tone. "She said she'll be back though, so let's give her a moment."

It's two minutes before she returns, striding more confidently toward the picnic table and reclaiming her seat. This time, with an envelope in her hand. She stares at it, her eyes a cloudy mix of emotion, before sliding it across the wood.

"Your mother once said you might have questions about your family, and despite her faults and errors, she tried. For both you and Alex, she tried her best—with what little she could trapped in her lifestyle. This is a letter," she stabs the envelope with her index finger, "from her. She gave it to me with you. Said if you ever inquired, to let you read this." She sighs, long and heavy, lifting her eyes to me again. "Since Alex came into your life, I've been tempted to hand this over, but Nattie, I really wanted you away from the Millers. I hoped your new relationship with your brother wouldn't spark these questions but," she smiles sadly, "I'm also not surprised since I know you."

I stare at the envelope, unmoving.

My mother's words.

Mom. A lady I've never known. A complete stranger, leaving a letter written specifically *for* me. As though she knew her fate; what would happen to her after leaving me with Jolene.

"Natalie," Tristan's gentle whisper jolts something into me—life. Encouragement. Determination to see this through. My mom potentially gave up her life to save me from the darkness Alex had to be raised amidst of, and the least I can do is read her final words to me.

The small envelope is heavy in my hand. Or maybe it's because my numb fingers have stopped working as I manage to slip a finger between the paper's edging and pull the envelope open. A folded-up paper rests inside.

With a staggered, difficult breath, I slide it out, unfold it, and read the unfamiliar scribbles.

Natalie. Daughter. Baby girl.

If you're reading this, it's because I'm not there to warn you myself. It's because Jolene listened to my final request and has given this to you to answer the questions you're asking. It's because your father has never come for you.

He's a bad man, Natalie. I'm sorry.

A whirlwind romance which turned into a quick engagement. I thought he was simply a rich, kind, handsome man, and it wasn't until after we wed, I learned how bad he truly is. How people die around him. How he has no care for life.

I've tried to run. Twice, but he's obsessed with keeping me docile and by his side.

The first time, he beat me.

The second time, when I gave birth to your brother, but he found me before I made it off the property.

Your father didn't want children, but when I was pregnant with your brother, it seemed to wake something up inside him. I hoped then that we'd be a normal family and he'd be the hero rather than the villain he designed himself to be.

He took him from me, Natalie. I tried to save Alex, but your father stole him away from me. My baby, one-year-old and innocent, is being kept and raised solely by your father. He plans on moving them away from the city, and forcing me here, trapped in his mansion.

Getting pregnant with you wasn't planned, but once I learned of it, I couldn't allow him to steal another child from me. Especially you, baby girl. A girl. I'll die before I see him do the same to you as he's done to me.

He won't touch you.

You've no doubt grown to be a beautiful, healthy woman, cared for by my own sister. I owe her more than I can say, and I'll never be able to repay her for the life she's provided for you. But now you're asking about your father or your brother. Don't go down this path, Natalie.

Don't.

Stay away from them. Run away. Move. Whatever it takes. Alex isn't the son I birthed. After years under your father's thumb, he'll be different. Twisted.

I'm begging you, baby girl, stay away from the Miller life.

For me, for Jolene, but most importantly, for you.

I've often been sorry I fell in love with him, but I can't be—not really. Because I got you—even if I'll never get to know you.

I love you.

Mom.

The letter flutters from my hand, caught by Tristan at the last second, who lays it face-down on the table. I stare at it, spotting the tear stains that have fallen upon my mother's words. A last letter—a message written when she knew my father wouldn't allow her to live any longer.

She knew. She knew about Alex's future darkness. One woven by her husband, and she tried to save us both from it.

She saved me but condemned Alex. Literature often speaks about whether a person can be born innately evil or if it's learned behaviour —it's the whole nature versus nurture debate. I've never been able to write a convincing essay because I've never had a firm stance on the matter.

But I do now. If Alex was raised as I was, away from a murderer and with Jolene who's been a godsent, he'd be different.

Alex was condemned to this life, and revelled in it, soon taking our father's place. For the briefest second, I feel sympathy for him and the life he was raised in.

But despite nurture, a person still has choices—autonomy. He could have chosen to *not* rape and murder woman. He could have changed the direction of the Miller name.

I don't feel the sobs, or the lack of breath rattling in my lungs until Tristan wraps his arm around my shoulders and tugs me into his side. My face falls into his chest and into his pleasant scent.

A delicate hand rests on my back, and after a second, Jolene's weaker form presses into my other side, hugging me.

It's between them, I cry. For myself. For Alex. For the women he's hurt. For Mom.

I cry until my eyes burn and my body stops working. I cry until I have nothing left.

I cry for a lifetime of pain my father created.

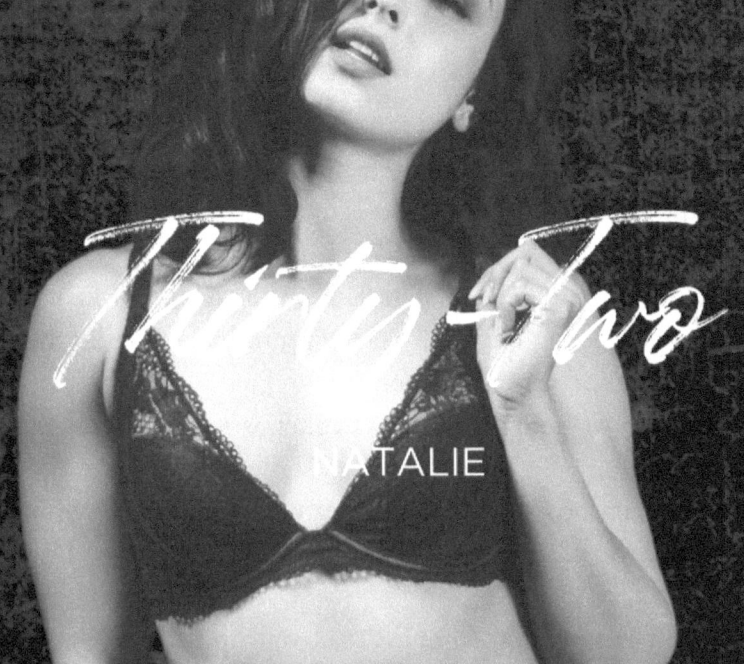

Thirty-Two

NATALIE

AFTER LEAVING JOLENE, Tristan snatches my hand and yanks me into a hard hug. We stand there on the sidewalk for long moments, just holding each other.

"Are you up for going somewhere else or do you want to go home?"

I pull back, peering up at him. By now, I've cried so many tears, I forget why I'm even crying. Mom's letter is heavy in my pocket. I nearly asked Jolene to keep it still, so I don't obsess over the words, but now that I have that piece of her—a piece of a mother I hadn't realized I wanted—I refuse to let it go.

"I'm okay. Now." I smile weakly, an attempt to show him my true emotions. He releases me, all except my hand, and turns us in the opposite direction of home. "Where are you taking me?"

"Right here." He stops in front of his cruiser.

I lift my brows. "Is this where you arrest me and tell me this is more of a set-up than you've admitted to?"

Tristan opens the passenger door, gesturing for me to get in. "Yep. I'll be placing you inside my own personal jail, designed specifically for your pleasure only. Get in."

I do, instantly settling in the soft, comfortable seat as I watch Tristan stride around the front of the car and get into the driver's seat. He starts the car, rumbles purring beneath me, and pulls away from the curb.

All sorts of things light up and flash on the dash, but he ignores them all, even twisting the knob on the funny-looking radio thing a woman's mechanical voice emits from.

"Where are we going?" I ask, watching as we pass through the town's streets.

"Elena mentioned the other day you were wondering why we're going through the effort with your brother."

"Yeah."

He briefly glances away from the road, only to tell me, "I'm going to show you instead."

He says nothing more on the topic, not as he continues to drive out the town and down the highway, heading toward the city. My eyes follow the off-ramp Billy takes toward Alex's house, but we continue past, pulling off at the next exit.

Tristan navigates the roads expertly, obviously having taken this path many, many times. And when we pull up to a facility, not dissimilar to the one Jolene is in, I blanch, twisting toward him again.

"What—"

"Not yet." He parks the car, and I scramble to follow him out.

The facility's sign reads *Cortville Gardens* and I note the single-floored building, pretty front, and well-maintained lawn. Coming from someone who priced out multiple different facilities, all appearing like this one does, I know whoever is here isn't staying for cheap.

Tristan strides through the front doors, stopping for a moment at the front desk, and signs our names on the visitor clipboard.

"Zelda. Marie." He nods at the two middle-aged women behind the desk and gestures to me. "If it's okay, I brought a guest along."

As one, they both glance at me, a tentative smile stretching their face. "Of course, Tristan. She'll enjoy that."

She'll? Tristan walks away, leaving me to follow along and discover the mystery.

He heads down the long hallway, nodding his hellos at any passing person in scrubs we see. They return the hellos, most of them using his first name. Only when we reach the end of the hallway do we stop.

He knocks once, before opening the door and popping his head in. "Cheryl!"

"Oh, Tommy!" a cheerful voice exclaims from beyond. "Come in. You've surprised me."

Tommy? What the hell is going on here? After another scan of the hallway, I follow him in, stopping short at the small room. It's similar to Jolene's. A bed pushed against the wall, a small closet boasting colourful clothing, a TV set up on the table across from the bed, and in the corner, a rocking chair.

Where a lady sits, her dark hair tied messily in a bun. Age lines mar her face, but she's still young—the age my mother would be, had she been alive. She—Cheryl, according to Tristan's greeting—leans forward in the rocking chair and lays the knitting down in time for Tristan to cross the room and drop a kiss on her forehead. Obvious adoration passes between their gazes, but only for a moment before she's glancing at the door.

"Tommy, that isn't Lisa. Who is this girl?"

Lisa? Who are *these people?*

"No, this is Natalie. She's staying with me for a while. Lisa is fine though. I thought you'd like to meet her."

Something between curiosity and wariness brings her closer to me. "Hm. Sure. Natalie, is it? Well, if my brother says you're a good one, then I suppose you're a good one. Don't you be taking Lisa's spot now though. She's been too good to him."

Brother? These two are *clearly* not siblings and I whip my gaze over her shoulder toward Tristan, who's already shaking his head, a plea in his gaze. He doesn't want me to say anything.

So, forcing a smile on my face, I continue his lie. "Of course not. He's been helping me. It's nice to meet you."

Satisfied with my response, she turns around, her bun bobbing as she walks back to Tristan and retakes her seat. I remain by the doorway, back pressed into the wall as I observe... whatever it is I'm observing.

"You haven't been around too much, Tommy. Will you stay long?"

"Ah, we can't. I'm sorry. I simply wanted to check in. Has everything been okay here? Still taking your meds?"

She waves her hand. "Yeah, yeah. You worry too much. Well, if you're not here to watch our show together then you may as well scoot along then."

Tristan grins, not seeming thrown off by her comment. "I love you too. Hug me before I go?"

Her scowl drops again and she opens her arms wide, accepting his hug. My eyes bubble with tears; I'm not sure why it feels like the most appropriate response right now.

When they part, Cheryl glances over at me again with a single nod. "Remember what I said, Natalie. Have a nice day the both of you."

Tristan walks by me, leading me out the door, but the moment it's shut, I speak.

"Tristan, what—"

"Outside," he cuts me off, his large legs eating up the shiny, smooth tiled floor as he leads me down the long hall again, past all the doors identical to Cheryl's, and checks us out. *Finally*, when we're back in the car and I feel my insides combusting with the unanswered questions I continue to try to ask, I blurt the rest out.

"Tristan, that answered *nothing*. Who is that? And who's Tommy?"

"Tommy is her brother. My uncle," he answers my second question.

Which, in turn, answers the first one too. "She's your mother," I breathe, eyes drifting to the side as I make sense of the interaction they had. I *see* it now. They have the same hair. The same mannerisms.

"Yes." He pauses, then swallows roughly before unleashing a childhood I never could have imagined. "The man who conceived me never wanted to be a father, so when my mother announced she was pregnant, he broke up with her and left. She managed to do the whole single-mother thing, and was damned good at it too. I never was hungry or cold. Although I was too young to remember, I know she worked her ass off. Multiple jobs, etcetera. I was often cared for by my uncle Tommy and his wife, Lisa, when Mom worked late nights."

Causing the names Cheryl referred to, to make much more sense. She knows her sister-in-law to be Lisa and wondered who I am.

"Anyway, we didn't live in the best of neighbourhoods, and one night we were broken into. Mom heard them coming and—" He pauses, taking a deep breath. His knuckles go white around the steering wheel. "She rushed into my room and practically threw me from the bed, told me to hide inside my closet. Taking the TV wasn't enough for them. Or the bit of money Mom was saving up in case of emergencies. No... They..." He trails off, leaving me to fill in the gaps.

I think I do, seeing now why the thought of rape and murder is so personal to him. His mother is physically fine and still alive, but it doesn't cut out the other option. I open my mouth, but he manages to continue his story.

"Think of the worst thing you could ever imagine, Little Bird. Then double it—*triple* it. They had no idea I was there, a thin door away, but I could see everything they were doing to her through the crack. My knuckles still have scars from where my teeth sank into them so hard, to prevent from crying out. I felt helpless, sitting in the closet while she was—I mean, I didn't know what they were doing exactly, of course, but even then I knew, they were hurting her."

My hand goes to my heart, rubbing at the pain I have for him. "Oh, Tristan."

"It took me ten years before I stopped having nightmares. After that day, my mom broke inside." A staggering breath blows through his lungs and his hands loosen, lessening the white on his knuckles. "Doctors say her mind snapped and went to a place she was last safe in. She thinks she's twenty again—years before I was born. Due to genes, I look a lot like her brother, so when I visit, that's who she thinks I am. Uncle Tommy."

Oh my God. For most of Tristan's life, he's been visiting a mother who doesn't even know he exists, forced to pretend to be a man he isn't —to maintain a relationship with her in ways that are different from what he should have.

"Why can't you tell her?" I ask in a small voice.

He laughs humourlessly. "Doctors fear it'll worsen her mind, by being forced to remind her of that time. Her body decided life before that moment was better, so by dredging it up, we'll only harm her. My aunt and uncle raised me after that, and I had a good childhood, but it wasn't complete, you know?" He huffs, shaking his head, and his hands fall away from the wheel. "Of course you do. Look who I'm speaking with. But it's why Tommy and I can never visit together."

It'll confuse her. "Tristan..."

"So you see why seeing what Alex is doing is worse—why it affects me so much. I like to pretend what happened didn't happen, and it's Ryker who had the initial idea to help Alex's victims, but it doesn't change the fact."

"Of course." I rub at my face, thinking of more words I can say. Instead, I reach over the console and lay my hand on his leg, rubbing it up and down. "I'm so sorry, Tristan, about what happened. Thank you for sharing that with me. Do you still get nightmares from it?"

"Not really. I used to, but Tommy and Lisa put me through a lot of therapy as a child, and it truly did work. It's really rare I dream about it now."

"That's good," I comment, having nothing else to say.

After a few beats of my heart, he glances over at me, a sad smile present. "I want you to know everything about me. I want you to know all of me, to know what you're getting."

The L-word he previously spoke hovers between us and while I haven't said it to him or even myself, I do feel it. I know I do, but now isn't the time to bring that into the car with us. Not with such a heavy history between us.

"Besides," his crooked smile wipes away the horror of the past, "at our wedding when the strange woman starts calling me Tommy, I need you to understand why."

Wedding. "You think you're marrying me one day?"

"I *know* I'm marrying you one day."

Thirty-Three

TRISTAN

TWENTY YEARS AGO

"TRISTAN, OUT OF BED *NOW*!" Mom's frantic voice, along with her firm grip on my arm, hauls me out of bed and pushes me toward my closet. I stumble, eyes still filled with sleep and I try to right myself.

"Mommy," I groan, rubbing at my eyes.

"In the closet!" Her hand on my back shoves me in the small room and the last thing I see is her feverish expression. Mommy is scared, but why I'm not sure.

At the same moment, a bang comes from close by and I flinch, stepping into the shadows. Thanks to the slats on the door, I can see through them, and I watch as Mommy remains still in the middle of the room. I want to call out to her, but she seems scared.

If she's scared, I think I should be too.

Our neighbours are sometimes loud, but never this loud. Another crash comes, followed by heavy footsteps and two large men enter the room. I don't recognize either of them, and since Mommy doesn't speak, I think she doesn't either.

"Well," the larger of the two growls, "what are you doing in here, all alone?"

Mommy whimpers, her hand jutting out to the side to gesture toward the rest of our home. "Just get out. Take what you want."

I lower myself in the shadows, willing my breathing not to be too loud.

The men share a look before they smile, but it's nothing like the smiles I'm used to. These ones make me feel cold inside, though I don't know why.

"Well, since you're giving us permission."

Don't take my toys! I crunch my legs up, putting my hand over my mouth to prevent from yelling at the scary men. And then at Mommy for allowing them to take our things.

I mean, stealing is bad. It's what she's always telling me.

Lost in my thoughts over my toys, I don't see when they grab her, but suddenly, Mommy is on my bed, with the man who spoke on top of her. She pushes at him, crying out, but the other one does nothing. Only looks on.

I push to my knees, wanting to help her, but as if Mommy knows what I'm about to do, she meets my eyes between the slats. I don't know how she can see me, but she does, and the warning in her eyes is the same as when she tells me to use crosswalks or stay away from the stove when she's cooking. So I fall back on my bum, pressing my back against the closet's wall.

But then she yells again and fights the men on top of her. I hear one's belt buckle, and then the other's as he moves toward her head, shoving himself into her face.

I close my eyes.

Because I have no clue what they're doing to Mommy, but based on the noises she's making, I know she isn't enjoying it. My head drops into my knees, my fist going into my mouth so every time Mommy cries out, I bite my knuckles.

I bite my knuckles a lot.

By the time the noises stop, my hand is a bloody mess.

The men laugh, though I don't know what's amusing about hurting Mommy. Their loud steps take them from the house, but even long after they're gone, I don't move.

The closet is safer than what's beyond this door.

Even if Mommy is still lying on my bed, her legs spread, blood dripping down one. She doesn't move, and I want to check her, but instead, I crawl deeper in the shadows.

I don't know how much time passes before a police officer finds me in the closet. She smiles gently, and it's a smile more normal than those men's. Her hand reaches toward me. "It's Tristan, right? Can you take my hand and we'll get out of here?"

"Mommy."

"I know. My friends are helping her. Take my hand so we can bring you to her."

I do, and they bring me to the hospital and put me in a chair beside the bed they have Mommy in. Her eyes are shut, seeming like she's sleeping, but tears stream down her face, so I know she's awake.

She's sad. I wish I helped her. I wish she wasn't so sad.

Little did I understand at that time, how treacherous the world truly is. How many villains enjoy doing the same as those men did to my mother. How they all need to be stopped. And how what I witnessed that day, it not only shaped my present but also my future.

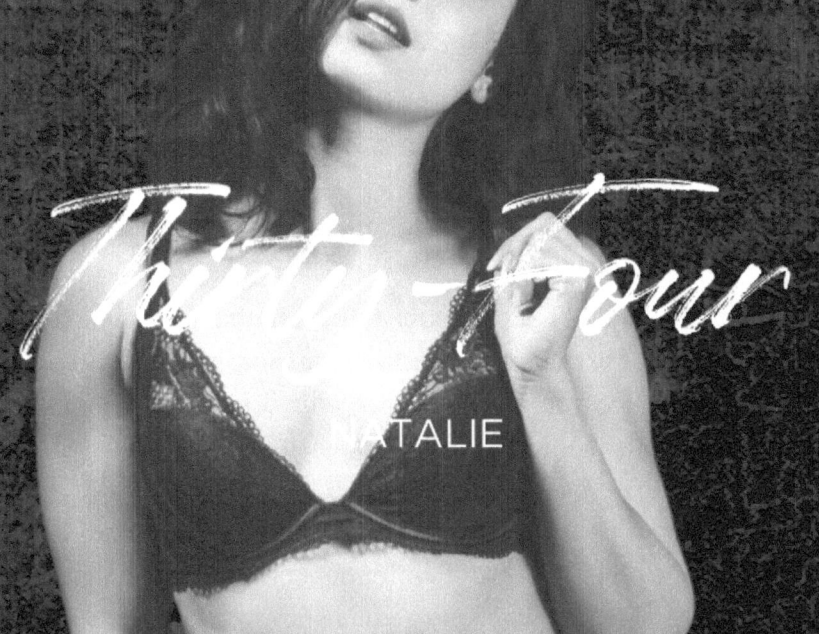

Thirty-Four

NATALIE

BIRDS CHIRP overhead on their way to anywhere that isn't the university's grounds. Lucky damn birds. *Take me with you.* With exams creeping up, I need to put aside any of the Alex drama and focus on what matters—graduating.

"You know how cute you are?"

Tristan's voice, like melted honey, oozes with desire, breaking my focus and forcing my gaze away from my textbook.

I smile sweetly, but my next words are anything but, "You know how annoying you are? I love you and all, but I *really* need to focus for the next while. Until I graduate, I'm off-limits to you and—" I stop, my mind finally catching up to my mouth.

Holy hell, I told him I love him. This is *not* the way I hoped to do that, so off-handed and uncaring.

His grin implies he doesn't care, and he's on his feet, moving to my side of the picnic table instantly. His head buries in the side of my neck, his nose nudging my hair away. "You realize what you just said, right?"

"Yeah, well..." I twist to face him, knocking his head away from mine. "You didn't even tell me to my face. You said it to my aunt, so this is payback." I resist sticking out my tongue, like I really want to.

Tristan growls, getting closer to me. To anyone looking by, we probably look like exactly what we are—a couple in love. "I've told you countless times."

I scoff playfully. "Right. When? When I was sleeping? It doesn't count, and you know it."

Suddenly I'm on his lap, his arm snaked around my waist, keeping me tight to him. His pupils dilate, seizing my entire breath with a single claiming look. "Do you not remember when I said you're mine and I'm obsessed with you. A man telling a woman he's obsessed with them is the same as saying he loves you."

My hand pushes between us, gaining a few inches, so he can see my exaggerated eye roll. "Well, *excuse me* for not knowing the difference."

He grins. "Well, now you know. And I know you love me too."

"Does that make me crazy?" Suddenly my skin itches and I long to rub at it. "I mean, Tristan, we've known each other for, like, a week."

"And?"

Of course, he doesn't see the issue. "And it's quick."

"And?"

I huff, but this time it's not playful or anything. I focus on him, studying his expression—his very passive and confused expression. He's serious about everything he's asking.

"And it's not normal. Even you have to know that."

My head is wrenched back, body bowing into his chest as his quick grasp of my hair leaves me at his mercy. "If we're not normal, Little Bird, I thank the stars. Because if normal means we'd have to go out and do that slow ass dating shit where I have to impress you and stuff, I'd be bored by day one. You excite me. You're made for me, and I for you. So yes, it might not be normal to fall in love after a week and a half, but you and I will never be that." Then, as if to reinforce his words, he presses his lips to mine, overwhelming my senses in all the ways he knows how.

And I let him for a long while, before fighting against his hold and pulling back an inch. "Tristan, we're out in public."

He releases my hair, letting the strands slip through his fingers as I right myself. Still, he grumbles. "Like it's ever stopped us before." His eyes flick over my shoulder, toward the library, and my insides warm with the reminder.

"Yeah, speaking of, now I know why my stalker was able to get a hold of my phone number."

"You have no idea how hard it was to avoid finding you and helping you finish on my tongue."

I shiver, picturing it. Imagining him crouched on the ground, lifting my leg over his shoulder, baring my core to his mouth.

"You're imagining it right now." His voice yanks me from my fantasy, the very one he's correct about. "I can tell because your pulse sped up and your breathing got heavier. We could make it happen."

Oh, how I want to, but I was serious about studying. With the strength of every nerve in my body, I turn and face my textbook once more. "I was serious, Tristan. I do need to study hard so I can graduate on time. And you should probably go back to work."

"Except Chief and Alex—both my bosses in this instance—haven't given me the right of way."

If he thinks he can play that game... I lift my phone and click on Alex's name, ready to carry on a seemingly normal conversation, and not let on that I'm working with the very people trying to put him behind bars.

ME

Hey. No one's bothered me in over a week. I think I don't need a bodyguard anymore.

ALEX

I'll make the call then. Only if you're sure though, and you feel safe?

ME

> I do. Thanks. I'll let you know if the need for him arises again.

I lower my phone, spotting a very annoyed looking Tristan. His annoyance deepens when his own phone chimes, but he barely glances at it.

"You're mean."

"Believe me. It'll be healthier for both of us if I can focus and get this done. You can have me in the evenings. Now, lunch is over, so you better get back to work before you're stuck making up those hours." I toss everything messily into my bag and flounce off, an extra skip to my step that I know makes my ass shake more than usual.

He knows it too.

TRISTAN

> I'll be home late because Chief has me here doing extra paperwork on your "stalker" since no one was caught. This is because SOMEONE insisted on sending me back to work.

THE MESSAGE that made me giggle only hours ago burns on my screen, a visual reminder of how late it truly is. To the point, I'm readying for bed and he still hasn't been by.

Perhaps this is more appropriate. Tristan and I have spent every moment together since meeting. Not that I still don't miss him and want him here, but if he's opted to continue to work or even to stay at his place tonight, I won't be crying over it.

A text would have been nice though.

For the first time in days, I fall asleep in my own bed, and my goodness, home is nice. The saying, home is where your heart is—

well, it's true. *My* blankets fall around my body, snuggling me into *my* mattress, just the right mix of firm and plushness. And when I fan my hair out on *my* pillow, I know I won't be breathing in Hawke's scent.

And that's how I drift off.

Until the telltale unlocking of my window, and the shadowy figure climbs through. He keeps the lights off and shuts the curtain, bathing the room in complete darkness.

For once, my heart doesn't beat in fear, but rather excitement. My thighs squeeze together because if he's come up this way, it's for one thing only.

"You remember I gave you my spare key, right?"

"You remember, Little Bird, I do what I want, right?"

His voice, deeper now than during the day—*how did I not hear how truly similar they are*—sends shivers down my spine and I hold the blanket tightly, squeezing it eagerly.

"You missed me." It's a statement, not a question.

"Of course."

"It's been way too long since I've had you, Little Bird, and I won't wait a moment longer. Lie back."

First, I pinch my shirt between two fingers and begin to pull it up my body, saving Tristan the work. His responding growl halts my movements, as does his own hand moving mine away.

"I didn't say undress. I said lie back."

I nod, though he probably can't see it, and follow his instructions, watching as the barely-there outline of him approaches. The bed dips with his weight and I feel the roughness of his jeans against my bare legs after he pulls the blanket away from my body, nestling himself in the space there.

"Tristan—"

His mouth latches onto my nipple from overtop of my tank top, wetting the cotton as he massages the small bud. My other one feels neglected so I lift my fingers to pinch it, only to find my hands pinned above my head, dark eyes casting flames down below.

"Nuh uh, Little Bird. You know how I like my control. You think I've unlocked your cage, but, baby, I'm simply moving you to another one."

His hair brushes my skin again, making me squirm to feel more, and his teeth bite down through my tank, sinking into the skin there. He clamps down, teeth biting even deeper, until a strained sound comes through my mouth.

"Tease," I murmur, a smile pulling at my lips. Because, let's be honest, even when his teasing is cruel, I love it.

"Mhm," he mumbles against my skin, and then worsens the torture by rubbing his jeans against my panty-clad front. The rough folds are nothing to the thin cloth and I feel *everything*.

"Tristan, inside me." I gasp, arching my back into him. "You want me as much as I want you."

"Ah, but there's where you're wrong, Little Bird. You forget, during all my nighttime visits, they were mostly about you. I was learning your cries of pleasure, your begs for more, the way you whimpered when you thought I wouldn't give you more. And right now, is no different."

Should I really be arguing with him? The man who wants to do all sorts of things to make me come.

His hands grasp my shorts and I lift my hips, welcoming him to slide them from me until the warm air of my bedroom hits my core and my legs fall open. I'm expecting his tongue, or his fingers. Something that's different than what I get.

Cold rubber.

I flinch. "What—"

Vvvvvvvvv.

My soul leaps from my body in that instance.

"A vibrator?"

The rubber shifts, becoming slick from my folds as Tristan expertly moves it around my clit.

"A throwback to our first night, when I found you here playing with yourself. It's why I was so late. I was out shopping."

He could have been at the moon for all I care now, because the vibration playing with my clit shoots sparks into the very depths of my soul and my hips move, chasing the high he's creating.

He slides it around again before pushing it into my core.

"Oh!"

It's as thick as his own cock, but combined with the vibrations rocking my interior, it's more intense.

"What I like about this toy is how I can so easily control your orgasms."

I hear the threat underlining his words. "You do that, I'll never suck your dick again."

Tristan's warm chuckle drifts over the bare skin of my thigh. "It's not all I purchased."

"No?" I manage between breaths.

"No," he reaffirms. "But we'll save the other items for another day."

I huff, disappointed, but the feeling is soon replaced by the high tide rising inside me, bringing me to the brink.

"Tristan, I'm—"

The vibrator rips from me, leaving my core to clench onto nothing as the high dwindles back into a low. Instead, he places it on my clit again.

"You're a dick."

"Yep."

And he continues to be so, all night long. Dragging me to the edge, only to pull back at the last second, until finally, he grants me mercy and I scream his name into the room.

Thirty-Five

TRISTAN

TWO MONTHS LATER

THANK fuck Natalie's last name is Miller or else I would have missed her. Damn Chief and his habit of talking for so long. Something about me not being around lately and missing out on the other guys' antics means I'm forced to listen to recollections of it. *Still*. Even two months after I've returned to work.

Thanks to some illegal speeding, I've made it to the university's graduation ceremony in time for the M's to begin being called. I wish I could have arrived earlier, as I spot Ryker up in the front row in a prime spot. Lucky fucker.

Also a lucky fucker who deserves it. The bastard missed his own graduation for Elena and had to get his GED through the prison. Being front and centre for his girl is the least the universe owes him. Hell, if it wasn't for Hawke's brilliance, it'd be Brent in his spot still, pretending.

But Hawke's a damn good lawyer. Even if I don't envy him with the shit he's dealing with right now.

It's over.

It's been an insane two months, but now it's Brent and Hawke's turn to go through Hell.

Brent being one year younger than the rest of us, his graduation is next year. But I wonder if it'll be pushed back, with his recent life developments. I don't see how he can be focusing at all on his school work.

I used to wonder how Ryker could love someone so much he'd attack someone the way he did, would spend a chunk of his early years in prison. But as the announcer says my girl's name— my Little Bird—I know why he did it.

I'd do it for her, and so much more.

It's why I was so fucking pissed when finding her at that party. When learning what the hell her own brother wanted to do to her. Murderous rage kept me concentrated on finding her, but all I truly wanted to do was search for Alex Miller and strangle him. If it meant having my badge stripped from me and going to prison, then so be it. My Little Bird would be safe from his clutches and that's all that matters.

Not that any of it is an issue anymore.

"Natalie Miller."

I move into a better view of the aisle, hoping when Natalie looks across the sea of faces, she finds mine and knows I didn't abandon her. I ensure my claps carry over those of everyone else's, my cheers definitely reaching her ears.

My Little Bird all but flutters across the stage, her smile so large and bright and *proud*. And damn, I'm proud of her too. I wouldn't have the patience for a degree like she did, so hell yes, I'm proud of what she's accomplished.

She accepts her diploma and glances to the side, her eyes instantly locking on mine in the back. Even from here, I can see the red in her cheeks, the damn fear of being noticed eating her up inside. But she's strong, and walks on, exiting the stage.

I slip to the side. With her name called, I have no further reason to stand here. Not when my girl is walking around in a graduation gown that's dying to be tossed over my shoulder as I fuck her raw in a back room.

I reach the side of the stage in time for her to exit from it on her path toward the graduates' seats in the front. I snatch her arm, yanking her away.

"Tristan!" Her wide smile holds no scorn for me. "I have to go sit with the other graduates."

"Nah, we've already determined you and I are not typical. Sitting there, following those rules, they're for normal people. Not us."

I pull her along, out of the university and straight to my squad car, opening the passenger door.

She stops, her brows lifting and arms crossing. With the graduation gown, she doesn't look half as menacing as she's going for.

"Come on. We're going for a bit of a drive."

"Where?"

"Don't worry about it. Get in."

Once she does, I drive us to our future.

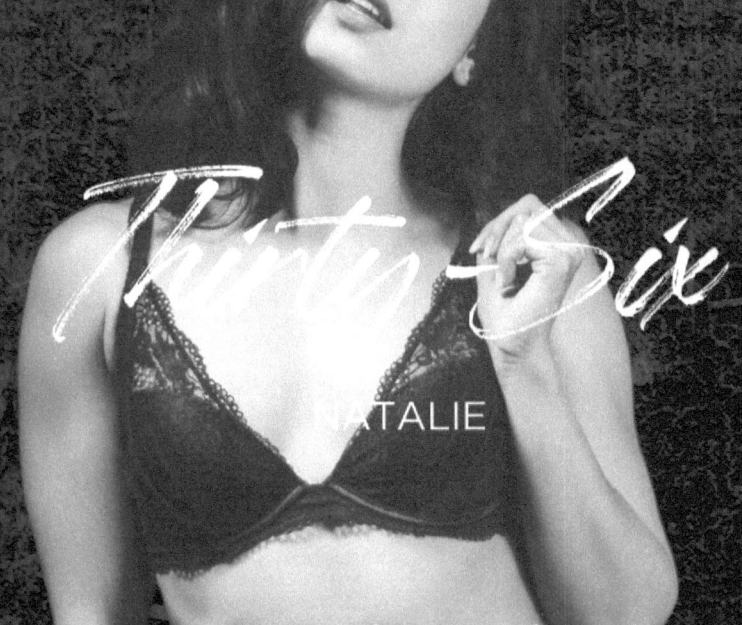

Thirty-Six

NATALIE

GIVEN Tristan's track record of surprises, I fear not knowing where we're headed. He drives to the edge of town, stopping at a small park made up of only grass and a couple trees.

"What are we...?"

But he's already gone, exiting the car and grabbing something from the back.

I follow along, but not before undoing my gown and leaving the clunky uncomfortable thing in the passenger seat. Something I should have done a while ago because the look Tristan gives me upon seeing me in my pink sundress makes my panty-less core go damp with desire —a surprise for him later.

His heated look doesn't keep my attention for long. Not when he's holding a basket.

"What are—"

As standard Tristan practices go, he walks away, leaving me to follow along as he leads me toward the shadowed mark on a specific area of the ground from blocking the bright sun overhead. He lowers to his knees, the scene looking all sorts of wrong with him in his uniform, and begins unpacking the basket.

First a blanket.

Then containers of food. Fruits. Sandwiches. Cans of pop.

"We're having a picnic?"

Tristan's lashes flutter as he lifts his eyes to mine. "You said so yourself, we never went on a date. Our relationship progressed quickly. No regrets, but I think we should experience at least one date before our wedding, no?"

I still. He isn't... *That* is most definitely too soon for me. Dating is one thing, but marriage...

"Relax," he comments, smirking. "It wasn't a proposal. Not yet anyway."

I lower myself, tucking my legs underneath my body and watch as he builds me a plate of meats, cheeses, mini-sandwiches, and fruit.

"Happy graduation, Little Bird. I'm really happy for you."

"Thank you." Warmth blooms in my chest, and I gesture to the spread he's set out. "And for all this."

"Anything for you." The way he says it is an absolute promise. "So, speaking of marriage, when can I propose?"

I bite my lip, staring down at the handful of grapes. I had planned on telling him today anyway, and now seems like the best chance. "The day I graduate with my master's degree?"

Tristan freezes, a slice of meat halfway to his mouth. "Masters? You want to return to school?"

I lay the plate on the ground, hands clenching in my dress as I roll the truth around in my mouth. "Remember when I said I was strangely enjoying English Lit? Well, if I do an MA in it, I think I may also go for my PhD... so I can teach. Turns out, I like the academia lifestyle."

Tristan's silent for a moment, but finally, he grins, leaning over to press his meat-flavoured lips to mine. "My smart girl. You'll be an amazing professor. I can't wait for you to be done with your MA now."

I furrow my brow playfully and fight the smile wanting to take over my expression. "You're strange."

But he's my strange.

And I love him for it.

He loves me.

Alex returned family and safety back into my life in more than one way. If it wasn't for him, wasn't for our shared genes, I would not know Tristan.

A fact I can't even pretend to imagine at the moment.

Our story may be fucked-up, but it's ours, and that's all I care about.

And to think, it all started with a single message from my stalker.

Thirty-Seven

BRENT

TWO MONTHS AGO

TEAGAN.

With red hair.

Who looks like an older version of the one I remember.

Impossible. Yet who else could it be? The world is huge and there's hundreds of thousands of places for her to go, yet she ended up in the same area she began in. The chance of it is way too great.

I'm the good guy. Who I was in high school, and hell, even after, left people with that persona of me. I'm okay with it because good guys finish last. The good guys are quiet and content with whatever gets tossed at them. But also, it's the good guys who become friendly with everyone in the whole school.

Natalie mentioned her working nights, and there's few jobs that allow for that. Given her connection with Alex, I don't believe she would have the education to work inside a hospital or anything of that professional calibre, so I marked that off my list of possible places where I could find her. Bartender, waitress, and stripper made it to the top three of that list. Jobs existing inside places that remain open late.

With Hawke and Tristan's help, we managed to gain a list of any clubs in Cortville, then it was a matter of looking into each one.

Tristan pulled employee records and found her by her stage name. A name that could only indicate one person.

A fucking strip club.

My girl works in a place where men grope her, treat her like garbage when she's always been a queen above them. Hell, a queen above *me*. I've continually wanted to be her slave, and she knew it too. It's why she was able to toss me away so easily.

Unfortunately for her, things change. People change. And I'm no longer her friend.

I'm her motherfucking enemy. The living embodiment of the nightmares that plague her at night.

Natalie claims she's being controlled by Alex, but my girl is too smart to be a kept woman. She's always paved her own path, fought when times were tough, and only ever cried in private. There's no way she's only a victim here.

So, as I watch her enter through the back door of the club, a large bouncer moving aside to let her slip past, I whip out my own phone and dial the number I've never once forgotten. Not since the moment she gifted me with it in the seventh grade.

I have no way of knowing if she's retained my number, but Teagan was always very adamant about forever keeping her number the same, no matter how many cell phones she goes through.

For my first text, I leave it simple:

Hi.

I'm not expecting her to respond, whether she knows it's me or not. But I do wait for the tiny line of text to appear under my message. And when it does—when it says *delivered*—I know, it's the beginning of more.

But first, I send anther text. This one to someone who'll ensure she doesn't take off when I approach her.

Game on, Cherry-Girl. Game fucking on.

Thank you for reading! Vicious Texts (Captive Writings #3) is now available. Continue onto the intense second chance/hate-to-love/friends-to-lovers romance between Brent and Teagan that solves every question you have.

Order your signed STORE EXCLUSIVE hardcover Captive Writings omnibus from my online store. It has a different cover and formatting from the regular paperbacks. Scan to order

More Books

Fractured Ever Afters

A 6-book (& 2 novellas) mafia romance series of interconnected standalones based on fairytales, featuring the Montreal mafia and the New York Famiglia.

The Desire in Deception (Prequel Novella)

The Hunt in Elusion

The Craving in Slumber

The Beauty in Scars

The Freedom in Captivity

The Sound in Silence

The Obscurity in Wishing

The Bonds in Christmas (Epilogue Novella)

The Bratva's Elite

A 4-book mafia series of interconnected standalones featuring the Russian Bratva.

Merciless Queen

Deadly Knight

Defensive Rook

Violent Pawn

Captive Writings

A new adult suspenseful romance series that progressively gets darker with each book

Ruthless Letters

Obsessive Messages

Vicious Texts

Burning Notes

Twisted Holidays

A series of dark romance holiday novellas

Silent Night

Egg Hunt

Fright Night

Be Mine

Midnight Kiss

Lucky Clover

Black Magick

A 5-book paranormal romance series of interconnected standalones featuring witches, vampires, shifters, mortals, and demons.

Dark Flame

Dark Mist

Dark Storm

Standalones

A Vampire for Christmas

Audiobooks

Silent Night

Acknowledgements

Megan, your continued support with this series means the world me. Thank you for all you do! There's not enough words for how much you help me and keep me grounded through all this.

Ashley, I always love our friendship and thank you for your help with the title of this book.

Thank you to Garnet Christie and Lee Jacquot. I love your ongoing support and having you two on my team.

To my betas, Megan and Colleen: Thank you for going back and forth with me through this book.

Thank you to The Next Step PR. Colleen, Jill, Megan, Anna, and of course, Kiki - you're all amazing. Thank you for everything you do. You're the best team to have!

Thank you to Rebecca Barney from Fairest Reviews Editing Services. You never cease to amaze me with your editing skills.

Thank you to Cat Imb of TRC Designs for giving Tristan his gorgeous cover!

Thank you to all the bloggers, bookmakers, and bookstagrammers who helped with the release of this book. Your help doesn't go unnoticed. Thank you for continuing on this insane trip with me.

And thank you to all the readers who took a shot on this book. My dream would not be possible without YOU—you who picked up this book and took a chance. I hope you loved Tristan and Natalie... but the ride's taking off with Brent and Teagan ;)

About

USA Today Bestselling author M.L. Philpitt writes both dark romance and paranormal romance. When she's not writing made-up realities, she's reading them. She lives in Canada with her four pets and survives life with coffee and an obsession with fictional characters, especially the morally grey kind. By day, she masks as a therapist.

TRIGGER/CONTENT WARNINGS

- Stalking
- Dubious consent
- Non-consensual sexual encounters
- Explicit sexual content
- Orgasm denial
- Manipulation
- Reference to slavery/trafficking
- Reference to murder
- Non-consensual sex (referenced in a memory; not to either main character)
- Physical violence